TAKE 'EM OUT
SOLIDARITY ACADEMY
AMBER NICOLE & ALISHA WILLIAMS

Nicole, Amber & Williams, Alisha

Take 'Em Out

Editing: Emma Luna at Moonlight Author Services

Cover Design: Alisha Williams

Formatting: November Sweets

We dedicate this book to our families. Thank you for your continued support and for helping us with the kids as we went into our writing bubbles. We love you all.

To anyone who has ever been mistreated or kicked aside, don't bite your tongue. Find your enemies weaknesses and Take 'Em Out!

AUTHOR'S NOTE

Hey, everyone, Alisha and I wanted to thank you all for continuing to support us through this new adventure of ours. All your kind words and reviews mean the world to us and give us the motivation to keep writing you all amazing stories.

So if you wouldn't mind leaving a rating or review that would be incredible.

Take 'Em Out is book two out of possibly four, of our dark, cheerleading academy, why choose series.

What that means is Rylee our FMC has more than one guy and will continue adding to her harem as the series progresses. All characters are over the age of eighteen as well.

Each book will end in a cliffhanger, but will have an HEA at the end of the series.

This series will be dark, and have heavy bullying in it. As well as MM scenes. As you know by now please check all warnings before proceeding and have some tissues on hand.

We are also not liable for any devices thrown or therapist bills, but we do allow yelling.

If you happen to find any edits (It happens we're all human) Please send them to ambernicoleauthor@ gmail.com

18+ preferred.

We love you all, and hope you continue to love Rylee and her men.

XOXO,

Amber & Alisha

TRIGGER WARNINGS

This book is not suitable for anyone under the age of **18** due to language and explicit sexual content.
Triggers include but are not limited to:
Severe Bullying
Drugs and Underage Drinking
Attempted Murder
Kidnapping
Assault
Grief
PTSD
Mention of Child Abuse
Attempted Sexual Assault
Please be mindful of your mental health & happy reading.

BLURB

Fool me once, shame on you.

Fool me twice, shame on me...

Isn't that how the saying goes?

At this point I don't even care.

I'm done trying to understand what went wrong and why those amazing guys from the summer became such nightmares.

It's time to put the pom poms down figuratively speaking and get into the ring.

They've messed with Rylee Moore for the last time.

Let's see who's played a fool now, boys!

It's time to take 'em out.

TAKE 'EM OUT

CHAPTER ONE

Rylee

"**G**et the fuck off me!" I shout, thrashing in my kidnapper's arms. I probably should be begging for my life, pleading with them that I'll give them anything they want. But, let's be honest, I have shit all to offer them, and seeing how these are Missi's goons, they probably know it too.

My heart pounds painfully in my chest, each breath is like a jagged knife ripping through the flesh of my lungs as I kick and punch. At least I try to, but someone is holding my arms and legs tightly.

"We should have gagged her first," a robotic voice snaps.

"I still think we should have used chloroform. It would have been a lot more effective for us staying discreet." I think someone else is talking, but it's hard to tell with the voice changers they're using. They all sound the same.

"And what? Make her sick? Fuck off."

Oh yeah, let's just have a grand old conversation. It's not like you're fucking kidnapping a girl or anything!

"Let me go!" I shout again, not giving up as I use all my strength to try and get out of their hold. *Stupid, Rylee. Why did you need food? You would have been better off starving for the night. Now look at you. Never learn, do we?*

"Not happening, sweetheart."

"I'm not your fucking sweetheart!" I snarl, bringing my head back and using all of my strength as I bring it forward hard. I hit someone as they shout.

"My fucking nose!" he growls.

"Try not to bleed on her."

"Fuck off!"

"Get her in the fucking van before the wrong people see us," someone hisses.

I struggle as they lift me up. A door slams behind me, and I resist the urge to cry. I'm not giving up though. Not until I take my last breath. Even then, I'll haunt these fuckers' asses!

An engine starts up, and my panic skyrockets. *What do they want with me? I've done nothing to anyone. Why the fuck can't people just leave me the hell alone?!*

"Would you calm the fuck down!" someone snaps, and I let out a snorting laugh.

"Calm down! You want me to, what? Just roll over and let you shove a bag over my head and kidnap me? You sure *you* haven't been sniffing something stronger than chloroform?" I sarcastically question, but I let my body go limp. There's no point in using all my energy right now. I'm not going anywhere while I'm locked up back here. So I'll rest, and the moment the door opens, that's when I'll fight again.

FUCK. I must have fallen asleep. My eyes open, but I see nothing, still blindfolded. My body bounces against something hard and warm as someone carries me.

I'm about to try and fight, to get away, when a very familiar scent hits me.

No way. No fucking way. Are the fuckers who kidnapped me my guys? Well, they're not *my* guys, but still. Why the fuck would they do this? Are they that desperate to get me to leave that they would go as far as to remove me themselves?

"You awake?" the voice asks. If this is one of my guys, based on the smell of sandalwood and citrus, this would be Mateo.

Come on, Rylee! Take him by surprise. Run for it! Your hands are free, for fuck's sake.

But, of course, my dumb ass plays dead. I wanna hear them out, see why they're doing this. And to be honest, I have no fucking clue where we are or how long we've been driving.

When Mateo takes me inside somewhere, I can hear the others talking. They still have their stupid voice changers on.

"Can we take this shit off now?" one of them asks.

"Not yet," another one says. "She can't see our faces. We need to get her to agree to go back home. I fucking hate all of this."

"She seemed afraid before. Maybe we scared her enough to go willingly?"

"Too soon to tell."

Mateo lays me down onto something soft. He's so quiet, I think maybe he left, but then I feel the bag being pulled off my face. I really want to take in deep breaths of fresh air, but I don't, concentrating on keeping my breathing even, as if I was sleeping instead.

"Chaos really does have a hard-on for you, doesn't it?" he says in his own voice. My eyes twitch to open, to see his face as his hand cups my cheek, his thumb brushing just under my eye.

I'm not sure if I should be offended by his comment or laugh at it.

"I really fucking wish life was a hell of a lot easier where you're concerned. More than anything, I wish you were the girl we thought you were," he says before I hear him walking away.

What the hell does that mean?

They all start to talk on the other side of the room, of wherever the fuck I am. Risking it, I let my eyes crack open.

Without moving, I can see that I'm on a couch. There's a fireplace facing me, some chairs, and a coffee table. Moving my head ever so slightly, out of the corner of my eye, I manage to see what looks like a toilet in another room.

If I can get in there, I should be able to lock the door behind me and give myself some time to think, without these guys breathing down my neck. I mean, it should have a lock, right? It's a bathroom.

I need to go now while they're still talking. Taking a deep breath, I open my eyes fully and jump up like a fucking jack in the box, sprinting toward the bathroom.

"Fuck!" one of them shouts, just as I slam the door shut and lock it.

My heart races wildly as I let out a sigh of relief.

"Open the door, Rylee!" they shout.

"How about you go fuck yourself, dick-wad!" I shout back, a massive grin on my face. I think I'm going crazy at this point.

They continue to pound on the door as I take a step back. With shaky limbs, I move to sit on the side of the tub.

"You gotta come out at some point!" one of them shouts before I hear footsteps moving away from the door.

"Holy shit," I say, letting out a breath. My heart hammers, and my hands shake as I take some time to get a grasp on what the fuck my life even is anymore.

Here are the things I know for sure. On my way to get food, I was chased and then taken. My kidnappers are the men who've been making my life a living hell, or at the very least, contributing to it.

Do I think they're going to hurt me? I don't know anymore.

Well, what the fuck do I do now? My body aches from the way they grabbed me and the ride here. All I wanna do is climb into a nice soft bed and go to sleep.

My eyes roam around the room, taking it in. This bathroom is really fucking nice. Not having anything better to do, I snoop around, seeing what's in here.

Opening a cabinet under the sink, I grin when I see all the different bath bombs and bubble baths.

I mean, if I'm locked in here, I may as well enjoy it. Giving a few of them a sniff, I find a nice vanilla scented bubble bath and go over to the tub. I turn the tap so the water is hot enough to steam. Letting the tub fill, I add the bubbles, then strip out of my dirty clothes and slip inside the water.

"Fuck, that feels amazing." I moan as I sink under the water, closing my eyes as I enjoy how it makes my sore muscles feel a hell of a lot better.

I'm so relaxed, I've almost drifted off to sleep when someone bursts through the door. I crack an eye open to see one of them, standing there with his chest heaving like he gave everything he's got to get through that door. He's still in one of those ghost face masks.

"Do you mind?" I quip, raising a brow. "I'm trying to relax. I don't need you perving on me, thanks. You can go," I say, closing my eyes before opening them again. "Could you get me something to drink? Oh, and something to eat, too. I'm starving!"

"You're kidding me, right?" he asks, his robotic voice giving away some of his stunned shock.

"Nope. I'm parched and very famished." I grin before my eyes light up. "Do you by any chance have any chocolate-covered strawberries? I've always wanted to soak in a bubble bath while eating them. I'll take a glass of wine too, if you have any."

"No! We don't fucking have any of that shit. This isn't some damn resort getaway!"

"You're telling me." I snort. "Your customer service is shit. Do you have any music on your phone? A little soft jazz would be nice."

"Are you for real? Like, did we hit your head a little too hard or something?"

"Not that I can remember." I shrug. "Although, I wouldn't make kidnapping your day job. If it wasn't night time, you guys would have totally been caught by the amount of yelling I was doing."

"I can't with you," he says, shaking his head before leaving, closing the door behind him. I hear them arguing on the other side of the door, and I giggle. Why not make the best out of a bad situation. I just really fucking pray it's them, because otherwise this is going to end up being a really awkward kidnapping.

The water begins to turn cold, and my fingers get wrinkly, so I decide to get out of the tub.

Just as I stand up, the door opens again. It's the same guy based on what he's wearing. We both just stand there. I blink as he moves his head up and down, getting a good look at my body as the bubbles slide down.

"Mind handing me a towel?" I ask, crossing my arms over

my tits. It pushes them up, not doing anything to help with his staring. When he does nothing, I clear my throat.

"Towel?" I repeat.

"Right," he says, coughing as he goes over to the shelf and grabs one. He hands it to me.

"Thanks."

"You know, for someone who just got kidnapped, you seem a little too... chilled? Should we be worried? Are you in like some kind of state of shock?"

"No." I snort. "I'm just not afraid." Okay, maybe I am a little, but they don't need to know that. Even if it is them, I know what they're capable of.

"You're not...?" he asks slowly.

"Nope," I say, popping the P as I wrap the big, fluffy towel around me.

"Why not? You've been kidnapped. Why aren't you begging for your life or something?"

"Not worth the time or energy. I know you're not going to do shit to me. Not after everything you've already done. I see the way you all looked at me when I lost my shit after the game."

He stills. Moments pass before he speaks again. "You know who we are?"

I give him a cocky smirk. "Yeah, big guy, I know who you are."

He lets out a huff before pulling off his mask. It's Donny. His blond hair is damp from sweating. "How did you know it was us?"

"Well, I wasn't fully convinced it was you guys until you

just revealed yourself." I laugh, and he curses. "But I suspected it was you because I know Mateo's scent."

He gives me a look that I don't want to deal with right now.

"Well, fuck," he says, then turns around to walk over to the door. "Guys! She knows!"

CHAPTER TWO

Adonis

Fuck! This isn't good. Rylee wasn't supposed to know who we are.

I stomp out into the kitchen where the guys are still arguing, and fight not to turn back for another peek at the girl who makes my blood boil and my cock rock hard. I bite my fist and groan. Lennox gives me a weird look at my entrance. I probably look like some pained baby giraffe the way I'm walking.

"What do you mean she knows?" Mateo snaps, and I

wince as he comes closer to me and pushes my back into the wall. "What the fuck did you do, Donny?"

I scoff and watch as his nostrils flare.

He's been more aggressive than usual the last few days as we plotted and planned. I think Lennox has been holding out on him, but I don't know why.

"I didn't do shit. I'm not the one who smells like a Magic Mike show," I growl as I shove him away from me. *Why am I the one who automatically gets blamed?*

Lennox moves closer and grabs Mateo's arm, pulling him back toward the island where Colt is sitting, watching everything.

Colt laughs and shakes his head, drawing all of our eyes to him.

"You think this is funny?" Mateo snaps, and I'm about to lose it on him. I get it, tensions are high, but he needs to chill the fuck out.

"Are you really so shocked? We got the jump on her at school, sure. But what did you expect to happen once we got out here, all of us alone in a cabin? I'm not surprised she figured it out so quickly, to be honest. Sooner than I expected, but it was bound to happen. The fact remains, she knows, and it's done now. We might as well go talk to her," Colt says as he stands from the chair and heads back to where I left Rylee, wet and sudsy.

And there goes my dick again.

I ignore Teo and Len, choosing to follow Colt instead. Rylee is still in her towel, sitting on the couch with her legs and arms crossed, giving us the evil eye.

Ignoring her mood, I plop down next to her then roll

onto my back and lay my head in her lap. Her soft lips part with a surprised gasp making me groan, this time loudly in her face. Seriously, she hasn't even touched me and my balls are ready to blow.

As Colt takes a seat on the coffee table in front of us, Rylee grips my hair in her fist as she tries to shove me off her, but that ain't happening. I roll toward her stomach and wrap my arms around her waist, shoving my face into her towel.

"What the hell are you doing?" she shouts, trying to push me off. I just sigh, relaxing for the first time in a long time.

I've missed her. We may have only had a few days together before things turned to shit, but these past few months of trying to hate her haven't worked. And after seeing her break down at the game... I just can't keep hurting her. I'm done fighting my feelings. I want her back, and I think the others do too.

Someone grips my shoulder and throws me onto the floor. I turn my head and glare up at a pissed off Mateo. Colt clears his throat, pulling Rylee's attention to him.

"I think it's time we all had a chat," he says, making Rylee snort.

"Have you all lost your damn minds?" she snaps. "You want to have a 'chat'? You're kidding me, right? You just kidnapped me. After everything you put me through, I still didn't think you would stoop this low." She shakes her head like she's disappointed with us. "Nah, I don't feel like listening to you. I think it's time someone answers my questions for once. If I'm going to be stuck here..." She looks around and frowns. "Wherever the fuck here is, then I want to be compensated for my troubles. Some chocolate-covered

strawberries, wine, and food sounds like a good start to me."
She huffs and recrosses her arms. I don't think she noticed
she was waving them around like a lunatic as she spoke.

Her demands don't go over well. Mateo roars like some
wild beast and gets closer to Rylee's face as she gives him a
slow smirk. My little Cherry seems to enjoy getting a rise out
of him.

Lennox is trying to control him, and me? I'm about to
whip my dick out and stroke him to the scene playing before
me. I never thought I would like a girl bossing me around.
But, fuck, Rylee could order me to prance around in a tutu
with an ice cream cone hat on my head and I would do it.
Especially if it meant I could finally slide in between her
sweet thighs.

"Fuck, Cherry, do that again," I moan, and she looks at
me shocked. Her green eyes are wide and a little glassy.

"Who the fuck do you think you are, little girl?" Mateo
continues to rant as Lennox tries to pull him outside. "You
do not order me around. We are the ones in charge here. In
case you forgot," he keeps shouting. I climb to my feet, ready
to knock his ass out, when Rylee stands and claps slowly.

"Oh, wow, what a big grumpy bear you are today. So large
and in charge," she taunts, and I watch as Teo tries to charge
at her. I don't know whether to clap along or make some
popcorn, but I'm waiting for the real show to begin. Because
if she keeps taunting him, he's going to have her bent over
his knee and her ass red. And fuck, if I'm not here for it all.

Who the fuck does she think she is? Acting like a brat and thinking she can get away with it. Well, she has another thing coming. I have put up with her shit for too long. I have too much on my damn plate to be 'kidnapping' her, and trying to keep her safe. Now, I have to deal with her being a whiny little bitch, thanks to shit for brains over there exposing us.

I stomp toward her and grip her throat tightly, lifting her slightly so her green eyes meet mine. Her eyes go wide as Lennox tries to get in my way, but I'm done. I ignore her towel dropping to the floor, exposing all her delicious curves, and growl into her face, our mouths only a breath apart.

"You are not the boss here, Rylee. So, shut the fuck up and be happy I don't have you tied up and gagged in the bathtub." Her nostrils flare, but I don't miss the way her eyes flash with heat and she rubs her thighs together. My dick is fighting to break through my jeans, and I know I need to get the fuck out of this cabin before I throw her back onto the couch and destroy her pussy. I bet it's probably dripping right now.

Colt says something, snapping me out of my haze, and I release her.

She falls onto her ass on the hardwood floor as she tries

to catch her breath while rubbing her neck. "What the fuck? You really are a crazy bastard," she snarls as she stands up. She doesn't care that she's naked and giving us all a show.

She knows what she's doing to all of us and is reveling in it. How do I know this? The fact that she gives me a cocky smirk, her eyes flicking down to the bulge in my jeans.

"Such a fucking brat," I mumble as I let Lennox finally intervene. Colt helps Rylee fix her towel as Len pulls me toward the front door. When the cool air hits my heated flesh, I take in a deep breath and flex my fists.

"Want to tell me what the hell is going on with you?" Len asks, and I scoff. Right now would be a perfect time to take up smoking. I need something to take the edge off before I really lose my shit. I stomp to the other side of the porch and lean against the railing, taking in the scenery. We needed somewhere secluded, and Adonis came through.

I don't think anyone will find us here, and if Rylee tries to run, all she will find is miles of forest and some bears. I growl just like the wild beasts nearby and shove off the railing, moving over to the porch swing. I shouldn't even be here. I need to be closer to my family. To keep them safe. I know my uncle has something planned, and the fact that I'm here trying to protect some ungrateful little bitch is making me murderous.

I should have just left her to Missi and her sick fucking plans. It's not like she's done anything to deserve my protection. She just had to mess with my head. Make me think that maybe I was wrong about Florida. Feel fucking guilty for the way we were treating her.

I grip my hair tightly and yank. Len moves closer and places his hand on my thigh, rubbing it gently.

He hasn't touched me in a few weeks, and just that small gesture is making my balls tingle. He leans forward and places a kiss onto my neck. I groan and grip his throat, pulling his lips to mine. We don't kiss. We attack each other's mouths with the pent up emotion and passion that's been missing.

Fuck. I need him. I push him away from me and stand, pressing his back against the white painted railing. He sighs into my lips, and I reach down to grip his ass. He's wearing dark sweatpants and I can feel the heat of his skin through the material. His cock jumps against my stomach, and I fight not to drop to my knees and suck him down.

Maybe later, but right now, I need to get rid of this pent up aggression, and his tight little ass is the perfect solution.

He groans into my mouth and I smile, kissing him deeper as I reach around and rub his cock. I pull away from his lips for a moment to catch my breath.

"Pants off, now," I order, then spin him so his stomach is facing the woods. He tugs the material down and I smack his tight little ass hard before gripping it in my palm. "I want you to bend over and hold your cheeks open wide, so I can watch as I feed you my cock," I growl. He shudders, following my orders.

I spit on his hole as he spreads it open for me, and rub my thumb along the rim to get him nice and slick. "This is going to be rough and fast, baby," I warn. "It's been too long since I've felt your hot walls clenching around me." I pull my cock out, give it a few tugs, then gently press against his opening. He groans and spreads his legs wider for me as I give him a few shallow thrusts.

I pull out and reach around, shoving my fingers into his mouth. "Suck. Get me nice and slippery so I can coat my dick in your saliva," I say as he starts to gag on my fingers. I pump my cock with my free hand. I'm already close from the perfect image he makes, all spread open for me, just waiting for my thick cock to split him open.

I pull my fingers away and coat my cock, then position myself against his tight little hole again, this time not stopping. I push through the ring and slam home. I give him a few seconds to adjust before gripping his hips and owning him once again.

"Fuck, baby, you squeeze me so good." I groan and he whimpers, releasing one of his cheeks to reach down and grip his cock. I smack his hand away and take over, giving him some quick jerks.

"Teo, please," he whines, and it's like a direct line to my balls. Him begging, me all breathless. I close my eyes and slow my pace a little to give myself some time. I don't want to rush this like I said. I want to stay here inside of him while he's wrapped around me. I don't want to go back to my corrupted family, or the little brat inside who makes me want to wring her neck.

I just want to stay here in my happy place. With the boy who means more to me than he knows. Out here in the middle of nowhere. Where it's peaceful for a few minutes. I open my eyes and lean forward, grinding deeper.

Lennox turns to look over his shoulder and I grip his neck gently, bringing his lips to mine. I fuck him nice and slow. I guess you could call it making love, but that's not my style. So, I'll say it's gentle fucking. He pulls away from me and pants against my mouth, giving me his lust filled hazel eyes.

"So beautiful," I coo, as he bites his bottom lip and wiggles against my cock. I pump his dick harder and watch as his eyes roll back, and he comes all over my fingers. He shakes and moans, and I know I'm about to fill his little hole full of my cum.

"Don't take your eyes off me," I grunt, picking up my pace. I smear his cum all over his hips as I take him hard and deep, really claiming him when my dick starts to pulse and he clenches me so tight that I see stars.

I lean forward and take his mouth once more as I spill inside him, muffling my moan and my desire to shout his name. I kiss him slower as I come down from my high and catch my breath.

I would have continued, but a door slams and reality comes back to me. The relaxation I just felt leaves immediately and my shoulders tense. I pull away from Len and fix my clothes. He groans, but doesn't say anything as he tugs his sweats back up. He leans in to kiss me again, but I spin away from him and stomp back to the other side of the house, ignoring the hurt in his eyes.

CHAPTER THREE

Rylee

Nice to see he's still a raging fucking asshole! Although, I do love getting under his skin. Dude should know he's just giving me power by reacting. And it's too much fun to resist. One thing he was right about, I'm a brat, but he made me into one.

"Are you okay?" Colton asks, his eyes filled with concern. He hesitates, but reaches out anyway, tilting my head so he can get a look at my neck.

"Fucking dick left handprints," Donny growls.

"I'm fine," I deadpan, stepping back and holding the

towel around my body tighter. I don't care that they seem worried about me. Where were those feelings when they fucking kidnapped me? When they tied me up and left me naked in a locker room? When Lennox's little, crazy bitch of a girlfriend tried to kill me on more than one occasion?

No, I don't want their pity, and especially not now.

I'm pissed, tired, and I just want something to wear. As much as I love how I affect the guys when it comes to my body, I don't want to be walking around them naked, or in a towel all of the time.

Letting out a sigh, I look away from Colt and Donny's pity-filled expressions and walk over to the window. "Where are we anyway?" I ask. It's still pitch black outside, but I can see the moonlight reflecting on what I'm gonna assume is a lake.

"My parents left it to me," Donny says.

"So you what? Woke up this morning and thought *'hey, you know what would be fun, a trip up to the cabin. And hey, let's kidnap Rylee and bring her along too'?*" I snort, shaking my head. They still haven't told me what the hell is going on, or why they brought me here in the first place.

"We didn't kidnap you," Donny mutters, brow furrowing.

"Oh no? Then what is it called when you shove a bag over someone's head, grab them, and then toss them into a van?" I ask, raising a brow as I wait for his response, because I'd really like to know.

"There's a lot more to it," Colton says, taking a step forward. He looks drained, like all of this is hard on him. *Well, it's hard on me, too, buddy.* This whole damn year has been so far.

"Then why don't you fill me in?" I ask, crossing my arms under my breasts. Of course the movement gets Donny's attention, his eyes darting down to my pushed up cleavage. Rolling my eyes, I leave it be.

"We will, when the others get back," Colton says. "We really do need to sit down and talk everything out."

I happen to agree with that. Maybe these shitheads will finally tell me why they went from blowing my mind one night, to ghosting me the next, to bullying me like I've fucked up their lives.

"Fine," I say, opening the window. "I'll tell them to get their asses back in here and answer my questions."

I'm about to shout out to them when the sounds of grunting and moaning hits my ears.

Are they... *are they fucking?* You have got to be fucking kidding me. Now is not the time to be balls deep in some-one's ass!

I'm not at all jealous that someone's getting laid and it's not me. And I'm not at all getting turned on to the image my mind is conjuring up as I listen to them fuck.

Keep lying to yourself, Rylee, and telling yourself what you think you wanna hear.

Closing the window, I turn back to the guys. "Ah, maybe I'll just wait until... they're done."

"Done what?" Donny asks, stalking over to the window and opening it. The sound of a deep guttural groan makes its way into the cabin, and my belly flutters. Betrayed by my own body.

"Lucky bastard," Donny grumbles, slamming the window hard.

"Look, can one of you give me your phone?" I ask, glancing from Donny to Colt.

"What? Why?" Donny asks, jumping in front of me. "You gonna call the cops or some shit?"

"No," I reply, rolling my eyes. Though I really should. "Serenity is going to be wondering why I'm not in the dorm when she gets back with Alex. And when she doesn't hear back from me after texting and calling, because I know she will do both, *she* will call the cops. She knows the shit you've done. She wouldn't think twice that my safety is in danger."

Colt and Donny give each other a look, having a silent conversation before Colton sighs and grabs his phone out of his back pocket. "Fine, but you sit on the couch so we can hear what you're saying."

"Fine," I huff. "This really does feel like some kind of hostage situation," I sass as I walk over to the couch. Sitting between the two of them, I try to ignore the heat of their bodies, the smell of their scents, as I take the phone Colt holds out to me.

"Thanks," I mutter, bringing up the new contact and typing in Ren's number. When I'm done typing out a message, I hit send.

> Me: Hey, babe, it's Rylee. I know you're going to walk into the dorm room and find it empty, but I just want you to know that I'm fine. I'll be back to school as soon as I can.

I see the dots pop up like she's texting back, but they disappear. A moment later the phone starts to ring.

"Hello," I answer.

"What do you mean you're not at the dorm? Alex and I were just heading back now. Where are you?" she asks, her tone sounding concerned.

I look up at Colt as he watches me with curious eyes, wondering if I'm going to blab about what they did to me.

"I need some time away from school. After everything that's been going on, I just need some time to breathe. I'm with... friends." That will probably be the biggest lie I've told her so far in this conversation. "But, I'm safe. I'll keep you updated, and I'll be back in a few days."

"What about school? About cheer?" she asks.

"It's only a day or two, I won't fall behind," I tell her, meaning it. But she's going to know who I'm with when she goes to practice and finds the only four guys missing as well as me. I'll deal with that then.

"Are you sure? You're okay? You would tell me if you were in any danger, right? There's not someone holding a gun to your head, telling you what to say, is there?"

"No, babe, there's not. I'm fine. Promise."

"Okay, but please text me soon, or call," she says, but I know she wants to ask me more. *"If you don't, I will be calling the cops."*

I can't help but smile. I love this girl. "I will. Just look after Alex for me, okay? Don't let him miss me too much."

"I don't know. He's going to be up my ass when I tell him. He's in the bathroom, then we're leaving the party."

"Maybe just tell him when you get back?" I ask.

"Alright. Be safe, Ry."

"I will," I tell her. "Love you."

"Love you, too."

I hang up and hand Colt his phone back. "You better not make me regret lying to her. Unlike you lot, I care about the people in my life," I say, narrowing my eyes.

Colt's face drops as he stands up and puts his phone back in his pocket.

"Come on, Donny, help me get the food from the van before it spoils."

"But..." Donny looks over at me then back to Colton.

"Now."

"Fine." Donny sighs, standing up to join him. He turns to me. "You stay here. Don't move."

"Where the fuck do you think I'm gonna go?" I deadpan. "I'm in a towel, in the middle of the woods, in the middle of nowhere."

"Good point." He nods.

"Speaking of being in a towel, did any of you bring something that I can change into?"

"I have something in my bag you can wear," Colton says.

They head outside, closing the door behind them. The moment the door is closed, I stand up and head into the little kitchen area. As I check the fridge to see what they have in there for me to eat or drink, I notice a set of keys on the counter. Picking them up, I see one of them is labeled 'Cabin'.

A slow grin takes over my face. I wonder if this is the only key they have?

Looking over at the door, my eyes find the lock. Wouldn't hurt to try. I laugh as I run over to the door, flicking the lock. My heart pounds in my chest as I hear them coming back up the stairs.

The door handle jiggles. "Open the door," Colton says. "This shit is heavy."

"I'm trying," Donny says, the door handle jiggling again. "It's locked."

"What? Let me try," Colt says. "What the hell?" They bang on the door. "Rylee. Can you unlock the door and let us in?"

"Nah, I don't think so," I say loud enough for them to hear.

"Rylee!" Donny shouts. "Open the door."

"No, thank you. I don't think I will," I say, giggling to myself.

"What the fuck is going on?" I hear Mateo's voice.

"The door is locked, and she's not letting us in," Colt says.

"Fucking brat." Mateo growls after trying himself.

He says something about the back door that has my eyes widening. I take off running toward the back of the cabin, finding the door and flicking the lock just in time as Mateo gets to the steps. I can see him through the window, standing there with the motion-activated porch light shining down on him.

"You little bitch," he sneers, his face morphing into anger.

"Sucks to suck." I cackle and turn around to head back into the main part of the cabin.

There's banging on the door, but I ignore them, opening

the fridge and finding a bottle of wine. "Well, isn't this my lucky day," I say, grabbing it.

I search for food, but don't find anything, so I open the bottle and head into the living room. Grabbing one of the magazines on the table, I flip it open and take a swig.

"Rylee!" Colt says, tapping on the window. I look over casually.

"Yeah?" I ask, taking another drink as I glance back at the magazine.

"Let us in, please," he asks, sounding defeated.

"Nope," I say, popping the P.

They argue for a few seconds more before Mateo speaks next, sounding really mad. "You're such an ungrateful brat! We try to save your ass and this is what you fucking do. We should have just left you to the dogs."

That gets my attention. Placing the bottle on the table with the magazine, I get up and open the door. "What the fuck are you talking about? How is any of this protecting me? You better fucking tell me everything, and right the fuck now, because I'm done with this and all these fucking games!" I yell.

I'm hungry, tired, and I just want to go to bed. I'm done with the games. I'm done with the secrets. They better start spilling their guts or I'll take their fucking van while they're sleeping and leave them out here for the wolves.

They all push past me, Colt and Donny bringing in the bags. Mateo stops before me. "Pull shit like this again and I swear to God, Rylee, I'm going to bend you over my fucking knee and redden your tight little ass so bad you won't be able to sit for a week," he threatens, getting so close to me that I can feel his minty breath feather against my lips.

"Is that a threat or a promise?" I ask, smirking up at him as his nostrils flare, his eyes filling with heat.

It's fun to poke the bear, but it looks like this one is about to snap.

This isn't how any of this was supposed to go. Hell, even I didn't know what was going on until the last possible moment. It was so last minute that it was either help them, or not be a part of it in any way. I should have gone with the more logical option, but I didn't want to leave Rylee alone with these guys, and not be here. Not that I think they would hurt her, but let's be honest, their choices up until now have been pretty questionable.

The plan was to get her here, convince her that she is in danger and that she should go home before she gets hurt. Missi is out of control, and as of right now, there's not much we can do about it. She hates Rylee with a passion, and is even desperate enough to resort to physical violence to get rid of her.

Although we may have stood by during Missi's reign of

terror, we never wanted Rylee to get hurt. At least, I know I didn't.

"You're a fucking brat," Mateo snarls.

"Yeah, yeah, tell me something I don't know," she says with a roll of her eyes as she turns her attention to me. "So, you got something for me?" she asks, raising a brow.

"What?" I splutter, brow furrowing.

"Clothes, remember," she says, gesturing to her toweled body.

"Oh, right. Yes. Here," I say, digging through the bag of clothes I brought with me and finding a T-shirt and sweatpants for her to wear.

"Must be fucking nice," she mutters. "You all thought so far ahead to bring a change of clothes for yourselves, but didn't think about what you would need for your kidnapee." She snatches the clothes from me and starts toward the bathroom.

"So fucking ungrateful," Mateo says, and that earns him the finger from Rylee as she walks away. Donny pouts and gives me a glare.

"What?" I ask, confused, looking around, and Donny sighs.

"Why would you give her clothes, man?" Len groans beside me. I roll my eyes, shaking my head and giving Donny a shove.

"I know I'm not the only one who was enjoying the show," Donny grumbles.

"Well." I huff out a breath, running my hand through my hair as I adjust my glasses. "We tell her everything?"

"At this point, I think lies are just pointless," Lennox says, and I nod.

We all move into the living room, taking different seats around the coffee table. A few minutes later, Rylee comes back out and joins us.

My eyes roam her body. I can't help but get hard at the sight of her in my clothes. The sweatpants are a little too big on her, so she has them rolled up around the waist. The shirt is baggy too, but it rests against her breasts nicely. And because she's not wearing a bra, her nipples poke through.

"Hey, boy wonder," Rylee says. My eyes snap up to hers, and I blush at the fact that I was caught staring.

"Here," Donny snickers, handing me a couch pillow to place over my dick.

"Thanks," I mutter, seeing I'm not the only one who needs one.

"So, who wants to spill first?" she asks, crossing her arms as she leans against the wall.

"Well, first, the reason why we brought you here wasn't because we wanted to harm you in any way," I start.

"Thanks for that by the way," she snips, making Mateo growl in irritation.

"I know you think we're the bad guys, and we really haven't done much to prove to you otherwise—" I continue, but she interrupts me again.

"You think?" She snorts.

"Let him fucking talk," Mateo snaps.

Rylee glares at him, then looks back at me with a wave of her hand. "Fine. Continue."

"Missi planned on doing something to you. Something

bad, something really fucked up. We couldn't sit by and let that happen, so we played double agents," I say.

"What do you mean?" she asks, more seriously now.

"Missi was planning on chloroforming you, tying you up, and dropping you off in the streets of LA to be gang-raped and possibly killed. She told us about it, and well... we had to act like we wanted in on it for her to tell us her full plan. She thinks we're her little puppets. But as you can see, that's not what happened. We never actually planned on doing what she wanted. We got to you first and brought you somewhere safe," Lennox says, gesturing to the cabin around us to drive his point home.

"Wow." Rylee sighs. "You really know how to pick them don't you?"

"What?" Lennox asks, confused.

"Girls. Dude, that bitch is bat-shit crazy. I don't care how good her pussy might be, it's not worth being locked to that cuckoo's nest."

"You don't actually think I like her do you?" Lennox asks.

Rylee shrugs. "You're dating her, aren't you?"

"Only for show," Lennox admits. Mateo snorts at that, earning a glare from Lennox.

"Whatever." Rylee rolls her eyes. "Thanks, I guess, for... you know, saving my life. Even after you set out to destroy it and all. What do you want, a cookie or something?" she asks.

"See. I fucking told you. We should have let the wing nut have her. She's so fucking ungrateful. Even after what she did to us, we still helped her, and look where that got us." Mateo explodes in a fit of rage.

"What I did to you?" she shouts. "Fuck you. I've never done anything to you."

"Oh fucking please." Mateo laughs. "You're joking, right? Like you didn't plan on using us for Lennox's money? You didn't plan on working with that sleazy ex of yours to blackmail him into giving you a nice payday?" Mateo shakes his head. "I know we hadn't known each other that long, but I thought that our time together meant more to you than that. Because I know it did to us. Clearly, we were fucking wrong."

Rylee's face goes pale, like she's seconds from puking. "What?" she whispers. "No." She shakes her head. "That's why you left that night? Why you've been so cruel to me?" She looks like she's about to cry, and my heart hurts for her. "You have it all wrong. That's not at all what happened."

"That's not what Colton and Donny said. They overheard the whole thing. You've been caught, Rylee. Just fucking own up to it," Mateo says with a sigh. He looks tired and sad.

"No. No, I'm not owning up to anything!" she shouts, looking at me and Donny. "What was the last thing you heard?"

"Ahh, pretty much what Teo said. We wanted to find you so we searched the hotel. You were in some closet with your ex talking about Len's dad, how much money he has, and about blackmailing him for fifty K," Donny says.

"God, you fucking dumb-asses!" she shouts, making Donny flinch back. "You should have stayed longer and you would have heard me turn him down. You would have heard me tell him he's full of shit and there's no amount of money that would make me do something so fucked up. I don't care that I didn't make a lot, or that I lived where I worked. I would never use someone to get money. I would never break someone's trust like that."

The whole room goes silent. I'm gonna puke. Fuck. Fuck, don't tell me that all these months of hurt and pain were because we didn't hear the whole conversation.

"Are you serious?" I ask her. "You were never going to go along with that guy's plan?"

"No!" Rylee shouts, throwing her hands in the air. "I'm not like that. No amount of fucking money would tempt me into becoming a horrible person." She shakes her head. "Now it makes sense why you guys have been so damn cruel since I came to school, if you assumed that's what I was going to do to you. And it was all for nothing. Months of treating me like shit, all for nothing. Are you guys proud of yourselves?" she snaps before turning around and storming over to the bathroom, slamming the door shut behind her.

"Guys," I say, breaking the silence. "I think we fucked up big time."

CHAPTER FOUR

Lennox

I stare off toward where Rylee just escaped to, trying to stop myself from chasing after her, dropping to my knees, and begging for forgiveness. If what she said is true, and I'm starting to think it is, then Colt is right. We really fucked things up.

Donny paces in front of us and shakes his head while mumbling a bunch of nonsense, and Colt looks like he might be physically sick, staring at the door.

"I need a fucking drink," Teo grunts, stomping into the kitchen. I slowly follow after him in search of some alcohol as well. I am way too sober for this, and with the way he just fucked me raw, I'm a little sore too. Not that it wasn't hot as hell. The way his strong body dominated me, and literally railed me into the railing.

I've missed him, but I wish he didn't just use me to once again forget the spitfire who heats his blood and temper. I know that's all it meant this time.

I grab a beer from the fridge and look for a bottle opener, avoiding Teo's gaze. It's not like I'm about to get shitfaced. There isn't enough alcohol here for that. Donny starts laughing in the other room, and Teo grabs my beer, opening it for me with a belt buckle he found in a drawer before chucking it into the corner of the room with a growl. I take a few sips then hand it to him to finish. We don't say a word, and I don't like it. We should be basking in the afterglow of our orgasms, not standing here barely looking at each other after the confession we just heard.

"I don't believe it," he finally grumbles, and I shake my head at how stubborn he is.

"I think I do, Teo. Things never added up that week. Even after Donny and Colt told us what they heard, I've always had some doubts. She didn't seem the type. And when she showed up at school..." I shrug, running my hands through my messy hair. I really need a shower and maybe some pain killers.

"Maybe this is all just a part of her scheme. She makes us fall at her feet, begging her to give us one more chance, then she rips our hearts from us once more, and steals your money in the process. I don't know about you, Len, but I can't afford the extra bullshit. I have enough going on with my family. I think we need to just cut ties with Rylee. She's on our team. We can be civil, keep her safe from Missi, but that's it." I glance out the window at the night sky and sigh.

What he's saying is true. He's not the only one being controlled and put through the wringer at the hands of their family. We all are. Him with his uncle, Donny with his grandmother, Colt with his mom, and me with my dad and the Kondoms. I know we should just let that week go, but I don't think I can.

It wasn't just a hot summer fling. Rylee felt like a part of our group. She fit so seamlessly before everything turned to total shit. Maybe there is a chance to get back to that and finally be happy again. She made us all happy.

Teo begs me with his eyes to agree with him, and I can see how exhausted he truly is. Donny joins us, and I'm still staring into Mateo's eyes when he cuts in with his goofy bullshit.

"How about we all whip up something to snack on, then we can get down to the nitty gritty?" Donny suggests as he moves toward the bags of groceries Colt brought inside. I sigh and take a seat, giving him my attention.

"What nitty gritty? I think I've been rubbed raw and exposed enough for one night," I mumble, and he gives me a huge, toothy smile.

"Well, now that we know my little Cherry isn't digging for gold, we can turn this kidnapping party into a super slutty slumber party," he announces with a wink. I'm about to smack him upside his head, but Colt beats me to it, muttering, 'idiot'.

"Get those thoughts out of your head right now, Don.

We have a long way to fucking go before I even think about putting my hands, mouth, or dick anywhere near Rylee," Teo snarks, and now I'm the one laughing.

He's so full of shit. He just destroyed *my* ass outside because he couldn't fuck *her*.

Donny pouts looking like a kicked puppy, and Colt comes over to help him cook. "I haven't been able to fuck anyone since Rylee," he whispers, and we all turn to stare at him. He's blushing and ripping up a paper towel. "I never even got to fuck her that night, and still she controls my dick." He looks so broken and down. I find myself climbing to my feet to give him a big hug.

Mateo gapes and is, for once in his life, speechless. Rylee enters the kitchen, coming to an immediate halt, realizing she missed something. Colt moves toward the sink and rinses his hands along with some chicken that he took out of the package.

Donny blows a raspberry on my neck, turning back into his goofy self. I chuckle, letting him go, dropping the subject for the moment. A lot of people see him as a prank-loving goofball, but Donny has a darkness inside, and a past that I wouldn't wish on anyone.

WE FINISH EATING the chicken salad they prepared, and when Donny suggests playing a game, we agree. He seems to be in better spirits now that Rylee's come back into the living room and isn't being so hostile. She's actually chatting with him. I forgot how much they bonded back in Florida. Things are still tense, but the bottle of vodka Donny found has helped.

We all take a seat in the living room while Donny pulls out some dusty board games from his childhood. He looks like a kid in a candy store being back here, and that makes me smile.

"So, we have Clue, Chutes and Ladders, Payday..." he drones on in the background as I look over at Teo. He seems relaxed and a little tipsy. He didn't say much at dinner, but he wasn't a total dick either, so I call it a win.

"You're right, these are childish. I say we play truth or dare," Donny shouts excitedly, but Rylee just scoffs, rolling her eyes. She stands and wobbles a little.

"I am the only girl here, so if you think I'm going to play that game with you, you've lost your damn mind." She slurs a little, making me worry that she's more drunk than I thought she was. She's been going a little too heavy on the wine. From what I remember, she doesn't drink much to begin with. She's clearly a lightweight. Donny pouts and gets on his knees for her, begging. She gives in with an annoyed sigh. It's hard to ignore him when he acts like that.

He has manipulation down to a science, even Teo can't ignore his puppy eyes. She mumbles under her breath and takes a seat closer to Colt. I find myself a little jealous that she's keeping so much space between us, but I guess out of the four of us, Teo and I were the biggest dicks. I'll have to do some major groveling if I ever want to be in her good graces again.

Donny gets back up on his feet and rushes over to the switch on the wall, dimming the lights. He takes his seat once more and looks at me. "Len, truth or dare?" I roll my eyes and pick dare, because I know I don't want to deal with any truths at the moment. We've had enough confessions for tonight. He gives me an evil smile, and I groan. "I want you to grab a banana and show us how good you take Teo. Really enjoy that treat, Len."

I splutter a laugh, not expecting that, but I do what he's requested. I notice Teo is getting turned on watching me, and I find I can't stop myself from picturing his thick length in my mouth, which makes me moan and squirm as my own cock hardens. Donny stops me, and I can tell the whole room is affected by how quiet they are.

Rylee bursts out laughing, and we all look at her. "Wow, that was amateur," she snarks, crossing her arms. I find my cheeks darkening and Teo snaps.

"Well then, how about you get on your knees and show us how it's done, princess!" Rylee rolls her eyes and gives us a little smirk.

"Truth or dare, Teo?" I have a feeling things are about to get a lot more heated when he grumbles "dare", looking at her all smug. She gives him a big smile and points to me.

"I want you to blow Len while I record it with Colt's phone," she says, and Donny whoops like this is the best thing since he discovered adult grilled cheese. Teo scoffs and stands up, stretching like he's about to do a backflip or something. His shirt rises, and I lick my lips when his tanned flesh is exposed.

"Phone, please," Rylee says to Colt, holding her hand out

as Teo drops to his knees in front of me and spreads my thighs. I swallow, nervous that he's about to do this in front of people. Let alone that it's being recorded. We may have had some kind of fucked up five-some on vacation, but we tend to keep our times together alone and in private. Well, besides the few times Donny's walked in on me bent over the couch.

I groan when his large hands run up my legs to grab the waistband of my dark sweats, tugging them down and letting my cock break free. I'm so turned on I'm leaking pre-cum, leaving a sticky mess on my shirt. I reach behind my head and tug my top off, then nod toward Teo's tank top. He gives me a naughty smile but takes his shirt off too.

I forget that this is a dare, or that people are watching, when he licks my tip clean and swallows me down. I drop my head back against the couch and grip his hair tight.

"Fuck." I groan breathlessly when he starts to swirl his tongue as he bobs back up to take a breath. He shoots me a wink, then runs his finger down under my balls, pressing on that spot he knows drives me wild. I jerk my hips up, thrusting my cock deeper into his throat, and he hums.

A sound has me bringing my eyes up to Rylee's wide green orbs. She can pretend to act as unaffected as she wants, but her eyes don't lie. She is beyond turned on by watching me grip Mateo's short hair and hold him down on my cock as I choke him. I don't take my eyes off hers as I start to fuck his face harder. I pull back, letting him breathe, then start again.

Mateo reaches around and tugs on my balls, and I know I'm about to come. I bite my bottom lip, eyes still glued to

Rylee's, and groan as cum pulses out of my tip while Mateo drinks me down. I loosen my grip on his hair and he pops off before licking me clean. Like the good little cum slut he can be.

People may see us and think that Teo would top me, but it's not like that at all. We are equal in everything. That's what makes us work. I just hate that we have to stay a secret.

CHAPTER FIVE

Adonis

Teo swallows Len down with a groan before leaning up and taking his mouth in a filthy kiss. I can't hold back a groan of my own. I'm not into gay porn, but, fuck, that was so hot. I feel like I should clap or tip them or something. But that would just make things awkward.

Rylee clears her throat, shuts the phone off, and grabs the bottle of vodka from the table.

She takes a few sips before looking at me. Her cheeks are flushed and her breaths are coming a little faster. I can tell she's trying to act unaffected, but the way her nipples are practically poking out of her thin shirt, and the way her legs are crossed tells me she is. I know she's wet.

Mateo breaks the kiss and mumbles, "Delicious," against Lennox's mouth, and I think my dick is about to shoot off like a damn rocket. I glance at Colt, but he doesn't seem to even be paying attention. He's been watching Rylee this whole time, with a weird look on his face.

"Okay, so who is next?" I ask, clearing my throat. I look at Rylee, and she's giving me a 'give me your best shot' look. I'm about to throw out a dare for her, but she surprises me.

"Truth," she says with a wink, and I blanch. I only have one question for her, but I don't want to dampen the mood, so I blurt out the only other thing that's been running through my mind.

"Do you think you could ever forgive us and give us another chance?" She blinks for a few minutes, brows pinched together as if she's having trouble focusing, which is completely possible since she's just about wasted. She frowns, then runs her fingers through her messy red hair.

"I don't know," she finally whispers.

I sigh, but accept it. She didn't say no, so I'll take that, as I still have a chance.

Shortly after that Colt gets dared to twerk along to a boring song, and by the time he's done, I'm crying from laughing so hard. I never thought someone could twerk to *The Lazy Song* by Bruno Mars, but he did it.

Mateo gets up to grab us another bottle of alcohol, but I'm done. I know my Cherry is waiting to dare me, and I need to be smart about it. She's been quiet for the most part, but I've seen her crack a smile or two. It could be from the liquor, but I like to think it's just like that week in Florida. She fits with us.

"Alright, last dare. Make it count, Cherry," I taunt with a big smile, and she scowls. I don't think she likes me using my nickname for her anymore, but tough titties.

Rylee stands from the couch and wobbles over to the coffee table. Her eyes are unfocused and she looks about ten seconds away from passing out.

"I dare you to jerk Teo off," she coos, blinking at me. I burst out laughing and she looks confused. I point between Mateo and Lennox.

"Sorry, Cherry, but that's one shark pond I'm not going to swim in. Len and Teo are soulmates," I say with a wink, turning down her dare and she shrugs.

"Okay, I guess you get a punishment then," she says with a dirty smile. I'm about to crawl over to her on my hands and knees and let her punish my face with her sweet pussy, but she stops me.

"I think doing my laundry for a few months would count. Actually, I think Alex would enjoy a few months of service too." She claps and looks like she's the happiest person on the planet right now, and instead of arguing like I planned, I agree. I've missed seeing her light up like that, especially because of me.

I still crawl over to her, then give her a shitty bow.

"I am at your service, my queen," I grumble, and she laughs, reaching out to touch my cheek. Her fingers trail down to my neck, and I gulp. "Okay, I think it's time for bed, little Cherry," I coo as Rylee pets me, turning me on again. I know she's wasted, but the feel of her fingers against my flesh is making me lose my damn mind.

"I don't want to go to bed," Rylee whines, and I glance over to Colt mouthing *help*. He nods and stands up, moving over to us. He's the most sober; considering his mom's disease, he doesn't drink much. He's also been pretty quiet tonight. I can tell all these truths being revealed are taking a toll on him.

Mateo and Len are off in their own little world, making out hard. I know if we don't leave soon then one of them is about to get fucked without a care of who could be watching. I've seen enough of my best friends for one night.

We help Rylee into my parent's bedroom, and I tuck her in tight. Memories flood me of the night we all shared a bed, and I rub my chest at the ache. I turn to go, but Rylee grips my hand and stops me from leaving.

"We could have been something, Donny. All you had to do was listen. Why wasn't I worth listening to? Why am I always thrown away without a second thought?" she asks, her words a soft, sleepy murmur.

I turn to tell her she's worth so much more, and that I'm so sorry, when a soft snore hits my ears, her hand dropping from mine. I glance back at my Cherry, cuddled on her side with her red hair a mess. She looks like an angel under the glow of the moon shining in through the large bay windows.

I sigh and exit the room, leaving the door open a crack in case she needs us. Colt stands out in the hall, looking just as wrecked as me.

"What did we do, Colt?" I choke out. "We need to make this right. She didn't deserve anything that happened. I think

I'm going to be sick," I groan, and Colt follows me into the bathroom as I lose my mind, along with everything in my stomach.

He rubs my back. "We'll fix this. I'm not sure exactly how, right now, but we will," he reassures me. I hope he's right. We have to. Rylee is ours. She was always meant to be ours.

AFTER MY STOMACH finally settled last night, I passed out on the floor of my old bedroom. Colt took the bed, and I don't know where Teo and Len ended up.

When I pull myself up from the carpet, I rub my eyes and look at all the drawings pinned to the walls. I haven't been back in this house in so many years, and I should probably be having some kind of breakdown, but I think having the guys and Rylee here with me is keeping my emotions at bay.

I leave my room and head to the kitchen. I'm the first one up, so I make a pot of coffee then go sit on the porch swing outside. I always loved coming here with my parents. I miss them so much, and their ghosts are all over this house. Even this swing I'm on. They would sit here and watch as I played in the yard.

Back when all my worries consisted of watching cartoons and eating snacks. Before I was scared to go into a house and be left alone with *them*. I'm glad *they* never brought me back here. That the memory of this place wasn't tarnished or tainted.

A door creaks closed and Len walks over to me with a blanket. He sits beside me and we watch the sun rise. Sighing, he lays the blanket over us both.

"Do you ever wish you had a time machine? Where you could go back and undo just one moment?" I know he's talking about Rylee, but if I had a time machine, there are a lot of other moments I wish I could change too.

I wouldn't let my parents get in that car. I would have never let *them* touch me. I would have stopped Rylee from leaving that morning, or made her take a day off.

I nod my head, and he rocks us gently on the swing as we watch a baby deer stumble out of the woods. I smile and take some deep breaths. I feel at peace here. I don't want to leave, but I know we have to. We have competitions coming up, and I need to get my grades back on track.

Plus, we still have to discuss all that shit about Missi. I glance at Len to see he's frowning at his phone.

"So, how pissed is Missi?" I ask him, and he grunts.

"She thinks we took her toy away from her, but she's happy that Rylee is finally gone. She says her *daddy* wants to thank us. Ugh, I can't wait to be rid of her psycho ass," he grumbles, shooting off a message to someone.

I laugh, and he turns to me, raising a brow. Shaking my head, I just sigh. "Lennox, you will never be rid of her toxic ass unless you stand up to your dad. You know it's the truth, brother," I state plainly. He nods, biting his bottom lip before giving me the blanket and standing.

"We better leave soon. We have a few hours drive ahead of us." I nod, and he leaves me to keep enjoying the little bit of peace I've found before we go back to the hell that awaits us.

WE CLEAN up all of our messes, and I even make Rylee laugh as we do the dishes together. I know she's trying to distance herself after her confession last night, but I wish she wouldn't. I'm all in now, and I hope I can convince her to forgive me. I knew on that beach in Florida that Rylee was it for me. I want to beat my own ass for not listening to the whole conversation that day, or not just confronting her right then and there. I'm waiting for the guys to beat me up. I deserve it.

We pack up the meager things we brought with us and load everything back into the SUV we borrowed for this getaway. I still don't know what's going to happen with Missi, and that makes me nervous. Maybe Rylee should move in with us, or one of us should camp outside her room, so no one can get to her. I know Alex is a good dude, but even he can't follow her into the showers.

Now me, on the other hand, I will volunteer to watch Rylee get all sudsy. I'll even offer to wash her back if she washes something of mine too...

"Earth to Donny!" Mateo snaps, and I tune in to what he's saying.

"Sorry, I was thinking about taking a shower," I blurt out, and Lennox snorts next to me.

"I'm sure you were," he mumbles. I know I'm about to blush when Rylee checks out my obvious erection.

"What I was saying is that we need to come up with a plan for Missi. She's not going to like that Rylee is still here," Mateo repeats, and I nod, looking over at Rylee. Her shoulders are tense and she's biting her lip.

"Do you really think she'll try to get rid of me again?" she asks. Lennox laughs, as if she was joking, but freezes when he sees how worried she is.

I reach over and squeeze her hand. "We won't let that happen, Rylee. I think you just need to stay with us until things blow over. I know Alex is strong, but he can't be with you all the time. There are four of us and only one of him."

Rylee snorts and immediately starts to argue. I sigh, but Colt is looking at me with a smile.

"We can't force you to stay with us, Rylee. But can you agree to let one of us hang out at the coffee shop while you work, and promise that someone will be with you if you're out walking at night?"

"Wait. You're serious? You actually want to keep me safe? This is a lot to think about. Two days ago, I thought I was being kidnapped and was going to die or be sold on the black market, and now you're all being way too nice to me? Talk about a mindfuck," she says, raising a brow like we've lost our minds. When we don't say anything, she shakes her head then groans. "Fine. I will make sure Alex or Ren are with me at all times... and Colt, if you want, you may sit at a table while I work," she grumbles, and I can't help myself, I lean over and kiss her cheek to show my gratitude.

She shoves me away and wipes my kiss off, but I'm still smiling. I think with some groveling, snuggling, kitty eating, and feeding, she will come back to me.

CHAPTER SIX

Rylee

The drive back was the quietest part of this whole trip. The van was somber, as if everyone knew what going back with me meant. It wasn't going to be easy for them, but I shouldn't care. They got themselves into this mess, and then they tossed me right into the middle of it too.

They're the ones who're going to have to find a way to deal with Missi, because I'm not going anywhere.

If the kidnapping went the other way, and we didn't end up clearing up a lot of things, I still wouldn't have left.

They're afraid of Missi and what she might do. Maybe I should be too, but I don't have a lot to lose. So I'm not leaving without a fight. Not after everything I've had to endure since getting here. I haven't run after all this time, and I won't start now.

"You owe me a new phone," I tell them as I get out of the van. I don't know what happened to mine, but I must have lost it when these fuckers grabbed me.

"We will get it to you tonight," Len says.

"Thanks for the ride, I guess. Normally, kidnappers don't drop off their victims at their door when they're done. I must be special," I snark.

"Fucking brat," Mateo mutters from the driver's seat, but this time it's not filled with hostility.

"Fuck you too, Teo." I smirk, flipping him off before taking a last glance at the others. Donny looks sad, like me leaving physically pains him, and the look on Colton's face tells me he has a lot to say, but doesn't want to voice it. "Any who," I say, trying to get out of this awkward moment. "See ya later, I guess."

"I'll be by to grab your clothes soon!" Donny calls as I start to walk away.

A smile forms on my lips and I shake my head at how eager he is. It's almost like the fucker is excited to be washing our nasty clothes. Because, trust me, Alex does not smell pretty after football. I'm not bad, but after practice, I'm not smelling like flowers either.

I've already missed class yesterday and today. I don't plan on leaving my dorm room until my first class tomorrow. So a shower and an early night sounds like the best option to me.

As I'm riding up to my floor, I finally have a free moment to think. What the fuck even was the last few days? My mind is still a tornado of thoughts, and I haven't even had time to really process them.

I've being tied up and left naked in a fucking locker room, forced to relive some of my past nightmares. I've had a bunch of crazy bitches write all over me, which still hasn't fully come off. Most of it has, but there are still faint markings.

Then, I finally lose my shit and blow up at the guys, while being televised, have a mini depressive episode, before going for a walk and I end up getting nabbed by said guys.

And on top of it all, I find out that Missi doesn't just want me gone, she wants me like dead and *gone*.

Oh, and let's not forget the whole reason why the guys have treated me like fucking trash for months, and made me public enemy number one, is because Dumb and Dumber completely misheard a conversation they were never meant to hear.

So, yeah, that's my fucking life. I don't know why I'm even surprised, nothing seems to be just normal in my life. Hell, I'd probably get suspicious at this point if my life was chill.

The elevator dings and I step off, heading to my room. The moment I open the door, Ren launches herself off my bed and practically tackles me back into the hall.

"I'm so glad you're back and safe," she says as she holds me in a death grip.

"Can't breathe," I choke out.

"Babe, let the girl breathe," Alex says, helping pry Serenity off me.

She grabs me by the hand and pulls me inside the room. Alex closes the door as Serenity shoves me onto the bed.

"What the hell?!" I huff as I scramble to sit, brushing the hair out of my face as I glare up at my best friend. But she's glaring down at me, arms crossed, eyes narrowed, looking at me like a pissed off mom who found out their kid snuck out at night.

"Don't 'what the hell' me! I'm not stupid, Ry! I know you weren't just off having time to yourself. I know you better than you think I do. So, where were you really?" she asks.

I can't lie to them. I've already done it enough, and it just isn't who I am. Plus, I don't owe anyone anything when it comes to keeping this a secret, so fuck the guys.

"Short story, Missi is an even crazier bitch than we thought. She planned to get rid of me for good, and so the guys played double agents to make sure she didn't carry out her plan," I tell them, bringing my legs up on the bed and crossing them.

"Wait!" Alex says, eyes bugging out of his head. "She was going to kill you?"

"No." I snort, then my brow furrows. "Actually, now that I think about it, knowing her, it's very likely it could have ended that way."

"Jesus." Serenity sighs, sitting down on Alex's bed. He pulls her onto his lap, wrapping his arms around her. They are so damn cute together. "So wait. That's where you've been this whole time? With the guys?"

"Not like I went willingly," I say, not making the situation any better.

"What the fuck do you mean 'not willingly'?" Alex growls.

"I went out a little while after you guys left. I got bored and decided to go get something to eat, and chose to walk rather than get the food delivered. Wrong move because I didn't even make it there. I was chased down then kidnapped by four assholes."

"They didn't!" Ren gasps.

"Oh, they did. I was pissed at first. But, in the end, they explained to me why they took me. I told them I still wasn't leaving. Then they agreed that they would deal with Missi so I could worry less about staying."

"And why did they go from locking you in a fucking locker room, to helping protect you from the very bitch who they've been helping fuck with you?" Alex asks, eyes hard. He's pissed, and I think Ren in his lap is the only thing keeping him from storming out of this room and beating the shit out of the guys for what they've done.

"Because I found out why they hated me." I let out an exhausted sigh, still in shock that all of this was over some stupid miscommunication.

"Really?" Ren perks up. "Why?"

"Back when we first met at the hotel where I lived, they overheard my piece of shit ex try to get me in on some fucked up scheme to blackmail them for Lennox's money. They didn't stick around long enough to hear me tell him to fuck off and that I would never do something like that."

Rolling over, I hug one of my pillows and lay my head to the side so that I can look at both of them.

Alex's brows raise so high they almost disappear into his hairline. "You're joking, right?" he says, before bursting out into a full belly laugh. "Wow. I mean, I thought I wasn't the brightest crayon in the box, but man! These fuckers have me beat. Oh, babe, what did you see in them back then? I know they're pretty to look at, but fuck."

I can't help it, I laugh too, and so does Serenity. He's not wrong. They were fucking stupid to just conjure up all that bullshit and make me out to be some villain before even talking to me.

I know we only knew each other for that one week, but like Mateo said, I thought it meant something. If it had, they would have been smart enough to ask me. But something I've noticed during my time here is that all four of them have a past.

What that past is, I have no idea. But it's fucked with each of them in some way. Maybe that's why they chose to believe the worst of me.

Doesn't matter how damaged they might be, we all have a past. Doesn't mean we can use that as an excuse to be shitty humans though. And it's not going to give them a pass from me getting the revenge I deserve.

They might look like they regret everything, like they wish they could take it all back. Well, mostly Colton and Donny, but still, it doesn't matter. It doesn't take away the fact that they did what they did.

I plan on dishing out my own payback. I'm tired of

letting people get away with thinking they can walk all over me and I'm gonna just sit by and take it. Not anymore.

Now, I just need to come up with a plan that takes all four of them down in one shot. Because something tells me, this needs to be an all or nothing kind of job.

I'VE ONLY BEEN BACK for two days before it's time for practice and I have to face the Queen Bitch herself. I thought we were going to be at the cabin for longer than two days. I still don't know what the guys have said or done regarding her, so I don't know what to expect when I walk into practice today.

Since they dropped me off, I've only seen Donny. He dropped off a replacement phone the night we got back. He tried to come into the room and talk to me, but Alex ripped the phone from his hand, shoved a bag of dirty clothes into his arms before slamming the door in his face.

The next day, I got ready and went to my classes. Thankfully, I don't share any of them with Missi or her friends, so the next couple of days that go by are surprisingly normal.

Now it's Friday evening, and that means *cheer*. I hate that I'm dreading it, because this is something that means so much to me, something that should bring me some shreds of joy. But it doesn't.

"I can't wait to see Missi's face when you walk into that room." Serenity giggles. "She was really cocky and smug as shit on Monday, and now I know why. I can't wait to see it wiped right off her stupid face."

"Me too." I laugh, lacing my arm through hers as we walk to practice.

"Would you two slow down!" Alex shouts, running to catch up with us. "I've already run too fucking much today."

"Lay off on all the cakes that used to be in the wrappers you have stuffed in your trash can and you will be able to keep up with us," I say over my shoulder, shooting him a grin.

"Listen here, woman," he growls playfully. "Those little cakes are like an orgasm in a wrapper. Don't take that away from me."

"But the real thing is so much better," I say, looking at Ren who lights up like Rudolph's nose. "I just know Ren here does it so much better."

"Rylee," she scolds me.

"Damn right, my baby does," Alex says, grabbing her around the waist, making her squeal with a laugh. "So hard I think my dick is going to fall off. I fucking love it."

"Ahhh! So you guys finally took that step?"

"What do you think we were doing with the room all to ourselves? You came home just in time. Ren only just got the smell of sex out of there." Alex chuckles when Serenity slaps his shoulder.

"Stop it!" she hisses.

"But am I lying?" he asks her with a cocky grin, making her blush harder.

"Come on, you lovebirds, let's go face the big, bad wolf." I sigh when we get to the gym.

"No matter what the witch does, I'm here," Ren says. I wrap my arm around her shoulder.

"Thanks, babe. I don't know what I'd do without you," I say.

"Hey, what am I? Chopped liver?" Alex pouts.

"Nah, you're the big brother I never wanted." I grin.

"Ouch!" he gasps.

"I'm only fucking with you." I let go of Ren. "But really, outside of my mom, I think you're the second most important person in my life. Serenity is just behind you, but you've been the best friend anyone could ask for. I know I can depend on you for anything."

"Damn right, you can!" he says, pulling me into a hug. "If you want me to kick their asses, just say the word. You know I'm dying to."

"Thank you." I laugh. "I'll keep that in mind."

"I'm staying with you both today. I don't care if it's a closed practice. There's no way I'm leaving you alone with that crazy bitch," Alex says as we head inside the building.

"Alright, team!" Missi's voice makes me cringe. Like nails on a chalkboard. "I'm so excited to get started on some new material."

As I'm stepping into the room, the guys are coming out of the locker room. "The fuck you mean new material?" Mateo asks.

"Well, since the trash took itself out, we need to re-work everything anyway. I thought we could just change it up since we're practically starting new," Missi says, preening like she's the queen of the fucking world. I really want to punch her in her stupid smug as fuck face. And if it wouldn't get me kicked out, and would give her exactly what she wants, I'd do it.

"You're not the Captain," Colt says, his jaw ticking. He's pissed off with her. But what else is new? She brings that out in everyone. "I am. How many times do we have to go over this?"

"Oh my God," she huffs. "I'm not changing everything. Just a few things to make it work since we're down one person. Change it up a little. God," she scoffs. "And about the captain thing, I think it's about time we do a vote. Everyone who thinks I should be the new captain, raise their hands," she says.

She looks around but the only people to raise their hands, alongside hers, are her friends. Everyone else is looking around awkwardly, like they would rather be anywhere but here.

"You're kidding me, right?" she shouts. "I'm so much better than him," she whines.

"Well, since you failed in that." Donny chuckles. "Can we move on, please?"

"We don't need to change anything," Colton says.

"Yes, we do," Missi says, stomping her foot like a child. "We're down a person, everything is thrown off."

Now is the perfect time to speak up. "Ummm, unless another girl is this trash you speak of, you're not down anyone."

Missi's head snaps in my direction as I walk toward the mat. Her eyes widen before morphing into pure anger. "What the fuck is she still doing here?!" Missi screams at the top of her lungs as she turns her attention to Len. Well, shit is about to hit the fan.

"Alright. Practice is canceled for today," Colton announces to the team, since our coach isn't here. I don't think anyone minds, given the way they all get up and rush out of the room.

"You know what? A night in sounds perfect. Let's go back to the dorm and have a *Scream* marathon," I say, turning to Serenity and Alex.

As much as I'd like to see Missi get her ass handed to her, I don't want to stay for all the insults she's going to be throwing my way. Plus, this is a mess the guys created, so they can dig themselves out.

"But it was just getting good," Alex says, sounding disappointed.

"I'm sure someone will tape it and show you later," I say.

Taking one last glance at the freak-out going on over there, I lock eyes with Donny. He gives me a small smile and a nod. Like he's telling me he'll be doing this for me.

"Come on," Serenity says.

The farther we get from the gym, the lighter I feel. But I'm not stupid enough to believe that this means anything good for me. If anything, she's going to be out for more of my blood.

CHAPTER SEVEN

Lennox

I am beyond dreading this practice, and the fact that I'm sober isn't helping things. "So, how do you think Missi is going to react?" Donny asks cheerfully as we change into our practice uniforms. He has been pumped to finally hand Missi her ass.

I shrug and pull my top on. "Probably going to have a seven meltdown on the Richter Scale," I mumble, and Donny laughs before smacking my back and going to chat with Colt. I take some much needed deep breaths as Teo comes over to me.

"Are you ready for this?" he asks and I nod. He knows how much this can blow up in my face if I don't handle things with caution. He doesn't agree with it, but I think he respects how delicate everything is right now.

My father wasn't pleased about my disappearance the past few days, or my avoiding his calls. My ribs still ache from his hit to my side. I slam my locker closed and give him a quick kiss for luck, then march out to the gym. Missi is on a rant about removing Colt as captain and taking his place. I know she's been trying to convince her dad too, but he knows that Colt is the man for the job. Trophies trump his little pumpkin.

I watch as Rylee enters with Ren and Alex. She seems to have a smirk permanently fixed onto her lips as Missi pleads with people to vote for her. Teo groans and rubs his eyes. He looks exhausted, and I know his uncle has been riding him hard for a new fight. We really need to do something about that asshole, but first we need to handle Missi. I'm sick of her shit, and I know the rest of the team is too.

Even if we weren't trying to make it up to Rylee, she's still a huge asset to the Black Widows. She was given this scholarship for a reason.

"You're kidding me, right?" Missi shouts, losing her cool. "I'm so much better than him."

"Well, since you failed in that," Donny chuckles, trying to move things along.

"We don't need to change anything," Colton says.

"Yes, we do," Missi snaps, stomping her foot like a child. "We're down a person, everything is thrown off."

TAKE 'EM OUT   67

I go to correct her when Rylee makes her appearance known.

"Ummm, unless another girl is this trash you speak of, you're not down anyone."

Missi spins toward her and I watch as her stunned expression turns to rage. She opens her mouth and starts her rant, but I'm over it. It's time to deal with this shit once and for all.

Colton cancels practice and I sigh with relief. At least not everyone is going to witness this. Though I'm sure someone will record it.

Missi rushes over to me, looking like a raging bull. "What the fuck, Len? I thought you were going to get rid of her. Why the hell is she not only still in my school, but walking in here like she's a part of my fucking team?" Her nostrils flare as she shakes with anger. "She's the devil. She needs to go," she shouts, and I cringe at the pitch of her voice.

"What you were planning was fucked up, Missi. We did what we had to, not only to keep Rylee safe, but to prevent you from doing something you would regret." Missi huffs and lets out an evil little chuckle before giving me a smirk.

"Oh sweet, sweet, Lenny. Who said I would ever regret a thing? To kill a snake you must chop off its head. No one would miss that pathetic waste of a human. I was only doing humanity a solid by getting rid of that slut," she says in a husky voice as she pats my cheek. I gape at the truly psychotic woman in front of me and sigh.

"No, Missi. You need to stop all the bullshit and think about what's best for this team. No more trying to remove Colton as captain, and making the Black Widows into the

Missi show. Rylee is a kickass flyer. She will help us win Nationals and maybe even Worlds."

She sneers at me, but I shake my head. Teo looks like he's about to rip her hand off my cheek, but I plead with my eyes for him to let it go. I know I need to end things, and I'm going to, but I need some more time.

"You betrayed me. You can make it up to me by taking me to the charity event. Your mother called me last week about dress shopping and I didn't even know about it." I watch as Teo shakes his head and storms out of the gym. His shoulders are slumped and I know that I need to just bite the bullet. Rip the Band-aid off and end this shit before I lose him and wake up one morning married to this bitch.

My hands shake and I take some deep breaths. This isn't going to end well.

"Missi, we need to have a talk, and I think you're going to want to do this in private," I warn her. She rolls her eyes and dismisses her friends. Donny leaves too, but Colt stays. He takes a seat on the bleachers and gives me a nod for support.

"Leave, dweeb," Missi growls at him and he just laughs, shaking his head and crossing his arms. "Whatever," she says with a frown, then looks back at me.

My stomach is churning and I may throw up on her GUCCI sneakers. *Huh, wouldn't that be the perfect way to get her to dump my ass?*

"So, you wanted to talk?" Missi says, raising a brow as she crosses her arms, waiting for me to talk. I nod and go right for the kill.

"I don't think this is working out anymore, Mis. The lies, manipulation, attempted kidnapping, and murder... I've hit my limit," I say with a sigh, rubbing my chin. I need a nap and a drink.

"Excuse me?" she says in a deadly tone. "This is about *her,* isn't it? I just told you that I would lay off!" she snaps, and I groan.

"No, Missi, this is about how I have to watch every little fucking thing I say, so you don't go crying to Daddy. How my own mother is calling you behind my back because my father wants to force me into a marriage with someone I can't stand!" I yell, taking in a few breaths. I need to calm down.

I need to get out of here before I turn into my father and actually hit a girl. Missi is now crying, but I'm done. I'm through with this fake relationship. I don't care what deal my father has with the Dean. It's over.

Missi shakes her head, reaching out to touch me. Shuddering, I step back. "Missi, I said no! You don't have permission to touch me anymore. We need to just end this here and now. I don't care what you tell my father, but you're fucking insane, and I'm tapping out."

Shit! I probably shouldn't have called her crazy, but it's true. I watch as she turns red with rage and lifts her hand, as if to slap me. I grab her wrist and stop her.

"How dare you!" she seethes, saliva spitting through her clenched teeth with every word. She looks completely feral. I take a step away and drop her wrist, shaking my head.

"Missi, just let it go. There are plenty of other men here to marry you, and keep you dressed in diamonds and whatever else you want."

She starts to laugh maniacally, and I'm done. I nod to

Colt to come with me, but he just waves me away, continuing to watch Missi tug at her hair and pace.

"I will have your heart for this, Lennox Crane!" she screams as I leave the gym.

The door slams behind me and I smile. My shoulders feel lighter. I start walking down to the little pond that's on campus. I come here sometimes when I just need to breathe or think. It's relaxing with the ducks that like to stop by and see if I brought them any snacks. I plop down on a bench and drop my head into my hands.

I may have finally ended shit with Missi, but I still have to fix things with Teo. He looked so hurt. I wish he would have stayed longer to see me end things with that bitch. I hope he comes home tonight so we can talk.

Plus, we need to make a plan for Rylee's safety. Missi is going to be going after her now, harder than ever. Shit! Why couldn't I have just kept up the ruse? I'm going to need to find someone who can keep an eye on Missi, and report back to me without her knowing...

I'm considering my options when my phone rings. I already know who it is, and I don't want to deal with this now, but if I delay it he will only make it hurt more.

"Hello," I say with a sigh.

"What the fuck did you do?" my dad roars on the other end of the line, and even though I know he can't touch me, I flinch.

"I'm assuming Missi called you?" I ask. I might as well just get the conversation started so I can hang up sooner.

"No. That little bitch wouldn't dare call me directly. I had to hear it from her father! You have put me in a bind for the last time, son!"

he spits, and I want to laugh. What about all the fucking times he's backed me into a corner?

"Well, I guess I'm sorry then. Maybe next time you should pick someone who isn't a psychotic bitch. I tried for months to like her, but she's too shitty of a person and I'm done," I grumble, fighting not to let my voice shake with the fear he instills in me.

Ever since I was little, I've been his punching bag. My mother took the brunt of his anger until people started to ask questions, but that didn't stop him. He could get away with it with me.

Oh, Lennox, he's fine! He just took a bad tackle at practice!

Stupid boy tripped going down the stairs. I told him to pick up his toys.

Took a nasty fall on his skateboard. We've confiscated that death trap now.

He always had an excuse for my injuries, and I was so terrified that I never told anyone the truth. Not like they could help me anyway. *Lennox the Lion* is beloved and richer than anyone I knew. Who would believe his son who was just having a tantrum?

"You will be sorry if you don't fix this. Now, go buy Missi something pretty and sparkly and fix this! While I try to talk her dad off a ledge! Do you hear me, Lennox? Or so help me!

"No, Dad, you listen to me for once!" I snap. "You might be okay with making your child miserable if it benefits you. But I will not continue to hurt the people I love!" I roar, and he's quiet for a minute, but I can hear him panting.

"And who is it you're hurting, Lennox? Is it the happy go lucky one, or is it Colt? I always thought he was a little too nerdy to be

your friend," my father says caustically. "*No, no. You wouldn't be this worked up if it was them. It's the misfit... Mateo, isn't it? How are you hurting him? Huh? I want you to tell me from your own mouth that my son likes to stick his dick where it doesn't belong.*"

A tear falls down my cheek and I wipe it away with a laugh. "You got me, Dad. I guess you've known all along that your son likes to take a cock up his ass. Let someone make him their little bitch, since that's all you've ever treated me as. Congrats. Now I'm going to hang up and go bend over for someone."

I end the call and let the emotions run over me as I sit here alone, wishing someone could hold me. Could love me for who I am.

I wait a few minutes to see if he'll call me back before giving up and walking back to the house. I take my time and grab a coffee, seeing if maybe I'll run into Rylee. She's not there, which makes sense since we were supposed to be at practice. I reach the house and my stomach growls.

A few girls say hi as I enter the front door, but I'm not in the mood to gossip, or for Missi to find me. I should probably talk to the guys about moving into our own place. Maybe in a few months we can convince Rylee to come too. I hope she doesn't think that we're through with her. I fell for her after forty-eight hours, and though I was angry and hurt, I still have those feelings.

I stomp up the stairs to our apartment, texting Teo. I wonder if he's home. We really need to talk. I want him to know, once and for all, what he truly means to me. I open the door and I'm immediately blindsided when I call out for Teo.

A fist hits me on my temple and I wobble sideways. It's dark and I don't know who hit me, but they smell like a brewery. I grip the wall and blink a few times. My head throbs and my vision is blurry.

"How fucking dare you hang up on me," the person who hit me growls, and I know I'm fucked. My dad is a beast when he's sober, but drunk... I've spent many nights in the hospital after being a punching bag for my alcoholic father's ass.

"Wow, really hitting me below the belt today, Dad. Couldn't even let me through the door before trying to knock me out," I goad him. I know that this is going to end up bad, but I don't care.

All my secrets are now out in the open, and even if he beats me to death tonight, I feel free. I just wish I could have told Mateo that I love him.

CHAPTER EIGHT

Adonis

L ennox and Missi start shouting, and as much as I
  wish I could stay and watch, I still need to finish
  Rylee's laundry. Since practice is canceled, I leave
the fight of the year with a pout and march back to the
house. I want to make Rylee happy, so I will be the best laun-
dromat that there ever was. I swing by and grab the bag of
dirty clothes, then head to the laundry room we have on the
second floor.

A few of the girls are around doing their own washing,
but I ignore them. They are gossiping about what happened

at practice, and I'm not in the mood to deal with it. Missi is finally about to get what she deserves, and I'm nervous about how things are going to go with Lennox and his dad, and also about Rylee.

Missi is going to be on the warpath. At least Colt said he will be with Rylee when she works. I still think she should just move in here with us. That way I'll know she's safe.

Ash and Lea leave the room and I turn on my Spotify app, cranking it loud, as I finish up Rylee's clothes. I'm not folding Alex's, he is one nasty mofo. Seriously, does this guy even shower? Some of his socks were so sweat-soaked they were crunchy.

Fucking nasty!

I shove his clean shit back into the bag, and finish up folding Rylee's stuff. I'm holding a pair of lacy pink panties and I'm struggling not to shove them into my pocket. I give them a loving caress and sigh.

"Next time, my love," I coo, then turn my music off and toss them into the basket I'm using to deliver her stuff.

Knowing my luck, Rylee will check all her laundry. Fuck, why does she make me so hard? Even her panties have me wanting to bust in my shorts.

I groan, then grab the basket and toss the bag on top before heading to the kitchen for a snack.

I'm starving. It's thankfully empty. I grab a pre-made sandwich then head toward our floor. I need to change before I drop off Rylee's stuff.

I'm almost to our door when shouting reaches my ears. I roll my eyes and keep walking. Seriously, if Len and Teo are at it again, I'm getting a new room. I'd rather sleep in Felicia's shoe closet than be a first-hand witness to their toxicity.

I thought they fixed their shit at the cabin.

I open the door and storm in, about to give them a piece of my mind, when Len's father punches him in the face, causing him to fall to the ground. He looks like a bear on steroids, and my hands shake. I clench the basket tighter and take a few breaths.

Len climbs to his feet, and I want to tell him to stay down, but my mouth won't open.

Len steps closer to his father, egging him on with blood running down his face from a split in his eyebrow.

"What now, Dad? You going to kill me because I'm no longer going to be your puppet?" Len screams, and I take a step back toward the door.

My back presses against the wood and I close my eyes to drown out the sound of flesh hitting flesh.

It brings me back to a time when I was little, and helpless from keeping *his* hands off me. When I tried to fight back, but I was only ten. The perfect prey.

"You know your place, boy. You will call Missi and apologize, or I will end you," Mr. Matthews shouts between hits.

My stomach turns and I know I'm about to be sick.

I slide down until I'm on the floor. The laundry basket is dumped next to me, but I don't register it.

All I can see is *him* coming closer to me. Telling me how beautiful I am. His perfect boy.

"Who's my good boy, Adonis?" His hand runs along my thigh as I quiver in fear.

A yell pulls me back to Lennox laying on the floor in front of me, telling me to get out of here.

"Go, Don, get out of here! Please!" he begs as I sit here silently crying and covering my ears with my hands, shaking.

"What's he crying for? You fucking him too?" Lennox's dad slurs, and I look up at him with a glare full of hate. I climb to my feet and take a step closer to the monster in the room.

The one my brother has nightmares about! Len grabs my ankle and holds me back. I look down at him and he shakes his head.

"Go, Donny," he grunts, climbing to his feet.

"Yeah, boy, get the fuck out of here before I show you just how I feel about guys who suck cock!"

I'm trembling as I grab the basket and throw the door open before hauling ass. I need to get out of here. Away from Len and his dad. I pull my phone out and call Colton. He will know what to do. He always knows.

My hands are shaking so bad and my breaths are coming too fast. I think I'm going to pass out. Colt answers and I struggle to say "home" before ending the call. I need to get away. I need to hide. Somewhere safe where he can't find me. I need her.

I storm into the dorm building and up the steps until I reach her door. I think I knock, or maybe I bang on the wood. I don't know. I'm having trouble seeing through my tears. I just need help.

"Please," I choke out as the door's thrown open. Rylee steps out, about to yell at me, but she stops. I shove her basket into her hands and she glances down.

"Adonis, what's wrong? I don't understand," she says, and I look at the empty basket in her hands. All of her things must have fallen out. I drop to my knees and pull the basket away, chucking it inside her room, then wrap my arms around her middle and let myself fall apart.

Right here in her doorway, with people watching me, I feel safe.

I stare down at him in shock, confused about what the hell is going on. Donny is clinging to my legs, crying about something I can't quite make out. But this isn't one of his normal over-dramatic stunts. No, he's genuinely upset about something.

I don't know why of all people he would come to me, but I can't just send him away, can I? I'm not that much of a bitch.

Looking up, I see people poking their heads out of their dorms. Nosy people who are always looking for something to record. Not wanting to give them the chance to whip out their phones, I run my fingers through Donny's blond strands.

"Do you wanna come in and talk?" I ask, my voice soft.

He doesn't say anything, but gets to his feet and stumbles

his way into my room. Closing the door behind him, I turn to see him standing in the middle of the room looking broken. His head is hung low, his shoulders curled in on himself. Something inside me feels for him. This isn't like Donny. I've never seen him like this. For some reason, that doesn't feel right to me.

He clearly needs someone, and I don't have it in me to tell him no. Putting aside everything that's happened the past few days, I let out a heavy sigh as he watches me walk over to my bed.

I'm only in a pair of sleep shorts and one of Alex's shirts I stole from him, but I get under the blanket and hold it open for Donny.

He doesn't even hesitate before crashing into the bed next to me. "Oouf!" I grunt as he knocks the air out of me. He snuggles into me, wrapping his arms around my body and pulling me close.

His hold on me is almost crushing as he lets out the smallest of sighs, like being here with me makes him feel the smallest bit better. My heart does a stupid little flutter.

Pulling the blanket over him, I bring my hand up to his hair as I start to play with the silky strands. "Do you want to talk about it?" I whisper. Anything louder just doesn't feel right at this moment?

He shakes his head, his face pressing into the crook of my neck. "Just don't leave me." His words are so quiet that if the room wasn't dead silent, I would have missed it.

Not knowing what to do or what to say, we just lay here. Eventually, Donny falls asleep. His soft snores fill the room as I continue to absently play with his hair, my nails lightly scratching his head as I stare at the ticking clock on the wall.

I don't even know I've fallen asleep until I hear the door open.

"Hey, Ry–"

My eyes flutter open to see Alex standing by the door, halfway inside the room. He looks at Donny, then me. His brows shoot up in mock horror as he goes to speak.

Quickly, I bring my finger to my lips as I give him a warning stare.

He glares back at me disapprovingly before closing the door behind him. "What the fuck, Rylee?" he whispers as he takes a seat on his bed.

"It's not what it looks like," I murmur back.

"Really?" he asks, raising a brow.

I roll my eyes. "He came to the door upset. I couldn't turn him away."

"Yeah, you could have," he says. "It's easy. Slam the door in his face."

"Alex." I sigh. "Look, he needed someone. He looked pretty messed up emotionally. And it's just not in me to be like that, no matter how much he deserves it."

"You're too nice, Rylee. After everything he and his friends did, you should tell him to eat shit. Maybe kick him in the balls. I mean, if you don't want to, I'll gladly do it," he says, and starts to get up.

"Sit down!" I whisper-hiss.

He listens, giving me a pout. "You're no fun."

I just give him the stink eye in return. "He will be gone by morning."

"He better. I love you, Rylee, and that's why I'm not going to just sit by and let you forgive him so easily."

"I wouldn't," I tell him. At least, I don't think I would. I have a plan and I'm going to stick with it.

"Ren and I wouldn't let you even if you planned to," he says. He glances at the back of Donny's head and gives him a glaring look before shaking his head. "You're too damn good for them, Ry. They will never deserve you."

"I know."

"Also, what the heck is up with the empty basket?"

Giving him a little shrug, I remember Donny handing it to me but there was nothing in it. "I don't know," I tell him. Whatever happened tonight had him shaken up, and I hate that I really want to know what it was that had him so upset.

There's something about these boys I just can't let go of. Like, if I dig deeper, maybe I'll find out why they are the way they are.

Alex gets ready for the night, before slipping into his bed and falling asleep almost immediately.

Of course, now I'm wide awake.

Feeling my arm going numb, I shift my body into a new position, trying not to wake Donny. "Rylee," he moans, still deep in his sleep as he tosses his leg over me. My eyes go wide as I feel something... hard pressed against me.

Biting my lips together, I try not to laugh. At least he's having happy dreams and is not plagued by whatever had him so messed up before.

"Oh, Donny," I whisper. "What am I going to do with you?"

CHAPTER NINE

Mateo

After leaving practice, I walk around for a little while. I need to clear my head and not turn around and storm back into that gym and reveal my relationship with Len. No matter how bad I want to, I can't do that to him.

He has enough shit on his plate right now. I just wish he would get the hint and choose me over Missi and his dad. I would protect him. I might be broke as shit, but I'd make him happy. I'd even let him keep seeing Rylee.

As for me and Rylee, I think some distance is needed.

I'm still not sure I even believe what she said. I've been burned too many times in my life to just take someone at their word.

I pass the coffee shop, but don't stop. I think I just need to get off campus altogether. I pull my phone out and call Ma. Her and my sister are staying at a friend's house for a few weeks, but I miss Nando. She doesn't pick up, so I send Brenna a quick text letting her know I'm swinging by the house, then I walk over to the parking lot for my bike.

The weather is okay today, so it should be fine to ride. Once I leave campus and hit the highway, I increase my speed and let the wind take away some of my frustration. I drive along the coast and enjoy the tranquility until the nice beachfront properties turn into smog-filled air and hustlers on the corner trying to sell you something.

One day, I am going to get my family out of this neighborhood and into one of those mansions on the water. I am going to give my ma a better future. One where she can relax and enjoy her retirement.

I pull up in front of the house and groan. The yard looks like shit. I haven't had much time to come by with all the Rylee drama. I park in the driveway and don't even bother going to the front door. I swing by the garage and grab the lawnmower and weed wacker, then get to work.

I'M DRIPPING with sweat when the black car pulls up on the side of the road and parks. Fuck! I do not need his bullshit today. Angelo climbs out and opens the back door for my uncle.

My Tio fixes his suit as he walks closer to me. "Ah, my boy. I was wondering when you were going to show up. I've had my guys watching the house." I turn the mower off and cross my arms. "Your ma seems to be away. That's not smart, Teo. Where is she?"

I shake my head and laugh. "Yeah, I'm not telling ya shit, Tio. What can I do for you? As you can tell, I'm a little busy here." I grunt, and watch as his calm demeanor switches into the big, bad boss. He used to scare me, but honestly, I think Missi is more terrifying at the moment. My uncle is too predictable, and I've learnt his tells. So when his fist swings up and toward my right cheek, I block him easily.

"Is that really why you're here, Uncle? To fight me in my front yard, where all these people will watch as I put you in your place?" I know I'm asking for a beating, and honestly, right now, I would welcome the pain.

He gives me a shark-like grin and nods to the car. "We have a fight tonight. I was going to call your cousin, Anthony, but I think you will take his place now." I laugh and he narrows his brown eyes.

I turn my back to him and grab the lawn shit. I was almost done with trimming the sides when he pulled up. I didn't plan to fight for him again, but maybe I need to beat the shit out of someone. Then I can go back home and deal with the Len and Missi aftermath with a clear head and an exhausted body.

THIS WAS A MISTAKE. My opponent wasn't made for my body weight or the way my blood is heated. I know this is going to be bad, but when his first strike hits my ribs, a red haze comes over me and I attack.

His blond hair turns dark, and his blue eyes become my uncle's eyes. I want to destroy him, and I don't stop until someone pulls me off his lifeless body. My past is coming back to haunt me, and I want to end him.

"What the fuck, Mateo?" my uncle roars, and I give him a bloody grin. Isn't this who he wanted me to be? Ruthless, unstoppable, a monster? The crowd is going crazy, and I don't fight it when Anthony pulls me into the locker room, or when Angelo starts using my ribs and chest like his personal punching bag.

I just smile and absorb the pain, and the numbness it brings. I don't think about Lennox and how I'll never be anything to him. I don't think about the clusterfuck that is Rylee. I zone out and let it happen until my uncle barks, "Enough," and they leave me there on the cold tiles.

I must have drifted off because a phone ringing pulls me back to the present and how fucking sore I am. I groan and crawl over to my pants that are still lying on the bench. By the time I unlock my phone, I've missed the call, but the text from Colt chills my blood and has me racing to get dressed.

I don't even feel the pain as I order an UBER and race back to school. When I reach the house, all the girls are in bed and it's quiet, but I know it won't be for long. I storm through the front door, not caring how loud I am being, and stomp down the stairs to our apartment. The door is cracked open, and when I enter, I'm ready to lose my shit again.

Furniture is smashed throughout the space and there is blood... so much blood. Colt is crying in the kitchen, holding Lennox in his arms. He looks up at me when I crouch beside them.

"He won't let me call an ambulance. He started to thrash and argue, but Teo—he needs help," Colt whispers and I nod.

My heart is racing and my hands are shaking. It's one thing to be the one always so broken and bloody, but to see him like this... I feel like my world is ending, and I would do anything to keep him safe. Even if that means my own demise in the aftermath.

"Help me get him into the shower and I'll take it from here. Where is Donny?" I ask, trying to keep my head straight and he shrugs. I lean closer to Lennox and move some of his hair off his cheek. His lip is split and there is a gash above his eye, where I think the most blood is flowing from. His eyes are closed as he sleeps, but they are a mottled mess of dried blood and bruises.

"Baby, who did this?" I ask him as he stirs, but I already have an idea. What I want to know is why? Lennox has been his perfect little follower. He does anything and everything his dad asks him to.

I glance over at Colt and he looks sick. "Can you grab me a wet washcloth and the first aid kit from my bathroom?" I grunt, and he climbs to his feet and rushes off. Lennox groans in pain and I want to burn the whole world down. This isn't a small fight, he's really fucked up. His eyes flutter open and he winces from the bright lights of the kitchen.

"Fuck," he moans. I continue to gently play with his hair, avoiding the small gash on his skull. Colt is right, he really should go to the hospital. But I won't force him. I lean my back against the refrigerator and sigh. I'm fucking exhausted, and I know in the morning, I probably won't be able to move either.

"I told him the truth," Len whispers and I look back down at him. One eye is swollen shut, but the other pierces me. "I told him about us. I couldn't keep lying to him and hurting you." He groans as he pulls away from me and tries to sit up. I help him, my hands shaking from his revelation.

My heart lurches as I see the aftermath of his declaration of love.

The sight of him broken, bloody, and defeated has me wanting to track that motherfucker down and read him his Last Rites.

Colt comes back and hands me the medical kit. Lennox won't stop looking at me, waiting for my response. But I don't know what to say. He finally told him, but at what price? He's laying here barely conscious. He's hurt because of it.

"Say something," he urges and I shake my head, then clear my throat.

"I always wanted you to tell him, to tell the world how much you cared about me, but not like this. It hurt me when you were with Missi, but seeing you like this hurts me more.

I'm so sorry you felt you had to tell him to keep me. So damn sorry," I rasp.

Colt excuses himself from the room and says he's going to bed. I don't blame him. Lennox's eyes fill with tears and he snorts. "I didn't just do this for you, Teo. I did this for myself. For us to have a future. To maybe, someday, be happy."

I grab the washcloth and start to gently clean off his face so I can assess all the damage done. It's not as bad as it looked and I sigh.

"One of my biggest regrets would be hurting you—in this life or the next. I'm not a good person, Lennox. I'm dangerous. I would never put my hands on you, but my uncle's influence is too powerful. I'm not going to have a happily ever after. I won't drag you down with me. I'm glad your dad knows now, so you can get away from Missi's claws..."

He shuts me up with a kiss to my lips. I groan and press my mouth harder to his until he winces and I feel like an asshole. I forgot about the split in his lip and it starts to bleed again. I press another softer kiss to his lips before licking the blood away. He groans and I shake my head with a small laugh.

"This won't end up with rings, a white picket fence, and babies, Lennox," I say with a sad smile.

"You don't give yourself enough credit, Teo." He grunts and I grab some cream for his cuts, then place some butterfly bandages on them. "I wouldn't have done what I did today if I didn't see a future for us. I see all of us—Colt, Rylee, and Donny—on a beach somewhere. Playing in the water, and bonfires at night. I see us happy and finally free."

I close my eyes and shake my head, trying to imagine what he's proposing. *This can't happen outside of his dreams, can it?*

"I would love to believe she'd want anything to do with us, but it's hard. She lied to us, but we fucked up too. Why would she want us now?" I ask.

He gives me a smile. "Well, considering we aren't in jail right now for kidnapping her, I'd say we have a pretty good shot at a second chance, Teo."

I blow out a breath with a nod. "We need to change some things then, Lennox. You've let all of this hiding and self-hatred fuel your addiction. We need to cut the bullshit, stop drinking, and work on getting Rylee to forgive us. I want our happy ending, but it's not going to be easy. So much is fucked up and twisted," I tell him.

Lennox thinks as he nods. "No more bullshit, drinking, or hiding. I can do that," he murmurs, wincing as he shifts his weight and hurts his side. I laugh and pull him closer to me so he can rest his head on my shoulder.

"Practice is going to be a bloodbath tomorrow," I groan and he laughs.

"Aren't we a pair? Both bruised to the nines, our bodies and egos." He groans and I hold him a little tighter.

"Donny is never going to let us live this down, you know?" I say and Len gasps.

"Fuck, he was here. He saw what my dad was doing and started to panic. I told him to run. That was hours ago; he should have been back by now." Lennox tries to climb to his feet but his legs are too shaky and his knees give out.

"Hey, it's okay. Let me help you and then we can call

him." I shuffle to my feet and try not to show how abused my ribs and side are, then gently pull Lennox up and over to the couch. I try calling Donny but it goes to voicemail. It's already three in the morning so I shrug.

"He's probably okay and just crashing at a friend's. We will find him in the morning, but right now, we need a shower, pain pills, and sleep—in that order," I grunt, and Lennox curls up closer to me on the couch.

My eyes are heavy and the warmth of his body against mine is putting me in a trance. Maybe I'll just rest here for a few minutes more...

CHAPTER TEN

Adonis

A light shines in my face and I groan, trying to move, but I'm being held down. My heart starts to race and I feel my breath starts to quicken until a soft breath hits my neck and I instantly calm. I open my eyes and glance at the sleeping angel on my chest. I want to hold her tighter, but she might wake up, and I don't want this moment to end.

The night before flashes back to me and I softly groan. I need to get back to the apartment. I never did get Len help. I'm a shit friend. He knew I was panicking and sent me away, but all I did was break down in Rylee's arms. I never told her that Lennox was in trouble.

I wiggle my arm under the covers and into my pocket for my phone. I'm surprised no one tried to get a hold of me last night. Oh, that makes sense. The phone is dead, and I really need to pee. I give Rylee a quick kiss on her temple and breathe in her scent before gently rolling over her and climbing from the bed. I tuck her in and she curls up into the pillow that I was using with a small sigh.

I can't help but to gently run my fingers through her hair before turning and searching for my shoes. I don't see them anywhere, and honestly, I can't remember if I was even wearing any. I laugh quietly and shake my head when piercing green eyes meet mine.

"Fuck," I gasp and grab my chest. Alex glances between Rylee and me, then frowns. I don't know what he's thinking about, but I should probably leave before he gives me the best friend special and hits me. I know I deserve it, but after the violence I saw last night... It's too soon.

I glance one more time at Rylee then turn and leave. The dorm is quiet as I sneak out and my stomach growls. I never did eat dinner. Sometimes when my emotions get the best of me, I end up skipping meals and that only makes things worse. Being locked up and starved as a child can cause irreparable damage, and now that I'm free, I eat... a lot.

I walk over to the small coffee shop and give the barista my biggest smile when she glares at me for not wearing shoes. I order two drinks and a bacon, egg, cheese, sausage, and ham croissant, with a large hash brown, and a breakfast burrito.

When she calls my name and hands me the tray with my food, I can't help but to do a happy dance. Walking back outside, I rip open my burrito and demolish it before starting in on the croissant. They always make them so hot, and I almost drop the coffees when scalding cheese drips onto my lip.

"Ugh," I whimper as I reach Rylee's dorm's front door. I quickly polish off the rest of my food, pull out some gum from my pocket, and make the walk to her room. I didn't get myself a drink, and I'm starting to realize that was a bad idea. I contemplate taking a sip of one of the coffees I'm holding.

No, Donny! You're trying to get brownie points right now. I sigh and lift my hand to knock, but the voices inside have me stopping and smiling. Rylee is defending me to Alex, and if my chest puffs up a little bit, no one is here to judge. I press a little closer and try to hear more. She's denying that she feels anything for me, but I know she's bluffing.

That girl held me like I was precious in my time of need, she even played with my hair. Not to mention she was wrapped around me like a Boa constrictor this morning. I know I still have a long way to go to earn back her trust, but the fact that she didn't toss me out last night proves that she has feelings for me.

I bite my lip and try not to do a little happy jig right there in front of her room. I have a chance! That's seriously the best news I've had in a long time. I try to wipe the smirk from my lips, then I knock on the door.

"Seriously! What the fuck now?" is shouted from inside and I laugh, holding up the tray of drinks as a peace offering when

Rylee throws the door open. She pauses a moment and her scowl lessens, so I'm calling it a win.

"These are for you both. I just wanted to say thanks for letting me crash here last night. I'll see ya later, Cherry," I say quickly then hand her the tray and turn to leave.

I'm about five steps away when I here Alex shout, "Yo, Adonis, where the fuck are my boxers?" And I lose it, laughing my ass off as I walk home.

Last night was a shit show, but today the sun is shining and my girl doesn't hate me as much as I thought. It's a damn good day!

I wake up on the couch, wrapped in Teo's arms. Someone must have covered us with a blanket, and I groan as I shift. My body feels like I was hit by a truck, and it's hard to see out of one of my eyes. I should have grabbed some ice before crashing, but that thought never crossed my mind.

Someone coughs from the doorway and Colt is standing there with a tray of coffees and a bag of something sweet. Probably donuts. My stomach twists at the thought of food, but I'll take a coffee. I gently remove Teo's arms from around me and sit up on the couch. He doesn't even stir and I shake my head, smiling. My lip cracks and I wince at the reminder of how much damage my father did last night. I'm surprised I'm even still alive.

"How are you feeling?" Colton asks as he hands me a coffee with two creams and hazelnut syrup. I shrug and he frowns. My hands shake as I set the cup on the coffee table and try to stand, but I'm dizzy all of a sudden. Shit. I probably should go get checked out. Knowing my dad's hits, I probably have a concussion at the very least.

"Can you grab me some pain pills?" I ask Colt and he hops up. "And an ice pack." I groan and he nods. Teo starts to move behind me and I flinch when he brushes my ribs. He groans and then sighs.

"Fuck, I'm sorry, baby," he says, then gently moves to sit next to me and grabs one of the coffees from the tray. I glance over his body and pause at the dark bruises on his cheek, eye, and ribs. Wow, aren't we just a pair.

Colt comes back with the stuff I asked for and a bottle of water. I dish out some pills and pass them to Teo, then swallow my own down, praying they work fast. Colt takes a seat on the coffee table in front of us and he looks nervous.

"I can't reach Donny. And from what you said last night about him having a panic attack, I'm starting to worry. I think maybe we should try Rylee's room. Her laundry is all over the floor, but I don't see a basket."

I raise my brow at that and nod. I never wanted Donny to be around when my dad is in one of his moods. Aggressive behavior from male adults is one of his triggers. He hasn't told us much about his childhood, but I know that he was hurt badly by people he trusted. We're all a little damaged. I think that's what makes us so close.

"Have you tried maybe calling Rylee?" I ask before trying to stand again. I really need to take a shower and get these nasty clothes off me. I feel disgusting, and I need to wash away the feeling of his hands on me. This time Teo helps me and I give him a smile of gratitude. He could do with a shower too.

"Yeah, but her phone seems to be off too..."

The front door bursts open and Donny is standing there with a shit eating grin on his face. Well, he seems perfectly okay to me.

"Good morning," he sing-songs then slams the door and marches straight over to Teo and kisses him on the lips. I blink a few times to make sure I'm not hallucinating, and Teo looks about to punch him.

"Donny, what the fuck?" Teo growls, then wipes his mouth off, but Don doesn't seem to care. Colton shuffles closer to us and grabs him, looking deep into his eyes. Probably checking to make sure he's not on drugs. Donny laughs and shoves him away.

"I'm fine. Chill. I just had a great night's sleep is all." He gives us one more smile before sobering up. "Holy shit. Are you guys okay? I... I forgot, Len. Your dad." His face turns pale and he looks like he's about to have a flashback.

I grip his hand and pull him into a hug, ignoring the way my ribs throb. "I'm okay, Donny. Take some deep breaths," I say softly and his shaking starts to calm down.

"I'm so, so sorry, Len. You told me to leave and I did. I was going to get you help, but the panic became too much and I found myself at Rylee's dorm." I give him one more squeeze then let him go.

"I'm fine, but I really want to take a shower. Let's all have a chat once I'm done, okay? I think there are some things we need to talk about. You guys left practice early and a lot went down... Holy fuck. I can't believe it was only yesterday," I say with a sigh.

Teo grunts and starts to lead me toward my room.

"Is one of those donuts for me?" Donny asks Colton and I shake my head. He's going to be fine if he's already thinking about food.

THE SHOWER HURTS LIKE A BITCH, but after the stinging goes away, it feels amazing. Teo left me alone and went to his own bathroom, for which I'm grateful. I knew the moment I was by myself I would break down.

I should be used to all this shit by now, but I think somewhere deep down inside, I still wish my dad loved me. I was always envious of my friends on the football team when they had fathers who would give them hugs and tell them how proud they were.

I would get snide remarks as he pointed out all my flaws, then in the privacy of home, I would get a few hits to the ribs and back. Win or lose, I could never make him happy.

I finish rinsing my hair, then turn the water off and get out. I'm going to have to call Coach and fake that Teo and I are sick. I know that she will freak out if she sees either one of us, and I can't lift any girls right now, or do any jumps. It's a hardship just trying to pull on some boxers.

I grab a pair of sweatpants and a zip-up hoodie and call it a day. When I reach the living room, Donny and Colt are in a deep discussion. I grab my lukewarm coffee and shuffle over to the chair. The guys stop talking and give me a glare.

"What?" I grumble, and Colt rolls his eyes.

"You should be in a hospital bed right now, Lennox," he snaps, and I can tell finding me half-dead last night affected him too. I sigh and run my hand over my damp hair.

"If I agree to go to urgent care later, will you drop the hospital? I can't go there or it will just set my dad off again." Teo chooses that moment to return, and I can tell he's on the verge of killing my dad.

"I told my dad last night about Teo and I. That's why he lost all control, and yeah, I'm going to be fucking sore for days and will have to miss practice, but I would do it all again. I'm sick of hiding shit, and I really don't want to be near Missi again."

"Wait, so your dad knows that Teo and you are…" Donny puts his tongue in his cheek and moves his hand like he's giving someone a blow job. I snort and roll my eyes as Colton leans forward and smacks him on the back of his head. He bursts out laughing and I find myself smiling.

"Yeah, Don, he knows we're together. So now all that we need to do is come up with a plan to get Rylee back into our fucked up wagon of misfits, and all will be right with the world again," I say, ignoring how Teo is glaring at me at the mention of our girl. He's going to have to get over his shit and accept that Rylee belongs with us.

"Hell yes! That's what I'm talking about," Donny shouts, then pulls out his phone and starts making a list of things we could do to make shit up to her. I stop him after he starts to rant about getting matching tattoos of 'Rylee, we're assholes'.

"Okay, I like the energy, Don, but nothing permanent. How about we start small and work our way up? Like leaving her little surprises every day?"

"That could work, but I don't think we should take any credit for it. Like leaving something at her door anonymously," Colt chimes in and I nod. My head is heavy and I blink a few times to wake up.

"Teo, what do you think?" I ask, bringing him into this conversation, because it won't work if we're not all on board.

"I think the princess is spoiled enough, but fine. I could see myself leaving her surprises, but I don't think we need to go crazy," he grumbles. "She fucked up too, and I don't see her bending over backwards to apologize."

Sighing, I shake my head. "You're misunderstanding. Our shit still outweighs hers, and I want us to be a family. She belongs with us. We just need her to accept it. This won't work if you're not into it, Teo. Rylee can smell bullshit, and she doesn't trust us. Can you just try, for me?"

"You guys are really serious about this, aren't you?" he asks, looking around the room at us. Donny is nodding and bouncing around like a hyper puppy, and Colton gives him a smile. He turns to me last and I reach out my hand for his.

"That week in Florida, before all the bullshit, are some of my favorite memories. And yes, it's because of you and the guys, but it's also because I fell in love with a red-headed temptress, and she opened our eyes to something incredible. Now I want that feeling back." I grunt as he pulls me to my feet to make us eye level.

I know he has trouble trusting people, and he's especially not good at forgiveness, but I hope he will at least try for us. We're all a family here in this basement apartment, and Rylee is our missing piece. She's sunshine and spice, and I want her back.

I know we've made mistakes, but even assholes deserve a little grace, right?

Teo growls under his breath. "I loved our trip. It was what we all needed, and I thought Rylee was our dream girl. I'll try, because you asked. I won't hesitate to put her over my knee if she's a brat though."

I chuckle with a shrug. It's better than nothing, though she may enjoy it too. I consider it a win.

"The two of you will be so much fun together." I grin. "I can't wait to watch."

Teo rolls his eyes and I grab him behind the neck, kissing him hard.

"Alright, enough fucking around, love birds," Donny snarks. "Here's the plan..."

CHAPTER ELEVEN

Rylee

Life has gone back to normal, for the most part. Practice is still tense. The death stares and snide remarks I get from Missi aren't missed. I know she's planning something, I just don't know what. I don't think she's going to risk hurting me again, at least I hope not. Too many witnesses, and evidence that can be used against her.

That still doesn't stop her from openly showing her hate for me. Not that I care. But the strangest thing of all is that I feel the safest now that the guys are my base for stunts, than

I have since I started at the school. We've had the least amount of fuck-ups, when it comes to me and the guys, than anyone else on the team.

That makes Colton happy. Every time things go perfectly, his face lights up with an adorable smile. He also does this little fist pump thing. I don't think he knows anyone notices, but I do.

When it comes to the guys, I've been noticing too much lately. It's like now that I don't completely hate them, and they are no longer out to get me, I've been paying closer attention to them.

Like the way Donny's cheeks dimple when he smiles one of his real smiles, not the ones he puts on for show.

Or the way Mateo watches Lennox when he's talking, the smallest smirk on his lips shows just how much he loves him.

Lennox is always watching, paying attention to what his friends are saying, like every bit is important to him.

But the biggest change that I've noticed is how they treat me. No more name calling. No more cold looks. They try to talk to me, ask me how I'm doing.

Donny has been doing a pretty good job at keeping up with mine and Alex's laundry, too. Although, I'm going to have to ask him what machines he's using because I've been noticing my underwear has slowly started to go missing. I know how easily smaller things can get eaten up by a washer, or get lost in the dryer.

Even with the way they've changed, I haven't forgotten what they did to me. The part they played in Missi's fucked up torture plan.

So that brings me to today. I'm going to the store after work to get everything I need for my first round of revenge.

After we got back from the cabin, I spent hours trying to come up with ways to fuck the guys over, to make them feel the pain I felt.

And although they deserve it, in the end, it's not me. I'm not going to stoop to their level. I don't want to physically hurt anyone. But I'm not going to just let them get away with it. I might not get to see them feel the same pain I did, but I can make their life as much of an inconvenience as possible.

So that means pranks. All the stupid, childish pranks I can think of. I've been grown up for way too long—longer than I should have had to be, so now seems like as good a time as any to have a little fun of my own.

I'm just about to close up from my Sunday afternoon shift, when Colton walks through the door.

"Hey," he says, giving me a shy smile.

"Hi," I say back. "We're just about to close. The best I can offer you is a baked good or a regular coffee."

"Oh no, I'm not here to get anything. I just wanted to give you this," he says, laying some papers down on the counter. "I was able to get access to the practice exam. I thought your best chance at doing well on finals was if we get a head start on it now." He pushes his glasses up his nose, and I have to tell myself to shut up when I think about how adorable he looks.

"Isn't that cheating?" I ask, raising a brow, my lips tipping into a smile.

"Maybe?" he says, blinking at me. "I didn't think of it that way."

"Thank you," I tell him. "I know it's been a while since we had a tutoring session, but I do think we should start them back up before I fall behind."

"I agree." He nods. "How about we keep our regular after-practice days, but maybe add in Wednesday night? You know, if you're not busy or anything."

"No, I think that would work." I nod.

"Perfect." He smiles, and *gah, why do I like making him smile?! Bad, Rylee.* "See you tomorrow?"

"Bright and early," I agree and he looks at me confused. "Math." I remind him.

"Oh, right, duh." He laughs. "See you later, Riles."

"Bye."

He gives me a little hesitant wave before leaving the shop.

Damn it! Why couldn't they have just stayed shitty guys so I can continue to hate them. But no, it was one big misunderstanding, and now I'm second guessing everything.

Donny asked me if I could ever forgive them and, right away, I wanted to say no. How could I? But as time goes on, I don't fucking know anymore.

No matter how damn nice they've been, I'm not letting that get in the way of my plans. Pranks aside, I plan on getting some big, juicy blackmailing material, just in case. I'd never use it, never share it with the public, but it would be smart to have something on them, just to save my own ass, wouldn't it? Can't hurt.

Only thing is, how the hell do I get close enough to them

to get that information? I may not be allowing myself to let them in my heart, but we could be... friends? Right?

"Now I just need to pick a color," I say to myself as I scan the shelf of hair dye. Donny is way too damn obsessed with his golden locks. I mean, his shaggy blond hair does look good on him, but still, there's more to life than your looks. Being knocked down a peg or two wouldn't hurt.

"What are you doing?" an amused voice comes from behind me.

I let out a frightened yelp as I spin around, coming face to face with Trevor from the football team. "Holy shit, dude," I huff out, my heart pounding in my chest. "Don't sneak up on people like that!"

"Sorry." He chuckles, his blue eyes gleaming with mirth. "Didn't mean to scare you. Just saw you and thought I'd come say hi."

"You didn't scare me," I mumble.

"Right." He smirks. He looks at the aisle behind me. "Please don't tell me you're going to dye that gorgeous red hair?"

"What?" My brows shoot up.

He looks at me, a slight blush taking over his stubbled cheek. "Sorry, I didn't mean to sound like I was telling you what to do. It's your hair, so you can do whatever you want with your body. It's just, your hair is really nice as it is."

"Oh." I laugh. "No, it's not for me, it's for Donny," I say, letting that little bit of information slip.

"Donny?" His brow furrows.

"Ahhh," I say, scratching the back of my head.

"Are you friends with them?" he asks, his smile dropping.

"No," I say.

"Good, I hate those guys," he mutters. "After everything they did to you, they need their asses kicked more than anything."

"I mean, I'm not going to argue with you there," I say with a grin. "Can I trust you with something?" He doesn't seem like someone to run and tell the guys what I'm up to. He sounds like he's not their biggest fan.

"Yeah, anything," he tells me, his face serious.

"I'm getting hair dye to put in Donny's shampoo." Now it's my turn to blush. I feel so stupid and childish right now.

His brows shoot up, a grin taking over his face. "Well, well, well. Miss Rylee. Are you getting some revenge?"

"Kinda?" I answer. "I know they deserve a lot more, but it's not who I am. But I'm also not someone who can just let this go."

"No, I like it." He chuckles. "But I feel like we can do better."

"We?" I ask.

"Well yeah, you think I'm not going to be your sidekick on this? I want in." He grins. I don't know this guy very well, but I know he's good friends with Alex, and if Alex trusts him, then maybe he's not too bad. I mean, he's nice to look at, so that's a plus. And he does seem really sweet. He was nice when we danced together, and really seemed worried about me after the game.

"Alright, I guess I could use the help. Got any ideas?"

He grins wickedly. "I heard from some of the girls on the cheer team that he's lactose intolerant. He takes pills everyday so he can eat whatever he wants and not worry about getting sick. I say you find a way to give him some dairy, after you've switched out his pills with sugar pills. Wait until practice and watch everything go to shit. Literally."

"Oh," I say with way too much excitement. "That's good. That's really good." I giggle.

"I thought so." He smiles. "Give me your phone."

"Okay...?" I say, pulling it out. "Why?"

"To add my number, silly," he says. "Give me until tomorrow before practice and I'll have the sugar pills for you. He likes to do his pre-practice workout at the gym. If you can get to his bag, you should be able to make the switch."

"Thanks," I say, opening up a new contact and handing over the phone. He puts his number in and I find myself watching him. He's cute, like really cute. Normally, I don't go for the football type, but there's something about him, with his shaggy black hair and dark clothes giving off a slight emo vibe. I'm here for it.

"Here you go," he says, snapping me out of my thoughts as he hands me back my phone. "I gotta get going, but I'll see you tomorrow around five."

"Okay, see you then. And thanks again," I say, putting my phone away.

"No thanks needed," he says. "I'm happy to be of

service," he continues with a wink, and my damn belly flutters as he walks away.

No, Rylee. Sexy men are what got you into this situation in the first place.

I can't believe I just agreed to help Rylee with this prank. I was only supposed to go to the pharmacy and pick up some more painkillers after that brutal practice. Fucking Alex. He's my best friend, but damn it if I didn't want to kick his ass after how hard he tackled me. He never goes easy, but I'd like to be in one piece before the next game.

As I was browsing the aisle, I walked into the one Rylee was in. I'm pretty sure I stood there so long I was borderline coming off as a creeper, but fuck, she's just so damn beautiful.

I've had a crush on Rylee since the first moment I set eyes on her. Alex and I were hanging out and I walked with him back to our dorm building. I was saying goodbye to him, because my room was one floor up, when I saw this stunning redhead pop her head out of the door, greeting Alex. Her smile stole my breath away. I've had a few girls that I've been really attracted to, but there was something about this one that was different.

I thought it was a joke when Alex told me he was roomed with a girl. Even though our dorm is co-ed, we hardly ever share a room with the opposite gender.

He quickly became best friends with her, and very protective of her. That made me want to meet her, to get to know her better, if she was capable of making meat-head Alex feel something other than wanting to get drunk and fuck girls. Although, that's not his life anymore since he met Serenity. Both of those girls have really changed him for the better.

So when I saw her at the party, I knew I had to take the chance and ask her to dance. Having her close to me like that, smelling her strawberries and cream scent, I felt like I never wanted to let her go.

I was going to ask her to go somewhere quiet to talk, but she ended up needing air and took off. After giving her some time, I went looking for her, but found her talking to Colton.

At that point, I'd heard some of the rumors going around about her and the guys on the cheer team. I never paid them much attention because, to me, that's all they were, rumors. But the way the two of them were looking at each other while they talked, it wasn't hard to see that something was going on there.

I tried not to let the disappointment get to me, but I had the urge to just get drunk and forget for the night. So I found the first girl who wanted to dance and distracted myself until I was too tired and finally I left alone.

After that, I kept my distance. It was hard because she was best friends with my best friend. They were always together.

Then came the game. I have never felt so much fucking rage than I did that night. How could people be so damn cruel to another person?! If Alex hadn't gone off on them like he did, I would have.

When Serenity was walking away with her, the broken look in her eyes, fuck that hurt to see. I was going to find her the next day, to see if she was okay, but I thought I'd give her some space. Then Alex told me she took off for a few days on Halloween and I've been waiting for a moment to talk to her since she got back.

And I just got that moment. I saw her, manned the fuck up, and went over to talk to her. Finding out she wanted to fuck with the guys made me like her a lot more. And I jumped at the chance to help her. Not just because I want to see the guys get their asses handed to them, but because this means I'll have an excuse to see her again and to spend more time with her.

As I walk back to my dorm room, I call my buddy who can get me the sugar pills. Thankfully, he agrees to help out. I just have to pick them up tomorrow before I meet Rylee.

My phone rings just as I get off the line with my previous call. Looking at the caller ID, I see it's Alex. "What's up, man?" I ask, answering the phone.

"Where are you? I'm outside your room and you're not here," he says, and I laugh at the pout in his voice.

"I'm just getting back from the store. Had to get some stronger painkillers for the fucking beating you gave me today." I groan, rolling my stiff and sore shoulder.

"Ah, you know you like it rough." He chuckles.

"Fuck you." I laugh.

"Why on earth would I fuck myself when I have a bombshell of a girlfriend who lets me do the honors?"

"Yeah, yeah, we all can't be as lucky as you to find an amazing girlfriend." I huff, rolling my eyes as I get to my dorm building and head into the elevator.

"You know I keep telling you to go out and find yourself a lady," he tells me. *"I can talk to Ren about maybe setting you up with one of her friends. She keeps good company."*

The elevator door dings and opens up on my dorm floor. I grin as I see him, his back to me, in front of my room door.

"Hello?" he says, and I mute the phone so it doesn't get any feedback. *"T, are you there? Fucking asshole, did you hang up on me?!"*

Trying not to laugh, I creep up behind him. "Boo!" I shout.

Alex lets out the loudest and girlish screech I've ever heard. I burst into a full belly laugh and almost fall over with how hard I'm laughing.

"What the fuck, man?!" he shouts, his eyes wide like he's seen a ghost. "Don't fucking do that shit."

"But you make it so damn easy," I say, stepping around him and unlocking my door. "Come inside, people are staring."

Alex looks around, seeing the few people who have popped their heads out to see what is going on. And of course Alex slips back into his cocky self, a grin taking over.

"It's because I'm sexy as hell," he says before looking at the girls. "Sorry ladies, I'm a taken man."

"Get in here." I snort out a laugh, dragging him inside. He chuckles and flings himself backward onto my bed. I'm lucky enough to not have a roommate, but my room is small as hell. Just enough room for a single bed, dresser, and a small desk. I could have taken my step-dad's money and gotten one of the pricey rooms. But I turned him down. It's his money, not mine.

"So, about what I was saying before. Why don't I set you up with one of Ren's friends?"

"Not to be rude, but most of her friends are on the cheer team. They're all nice enough, but not my type," I tell him. "They care more about getting a boyfriend on the football team, or one of the other sports teams, than the actual man they're dating."

"Not all of them are like that," Alex says. "Rylee isn't."

At the mention of her name, I look away. But not in time to hide the blush that creeps over my cheeks. I hate how easy it is to see my emotions on my face sometimes.

Alex shoots up into a sitting position. "Dude! Do you have a thing for Rylee?"

Letting out a heavy sigh, I turn to my best friend. "I love you, man, but sometimes you're blind as a bat."

"Am not. I have 20-20 vision," he snorts.

I shake my head. "Not like that, dumb ass. I don't get how you didn't know that I've had a thing for Rylee for a while."

"What?! You have? You never told me!" He gapes at me.

"Okay, fair point," I say, running a hand through my hair.

"Okay, so this is fucking amazing!" he says, his face lighting up. "Why didn't I think of this before?! You would be perfect for her. Dude, she's so sweet, caring, and funny.

Hell, if I wasn't madly, head-over-heels for Ren, I'd probably be with Rylee."

That earns him a death glare and he grins wider. "You so have it bad for her!"

"So what? She wouldn't want to go out with me. She's already interested in someone else."

"Who?" he asks, brows furrowing. "I'd know if she was."

"Colton... Maybe even Donny and the other guys," I say, taking a seat at my desk.

"Oh, fuck that group of guys." He waves off my comment. "Trust me, you're so much better than them. She needs a good guy, someone who won't hurt her, and will treat her right."

"Still doesn't change the fact that there's history with the guys."

"Look," he says. "I'm not going to lie, the shit between her and them is... well, it's messy. But I can tell you she *is* single, and I do think you have a shot. I mean, what's the worst that could happen?"

"She could say no? She could turn me down. She has four guys who clearly have a thing for her. I've seen how they've been with her since Halloween."

"Trust me, you have a better advantage than they do." He grins.

"How so?" I ask, raising a brow.

"I mean, yes, she already has four dicks with their hats in the ring, but I've seen yours." He wiggles his eyebrows and holds up his arm. "Forearm, baby! She can't say no to that."

I close my eyes, not even sure how to deal with this man right now. "Shut up. Just, shut up," I groan.

"But on a serious note, if you get the chance, ask her out. I approve. I think you would be perfect for her. Just try. I know you, you're going to hate yourself if you don't."

"Yeah, maybe," I tell him. I don't mention the prank. If Rylee wants him to know, she will tell him herself.

Alex leaves and I get the courage to text her. I'm glad I do because we spend the next few hours talking about a little of everything, and I've never smiled so much as I do tonight.

CHAPTER TWELVE

Rylee

I make sure I get out of my last class as quickly as I can so that I can rush home to drop everything off before getting my cheer bag.

Trevor is meeting me soon, and I want to make sure I'm there when he arrives. We texted back and forth a little bit last night, and I hate to admit how much I enjoyed it.

He's just really easy to talk to. No awkward silences. No leaving the other person on read. We didn't talk about anything personal, but I still felt like I got to know his personality pretty well.

When I get to the gym, where he told me to meet him, I take a seat on the bench near the building with the two milk-shakes I bought.

I can't wait to see the look on Donny's face when he realizes he's about to shit his pants. Cocky fucker deserves it.

"Hey," Trevor says, making my head snap up from looking at my phone.

"Hey." I greet him, standing up with a smile.

He looks around like he's scoping out the place.

"I got them," he says, discreetly showing me a bottle.

"Dude, this isn't a drug deal." I laugh, shaking my head.

His lips break out into a smile. "Kinda is. These are sugar pills. Still has the word pills in the title."

"You're crazy," I say, smiling wider as he passes me the bottle and I stick it in my bag.

"Any chance I can watch this all go down?" he asks with a smirk. "I'd love to see one of those guys get his ass handed to them in some way."

"I mean, normally we don't let anyone watch practices."

"Alex watches all the time," he points out.

"True," I say. "Sometimes the girls' boyfriends come and watch."

"Just say we're dating." He winks. "I bet that would drive the guys crazy."

"Already did the fake dating thing once and he ended up falling for my best friend," I say, raising a brow in amusement.

"No worries here. I don't have my eye on anyone," he mutters with a shrug.

"What about the girl you ditched me at the party to

dance with?" I ask, the words leave my mouth before I can think better. *What the fuck was that?*

Trevor's brows shoot up in surprise. "I didn't even know her," he says, a blush breaking out on the tops of his cheeks. "To be honest, I didn't mean to ditch you. I went looking for you and saw you talking to Colton. From the way you two were looking at each other, I knew I would have been interrupting something. I didn't want to get in the way."

"Oh," I say, blinking. "I—there's nothing going on with me and Colton," I mumble, but even that seems like a lie. The way he is with me, I'd be stupid to think I wasn't attracted to him.

"What about the other guys?" he asks, a look of hope flashing in his eyes.

I bite my lip, pondering my answer. There's no simple answer to that question, so I tell him the truth. "I'm not seeing anyone. No boyfriend."

His little smile makes my belly flutter. "Then would it be alright if I asked you out on a date?" he asks.

Trevor is hot, that much is clear. He's really nice, and we seem to get along great. I'm not really looking for anything serious, but I deserve to have a nice time with a good guy. "Yeah," I say with a smile. "A coffee sometime?"

"I'd like that," he replies with a grin.

"And about you watching everything go down. I guess it wouldn't be a big deal if you came to practice. I mean, you did play a big part in my plan, so the least I can do is let you watch it play out."

"Yes," he says, fist pumping the air and I giggle. "I'm so

recording the shit out of it. Get it? Shit." He wiggles his eyebrows and I snort out a laugh.

"You're such a dork." I roll my eyes, but my lips form a smile. "Now, wish me luck," I say.

"You got this. Meet me back out here and I'll walk you to practice."

Nodding, I turn and head into the gym. The person at the front desk looks up but I show him my badge. All the sport teams get free access to any of the gyms on campus, so this makes my plan easier.

Once I slip further into the building, to the main workout area, I find Donny running on one of the treadmills. Looking down next to him, I see his bag. Crap, it's too close to him. He would see me for sure.

But then, as if the universe is on my side for once, he starts to slow down. Once the machine stops, he grabs his towel and wipes down his face. Leaving his bag, he takes off toward the bathroom.

Letting a few seconds go by, I look around and find myself happy to see it's pretty dead. A few people are facing away from me, with what looks to be earbuds in their ears. Knowing I don't have long, I take off across the room. I put the drinks on the bench and grab Donny's bag. After moving a few things around, I find the pills. Grabbing my bag, I open the bottle and dump his pills into my bag, then take the sugar pills that Trevor gave me and put them into his bottle.

Looking over my shoulder, I make sure he's not coming back before quickly putting the bottle back in his bag.

Grabbing the drinks, I stand just in time to see Donny coming back.

"Rylee?" he asks, looking at me with a surprised look. "What are you doing here?"

"Oh, hey Donny. I was looking for Ren. She said something about getting a workout in before practice."

"That's what I'm doing," he says with a smile. "But I haven't seen her around."

"Damn, she must be at one of the other gyms. By the time I get to her, this milkshake is going to be melted," I say, pretending to be disappointed.

"Milkshake?" he says with enthusiasm. "What kind?"

"Chocolate chip cookie dough."

His eyes light up. "You know, I just so happen to love that kind. I don't mind taking it off your hands. So it won't go to waste."

"Really? Thanks." I hand it over to him. "I'd hate for it to be thrown out."

"No need. I got this one, Cherry." He winks, then bends over, grabs a pill from his bottle and pops it in his mouth. "I'm lactose intolerant. But I don't let that stop me. I just take these babies and I'm good to eat whatever."

"Smart." I nod. "Well, I better get going. Ren is gonna start calling me if I don't go meet her."

"Okay, thanks for the milkshake! See you soon."

"Bye." I give him a friendly smile and a wave goodbye.

Turning around to head out, a wicked smile takes over my face. This is going to be one messy practice.

"Let's go!" Rylee says as she rushes out of the gym, a wide smile taking over her face as she heads toward me. She laughs as she grabs my arm and pulls me away from the building.

"Did everything go as planned?" A weird burst of excited energy fills me as we head toward the building where the cheer team practices.

"Yup." She looks over at me with that smile that does funny things to my heart. I'm most definitely crushing hard on this girl. "Now, we wait."

"You're really excited, aren't you?" I laugh.

"I mean, maybe a little." She shrugs, but the grin doesn't leave her tempting lips. "They fucked with me. And even if I plan on putting the past behind me, I can't do that without getting a little revenge. I'm not bat shit crazy like Missi, and I would never stoop to her level, but hey, I can't let them get away scot-free, can I?"

"Nope," I agree. "They need a little dose of their own medicine."

"Do you think it's a little childish?" she asks me as we stop in front of the building.

"I do," I reply with a chuckle. "But I also think they deserve it."

"Me too." She nods. "Come on. He should be here any minute."

When we walk into the gym, I find Alex over by the bleachers talking to Serenity. Rylee grabs my hand and pulls me toward them. I try not to focus on how soft her skin feels against mine, or how much I like holding her hand like this.

"Hey, T. What are you doing here?" Alex asks, his brow furrowing as he looks between me and Rylee.

"Rylee here said I could join you to watch practice," I say, taking a seat next to him.

"She did, did she?" he asks, looking up at Rylee.

"I wanted to give him a front row seat." Rylee's face slips into a mischievous grin.

"To what?" Alex asks, his lip twitching with a smile. "And should I be worried about that look on your face?"

"Let's just say, things are about to get... interesting." Rylee laughs.

"Wanna clue me in?" Serenity asks.

Rylee leans over and whispers in Serenity's ear as I look past them to see Lennox, Mateo, and Colton watching us with matching scowls on their faces.

Smirking, I give them a little wave. Mateo's lip peels back in a scowl.

"No fucking way." Serenity gasps before she starts to laugh. "Oh, this is going to be good. I'm so proud of you, babe."

"What's going to be good?" Alex asks. "Come on! It's not fair if all of you know except me!"

"Just wait. Trust me, it will be better if you see it for yourself," Rylee says.

"You all suck." Alex pouts.

"Alright!" Colton shouts, clapping his hands. "Now that everyone is here, let's get this practice started, shall we?" Donny walks into the room, tossing the milkshake cup into the trash before walking over to us.

"Looks like you found her," Donny chuckles to Rylee before looking at Serenity. "Sorry about missing out on that milkshake, because damn it was good." He has a cocky smirk on his face like he won something.

Rylee's eyes lock with mine as she tries to hide her smile behind her hand. A matching grin tugs at my lips as I give her a wink, her eyes sparkling back with trouble.

"That's okay," Serenity says. "I'll get one after practice. Glad it didn't go to waste."

"No issues there," Donny says. "Come on ladies, let's shake them pom poms!" Donny whoops before bouncing over to the guys.

"Pom poms?" Alex asks. "Since when do you use those?"

"We don't, baby," Serenity bends over to kiss her boyfriend.

"What the fuck is he talking about then?" Alex asks. The poor guy looks so confused.

My eyes find Rylee's again and we both burst out a little laugh. The guy's my best friend, but he's not always the brightest crayon in the box.

"Don't worry about it," Rylee coos. "See you two after." This time she gives me a wink before heading out to join the team.

"Dude, what is going on? I feel so lost right now. And why do you get to be in on the secret?" Alex asks, grumbling.

"Because I helped her. Trust me, it will be worth the wait."

"It's not fair that the new guy gets to be in on the secrets," he mutters. "If you think you're going to swoop in and steal my best friend away from me, you have another thing coming."

"Hey, I'm your best friend too!"

"Yeah, but she's like my little sister. Not to mention, she's my girl's bestie too. Therefore making her a higher rank than you." He smirks.

"Gee, thanks." I roll my eyes.

The music begins and Colton starts to bark out orders like a drill sergeant. Here I thought he was the nice, quiet one.

"This better be good," Alex chuckles.

I can't wait to see that fucker get what he deserves. They should all be lucky that Rylee is such a good person because they deserve so much worse than what they are going to get.

CHAPTER THIRTEEN

Lennox

Mateo and I walk down the sidewalk, getting some fresh air for the first time in over a week, and I can't hold in my groan. "I am so fucking happy to be out of that apartment. I love you, man, but I don't know how many more zombie shooting games I could have handled. I was ready to go postal," I say, turning toward Teo as he laughs.

"That's cute, baby. You and I both know you enjoyed all the afternoons together in my bed, shower, and the kitchen counter." I step closer to him and place my palm over his mouth, ignoring him when he licks it.

"Shhh. Yes, I loved getting to spend some quality time together, but having to be sober the whole time made me antsy. At least the bruises have started to fade." I remove my hand and he gives me a look full of heat, but we don't have time for any pit stops. Colton will have our balls if we miss this practice.

"I think I'm going to go check on my mom and Nando this weekend. Do you want to come with me? I know your dad has been blowing up your phone about getting your things. I'd say we all go after." I pause and run my hand over my face, scratching my cheek. I didn't shave today and it's bugging me.

"Honestly, I don't know if I even want to bother. It's all materialistic shit. Everything that matters is in my room back at the cheer house. But I should probably go check on my mom," I say as we reach the doors to the gym.

"Whatever you decide to do, Len, you know the guys and I will be there with you. I won't ever let that man put his hands on you again." I give him a nod and grab the door handle. He stops me with his hand against the wood and I sigh.

"I know, and I don't regret telling him, Teo, but I don't want to see him ever again. He has tormented me enough. I just want to move on with you and Rylee, if she ever decides to give us another chance. I haven't heard anything back about the gifts we left her. Maybe she didn't get them."

Teo grumbles behind me and I ignore him. I know he wants to talk about my father. He's been trying for the last week, but avoidance is the best policy in my opinion. I will talk about things when I'm ready.

"I'll drop this shit for now, Len. But we will be going to that fucker's house and getting the rest of your shit," he growls, and I shiver. He steps back and lets me open the door, and I can't help but smile when the aroma of sweaty gym socks and the noise of my team bickering greets me.

I almost want to drop to my knees and kiss the shiny laminated gym floor. I have never been so happy to be back to practice. I wasn't kidding—being stuck in our apartment while we healed, and the bruises faded, was torture.

Mateo laughs at how wide my smile is and he takes my hand.

I suck in a breath and my cheeks blush. I know I came out to my father, but are we really about to do this? PDA at practice? Mateo must feel my hesitation because he drops my hand and shoves his into his pockets.

Rylee walks in, laughing with Trevor? They walk over toward the bleachers and our eyes trail to her. She sits next to Serenity and Alex. What the fuck is Trevor doing here, and why is Rylee holding his hand? A scowl forms on my lips and I fight the urge to march over there and demand to know what is going on.

Is she attempting to fake-date someone else? We apologized and have been trying to make things better. Is she giving up on us?

Trevor notices us glaring and gives us a condescending little wave. Mateo growls softly next to me. I wait for him to make a move, but he surprises me and takes some deep breaths, calming down.

Serenity starts to laugh and I really wish I could go over there and join them. Colton claps, announcing practice is starting as Donny walks into the gym, slurping on a straw. He tosses the cup and walks over to Rylee. He says something and the girls smile.

"Come on, ladies, let's shake them pom poms," he whoops, and comes over to join us. He's way too happy right now and I'm getting aggravated.

"Cutting it close, aren't we?" I can't help but snark, and he blows me a kiss. I roll my eyes and huff, crossing my arms. I'm still glaring at the group on the bleachers and Teo grumbles.

"What the fuck is going on over there?" he growls and I shrug.

Missi is talking smack about Rylee being a whore again, and I know she's doing it to get another rise out of me, but I told her where I stand. She just needs to accept it.

Colt turns the music on and starts ordering us into formation. I know Mateo and I being out 'sick' lately has made him antsy to try these new stunts and choreography. One of the best things about having so many men on our team is that we get to go wild with stunts.

It's one of the things I love best about cheer over football. Rylee stands in front of me and my eyebrows raise. I don't ask any questions though, because I don't want her to change her mind and choose Donny or Teo.

I gently grip her hips and position her to be lifted in the air. I wait for Colt's signal, then bend my knees and toss her up. Her ponytail waves in front of my face and the scent of her shampoo is strong. My mouth waters and my dick stiffens.

I shake my head and focus. Rylee is trusting me not to drop her, and I will be damned if my dick interferes with her safety.

Mateo comes over next to me and we catch Rylee in a basic cradle. She gives me a weird look but I shake my head. My ribs twinge and I bite my lip to hide the pain. I know I should still be resting, but I need this. I'll just pop some pills later and maybe soak in the hot tub.

"Okay, listen up," Colt barks and I turn to him. "I want to practice doing scorpions today. I have an idea for a new stunt. Rylee, you take the lead on this one."

"Are you ready for this?" she asks me, and I nod.

"Yeah. Let's start with the handstand to a cupie and wait till I have a good grip before switching to a liberty. From there you can get into the scorpion pose," I suggest, and she nods.

Rylee leans down to get into the handstand position when we are distracted by Donny and his antics.

He does a few backflips until he knows he's caught Rylee's attention, and then he starts to goof off and do a triple toe. Colton is about ready to strangle him but Rylee laughs.

"You didn't smile during that triple toe, Donny. Do it again," she orders with her hands on her hips and an eyebrow raised. Donny looks stunned, and for once, he's silent before he winks and opens his mouth.

"You just like seeing how flexible I am, baby. You know

all you have to do is ask and I'll give you a private show." He winks and Rylee rolls her eyes and turns back to me.

"You ready?" I ask, and she nods. "Okay, Teo, get on her other side. Donny, stop fucking off and get in front," I bark and he listens, grumbling about me bossing him around.

Rylee flips into a handstand and I grip her ankles with one hand and under her back with the other, helping to guide her into my palms for a cupie pose. Donny shoves closer to me until we're almost nose to nose.

I roll my eyes, and thankfully, Teo shoves him out of the way. "What? I just wanted to help," Donny whines, and I take some breaths trying to focus.

"Okay, Ry, you're good to switch into a liberty pose," I tell her as I carefully loosen my hold on one of her feet so she can lift one knee and balance.

Sweat drips down my temples and I grit my teeth. Fuck, I'm out of shape. One week of doing nothing and I feel like I'm weak.

"Hey, Rylee, let's do an elevator, okay?" I give her my other hand to step on and guide her down to the mats.

"What's wrong? Is everything okay?" she asks me and I shake my head. I'm lightheaded and my side is throbbing.

"I guess being sick took more out of me than I thought. Teo, switch with me."

Mateo moves in and grabs Rylee's waist.

I watch as they nail the perfect cupie to a scorpion. I smile up at Rylee and she has the biggest grin on her face. You can tell she loves being a flyer, and she's really meant to be one.

Donny starts to grumble and then his stomach starts to make the same noises. He looks ill.

"You okay?" I ask him, and he shakes his head. Mateo brings Rylee down and then the shit hits the fan. Literally.

Can we ever just catch a fucking break?

Practice is almost done and I'm starting to worry that the plan isn't going to work. That is until a loud gurgling comes from Donny, as I hold my scorpion pose before safely flipping out of it. The guys catch me and place me on my feet.

"Are you okay?" Colton asks as Donny's face pales.

"Yeah," Donny says, but he doesn't sound so sure about that. "Oh, God." He groans as his stomach makes another loud rumble.

"Dude, what the fuck?" Mateo barks.

Donny groans again as a loud fart rips from him. My eyes widen and I take a step back before the smell hits me.

"Eww, Donny, that's nasty!" one of the girls cries.

"Sorry," Donny says, his cheeks turning red. "I don't feel so good."

"God, you're so gross." Missi gags as Donny lets another one rip.

So, I guess it did work after all. But, I don't find myself

filled with the satisfaction of getting my revenge, as Donny looks sicker by the second.

"Oh fuck," Donny says, his eyes widen as he grabs his ass and clutches his stomach.

The girls are recording him now. Just in time for Missi to scream, "Did you just shit your pants?!"

He takes off running, chanting "no, no, no," as he heads toward the bathroom. Within seconds of Donny entering the bathroom, we all hear some not so fun noises.

The girls are laughing hard, so is Alex and Trevor. But not me. I bite my lower lip, a guilty feeling filling me. He looked really sick and, by the sounds of it, he's really suffering.

"Put your fucking phones away!" Mateo snarls as he grabs a few of the girls' phones and tosses them to the side.

"Practice is over. You all did well. Remember, we have a competition coming up. Extra practices on Wednesday to get ready for it."

The girls start to pack up and head toward the women's locker room as the guys head into the men's.

I follow after them when the door closes and listen in. "Are you okay?" Colton asks. More horrifying sounds follow along with some gagging noises.

"No. God, I think I'm dying," he groans.

"Do you think it's food poisoning?" Mateo asks.

"I don't know. All I ate today was an egg sandwich for breakfast and a burger for lunch," Donny says. "Maybe the eggs had expired."

"I just bought them yesterday," Colton says. "I made sure to check the date."

"Anything else you ate that could have caused this?" Lennox asks.

"I had a milkshake that Rylee gave me, but I took my pills before I drank it."

"Hey," Trevor says from behind me, making me jump. "That was awesome. I have it all on camera." He laughs.

"Dude shit his pants!" Alex howls with laughter. "God, that really was worth the wait."

"Come on," Ren says. "I can smell it through the door." She looks at me. "I'll see you later. And good work." She winks.

They leave and a sinking feeling fills my belly.

"Rylee," Trevor says, gaining my attention. "Why the long face?"

Donny makes some groaning sounds and I'm hit with another wave of guilt.

"I think I really hurt him," I say, biting my lower lip.

"So what?!" Trevor growls. "He fucking deserves it. Alex told me what they did to you in that locker room. It's fucked up, Rylee. He deserves so much more than the shits."

"I know," I say. He does have a point, but it doesn't do anything to make me feel better.

"He's going to be fine. Come on, let me walk you back to your room," Trevor says. "He has his friends. They will make sure he's okay."

"Yeah, you're right," I say, leaving the locker room door and heading toward the exit with Trevor.

As we go to leave, I look back to see the guys and Donny filing out of the locker room. He doesn't look good. His face is pale and his hair is sweaty as he leans against

Colton. "I'll go get the car. We should have something at home to settle your stomach. But if you can't keep anything in, we're taking you to the emergency room," Lennox says. Donny nods as the guys walk him to the bench close by the bathroom.

When Lennox walks past me and out the door, our eyes lock. The look of crippling guilt taking over my face does nothing to hide the fact that this was all my doing. Lennox says nothing as he breaks eye contact and keeps going.

Trevor takes me home and I spend the rest of the night trying to take my mind off everything. But as I lay in bed, all I can do is wonder if Donny is okay. No matter how much he might deserve it, I find myself regretting my decision.

Stupid boys. Why can't they just stay the fuck out of my head?

I feel like shit. Literally. I haven't crapped my brains out this much since the time I left my pills at home and went to the all you can eat buffet with Colt and Len. That day will forever be known as The Bathroom Explosion of Twenty-Twenty.

We have never returned to that place, and it's a shame because they had amazing desserts. Colton takes my arm and helps me into the car. I'm having trouble walking on my own and I know my cheeks are beet red.

Usually things don't phase me and I can just joke them all away, but Rylee witnessed this, and now she's not going to want anything to do with me.

I'm close to tears as Lennox drives us home. He seems lost in thought, but hasn't said anything. I clutch my stomach and groan as Teo barks to roll the windows down before I let another fart rip.

"Fuck, I'm never eating again," I moan and the guys laugh. "This is not funny," I growl, but it's weak at best. I just want my bed, and to never move. The small vibrations from the tires moving is not helping my current situation.

My phone buzzes but I ignore it. I'm being tagged in a ton of pictures, memes, and videos, and I just want to crawl into a hole and hide. Lennox pulls up to the house and lets Colt and me out, before going to park.

"How bad is it?" I ask Colt and he sighs before pushing his glasses up onto his nose. He usually wears contacts during practice, but today he didn't bother. I know they make his eyes itch. I think I'm going to surprise him for his birthday and get him Lasik. I know it's something he's been really wanting, but money's tight.

Moving into the cheer house, I'm happy no one seems to be home. I was just waiting for an ambush. Some of these girls can be ruthless. I hold onto Colt's arm as we head down the stairs to our apartment. He unlocks the door and helps me to the couch.

"No, I need a shower and then my bed," I groan, and he continues walking slowly until we reach my door.

"You don't need help showering, right?" he asks, his cheeks turning pink and I snort.

"I love you, man, but no. I'll go easy," I mumble and he nods, looking relieved. I mean, we have all seen each other naked, multiple times. I was there the day he got his dick pierced, but showering together... yeah, that's a Len and Mateo thing.

He leaves me at my door and I shuffle into my bathroom, turning the water onto cool. My stomach is still all in knots, and I don't think I can handle any hot steam. I rinse off and groan as a second... well, I guess this would be more like a fifth wave... comes over me. I make it to the toilet in time, and I want to cry.

This is going to be a long fucking night.

It's a few hours later when Lennox brings me some of Teo's mom's homemade chicken soup and some ginger ale. He plops down on my bed with me and I put on a movie. It doesn't take long until Mateo joins us and then Colton.

"I think I'm going to need a bigger bed," I joke as Mateo almost falls off the edge. He grunts and grumbles but Len tells him to be quiet.

I smile and look at my family. "Thanks for this, guys. I've never had someone to take care of me when I was sick before. Not since my parents died. I had to learn to rely on myself and become independent," I mumble, and I try not to let past memories cloud my mind.

"We're family, Donny. And we're always here for you. Even when you blow up the bathroom at practice," Lennox says and I groan. "What? Too soon?" he jokes, and if my stomach still didn't feel like I've been on a rollercoaster, I would have tackled him.

Colton pauses the movie and turns to look my way.

"I've been thinking hard about what happened, and I don't think it was the eggs. You said Rylee gave you a milk-shake–do you think maybe she put something in it?" He looks at me seriously and I laugh, waving my hand, shaking my head.

"No, this wasn't Rylee. I took my lactose pills like I usually do. Maybe I need to go to the doctor and have a check up." I grumble just thinking of that sterile room with the white walls and the man with the really cold hands. I fucking hate doctors.

I must shiver because Lennox wraps his arm around my shoulder and gives me a side hug. I've noticed now that he's no longer listening to his dad, he has become more comfort-able with showing compassion.

"If we need to go with you and hold your hand, we got you," he jokes again, and this time I say fuck the nausea and shove him, causing Teo to fall to the floor and give me a glare.

"If you weren't sick right now, man, your ass would be on the ground," he growls, then climbs to his feet and storms out of the room.

Lennox looks at me and I can't help myself. "Uh oh, we

made Daddy Teo angry," I whisper, and Lennox's eyes go wide before he bursts out into laughter.

"I heard that, Shit Stain," Teo yells from his room and I frown, then pout. Colton is now chuckling.

"That's not funny. If anything, call me Butt Truffles." I groan and cover my face with my pillow. "No, that's even worse. I'm just going to hide here until graduation."

"If this *was* Rylee, I think it's only the beginning," Colton mumbles and I sigh, lifting the pillow just enough so they can hear me.

"I don't think it was, but if she is trying to get revenge then we deserve it," I grumble and I feel the bed shift.

"If I fall off this mattress again then I am kicking all of your asses. And don't ever fucking call me Daddy Teo, unless I'm balls deep in one of your holes and giving you a hand necklace."

The pillow is removed from my face and Lennox looks like a tomato. I don't think he's even breathing. He swallows and glances at Mateo.

"Well, shit just got interesting." I can't help but comment, and Teo tells me to shut the fuck up and hits play once again on the movie we're not watching.

I MUST HAVE DOZED OFF. My phone buzzing on my nightstand table has me opening my eyes with a wince. Someone left the bright light on, but I'm all alone now. I sigh and open my messages. I ignore all the tags for the incident and click on Rylee's name.

> Cherry: Are you okay?

I blink a few times to make sure I'm not hallucinating, then smile. I read her words a couple of times before chuckling to myself as I reply.

> Me: No, I'm dying. I need a hot nurse to come save me.

The bubbles show and then disappear a few times, and I worry maybe I took it too far. *Fuck, Donny, you're so stupid sometimes.* I start to write a new text but she beats me to it.

> Cherry: Sorry, I left that uniform in Florida.

I laugh and sit up, resting my back against my headboard. I'm surprised she's checking on me. I mean, things have been getting a little better between us, but this shows that she still cares, and it has my palms sweaty and heart racing.

> Me: Damn, looks like a shopping trip is in order then. I'll also be needing a sexy baker, cowgirl, and parole officer.

> Cherry: In your dreams, lover boy. I'm glad you're okay, Donny. Get some sleep.

I send her back a mass amount of kissing emojis then lay back down with a sigh. It's too quiet. It was nice having all the guys in here earlier. It gets lonely sometimes. I just need to fix things with Rylee for good, so I'll never have to be alone again.

Waking up with her in my arms was like a dream, and I want that for the rest of my life. I will make her fall for me again, and this time, I'm not letting her go.

CHAPTER FOURTEEN

Rylee

I t's been a few days since the Donny prank happened and it's gone viral. I mean, someone even turned it into a meme.

At first, I did feel guilty, but when I found out he was fine, I remembered what they did to me and the guilt drifted away. He deserves it, and a little embarrassment will do him some good. Remind him that he's not untouchable, and maybe it will even humble him.

I don't plan on ending my pranks just yet. Yesterday, I made Lennox my next victim when he came into my work while I was there studying. The free coffee is what's keeping me going.

While Lennox was busy on his phone, leaving his drink unattended for a moment, I quickly switched the sugar with salt, then sat back and watched, with my camera ready, as he took a mouthful then proceeded to spit it across the room. His dramatics were hilarious as he started gagging and coughing.

And that video went right alongside Donny's on the anonymous TikTok account and Instagram that Trevor made.

Now today, my choice in victims is Colton. The sexy nerd who wasn't as smart as I thought, and jumped to conclusions that caused this downhill spiral.

I couldn't bring myself to do something as severe as I did to Donny. The thought of making someone hurt like that doesn't feel good. I'm not like them. It just doesn't sit right with me.

"Hey, Rylee," Colton says as I step into the class that he is a student teacher in.

"Hey, Colton," I reply, giving him a smile. "I just wanted to say I'm glad Donny is doing better." Taking Colton by surprise, I wrap my arms around him.

He stiffens for a moment before hugging me back. As good as he smells right now, I'm not meant to actually be all cozy with him.

Taking the piece of paper in my hand, I stick it to his back and grin before stepping away.

"Well, that was a pleasant surprise," he says, blinking at me as he pushes his glasses up his nose. I like that he doesn't seem to be wearing his contacts as much anymore. He looks cute.

"I'm just in a good mood," I say, giving him a wink before turning around, my skirt twirling with me as I find a seat.

"Alright, class," Colton says as he takes a step up to the front of the class. "Professor Storm is out sick today, so I will be teaching today's lesson."

Turning around, he starts to write on the white board.

The class instantly breaks out into hushed whispers. Students start to snicker as others take out their phones and snap photos.

Biting my lip, I try to hold back the laugh bubbling in my throat, but I'm unable to keep the smile from breaking out across my face.

Colton turns around, brow furrowing as he looks at the class in confusion. "Quiet, please. Class has started."

"It's okay, Colton." A guy a few rows behind me chokes out a laugh. "I'm sure you're a grower, not a shower."

"What the hell are you talking about?" Colton asks.

"Is that why you never wanted to be with any of the cheer team?" one of the members of the squad asks, the pity in her voice has me choking on my giggle.

"Okay. I'm missing something," Colton murmurs, his eyes landing on me. I'm not stupid, I'm sure they've all figured out what I'm up to at this point, seeing as how I was at the scene of the crime both times. And I'm not exactly trying to hide what I'm doing.

I give him a smile and a shrug of my shoulders.

"I think it's brave of you to show your support regarding your *little* issue." Another girl laughs. "It's okay, not all girls are after size; it's what's in the heart that matters."

Of course, that's when the tape on the paper decides to give out, making it float to the floor. Colton sees it and picks it up.

The look of horror on his face has the whole room bursting out into laughter as he reads the note.

I have a micro penis and I'm proud. #SizeDoesn'tMatter

"What the..." he whispers, his eyes finding mine again, and I give him a little wink.

I have to give it to him, he does a good job holding back his anger as he crumples the paper in his hand.

"Haha," he says, tossing it into the trash. "Very funny. Now, are we done with a good morning laugh, so we can get back to learning?"

Colton goes on teaching the lesson, but it takes a few minutes before the class starts to calm down.

His eyes keep wandering to me as he talks, only lingering for a second before he notices me watching him. I love how pink his cheeks get every time we lock eyes.

I'm gonna have a little fun with him.

Next time he looks at me, I shift in my seat so that my legs widen a little, making my skirt ride up a bit.

He stumbles over his words slightly before carrying on.

I bite the inside of my cheek to hold back the smile. Next time, I take it a little further, letting my hand slide up my thigh.

He does a double take as my hand slips under and over my panty-covered pussy. His eyes flick up to mine, and I bite my lower lip seductively.

Colton swallows hard, and fuck, if it isn't funny watching him try to hide the hard-on he's getting.

By the time class is over, I'm regretting the little tease show I put on for Colton. The way he reacted made my lower belly heat and my panties wet. I might not be his biggest fan, but I still find him insanely attractive.

"Time is up. Have your assignments ready by the next class."

The class gets up and starts to file outside of the room. I linger back so that I can pass Colton as he stands in front of the room, watching as everyone leaves.

"Don't worry, Colt. I can verify that your dick is, in fact, not micro size." I give him a slow grin as he shifts from one foot to the other. "Trust me, I felt... everything."

Colton's eyes flash with heat, and I love the way he looks at me with pure hunger.

Leaving him there with his dick tenting his pants, I walk out of the classroom.

Just because I'm not ready to forgive them, if I ever even will be, does that mean I can't enjoy them? What harm will a little casual sex do?

God, I can't believe I'm even thinking about this right now. I need to get laid. But I don't know anyone that I'd bother to give my time of day to.

I've been with Colton. And it was good. Better than good, it was amazing. He knew how to use his dick. I wonder what he could do if I was to sit on his desk and open wide for him.

I'm halfway down the hall when I pause.

He doesn't have any more classes in that room today. And it's his free time to grade papers, and whatever else teachers do when they're not teaching.

The idea of me on that desk for him plays out in my head. Fuck, the thought of his mouth on my pussy makes it flutter.

Before I can think better of it, I'm turning on my heel and heading back to the classroom.

I really hope this doesn't go south, and I end up making a fool of myself.

Well, that was one interesting class, I think as I let out a breath, running my hand through my hair.

Taking a seat at the desk, I grab the pile of papers and start to grade them. Or should I say try, because my mind can't stop thinking about Rylee.

We all know it was her who messed with Donny. And as much as I felt bad for him, he deserved it.

If Rylee feels the need to do these little pranks, then

we're going to let her. She's too good of a person, because anyone else would be dishing out what we gave her or worse.

It just shows how wrong we were about her. Without the hurt and hatred clouding the way we think about her, it's clear she's still the same person we met at the hotel.

Only, because of us, she's a little more damaged, and that's something I'm not sure I'll ever forgive myself for. But I plan on doing whatever I can to make it up to her.

Tutoring is going well, but it's hard to focus on the work we do when my eyes keep straying. She's so gorgeous. It takes everything in me to restrain myself from reaching out to tuck a piece of hair behind her ear when it falls forward as she works. To run my thumb along her crinkled brow to smooth it out when she's deep in concentration.

At least she's giving me the time of day outside of tutoring. She doesn't tell me to fuck off and go away when I show up randomly with coffee. She smiles and thanks me, and I get way too much joy from it.

But today? God she was so fucking tempting today. Do you know how hard it is to be in front of a class of students and hide how hard my dick is? Really hard. A lot of teaching over the shoulder as I faced the board. Not the best for my neck.

"What has you so deep in thought?" Rylee's voice makes me jump, my head snapping up from the paper to see her bending over the desk.

"I didn't hear you come in," I say, letting out a breath as my eyes fall to her breasts. They're right there in my face. *Focus, Colton.*

She stands up and my eyes follow her movements as she makes her way around the desk.

My heart starts to race faster as I push my glasses up my nose. On instinct, I push back my chair, giving her room as she steps in front of me before hopping up onto the desk.

"What are you doing?" I hate how unsteady my voice is right now, but there's this look in her eyes that has me all flustered.

"I wanted to give you something," she says, giving me a sexy smirk.

"Ahhh..." I say, not sure what she would have to give me.

She holds something out in her hand. I stare at it for a moment, my eyes flicking back to hers.

"Go on." She gives me a sexy laugh that has my cock twitching. "Take it."

Reaching out, I open my hand and she drops something in it. My eyes widen as I look at a pair of red lacy panties.

"Since you're the one that got them so wet, I thought you should have them," she says in a husky voice.

Fuck. Fuck me. Is this really happening right now? I don't even care if this is some sort of prank like the one she did before. I'm holding her fucking underwear—her wet panties. And I know they're hers because I got a little peek of the red when she lifted her skirt while she was teasing me before.

"Rylee," I say, my eyes flicking back up to hers.

"You know, Mr. John. It's not nice to leave me all worked up," she purrs. Leaning over, she reaches out and slowly takes my glasses off my face. My breath catches as my pulse starts to race. I feel like a nervous, sweating virgin right now.

But isn't that pretty much what I am? I've only had sex one time. I've never messed around with anyone else.

She folds the glasses up and places them on the desk next to her.

"I think you should be a good boy and do something to help me out," she says, caressing my face. My eyes flutter closed as I lean into her touch. She slides her fingers to the back of my head and grabs a handful of my hair. The sharp tug makes my eyes snap open.

"H-how?" I ask, the shakiness giving away how worked up I am. My cock is so hard it's pressing against my tight slacks.

Letting go of my hair, she brings her hands behind her and leans back on her arms before lifting both legs up and onto the armrests of the chair.

I let out a groan as her skirt rides up, putting her pussy on display for me. Is she really asking what I think she's asking?

Biting my lower lip. "I-I've never... pleasured a woman like that before," I admit, my cheeks pinking with embarrassment.

Her eyes light up. "Really?" she asks.

Swallowing thickly, I almost tell her that I've only been with her, but I don't. Something like that might be a little too heavy for her to hear, and I don't want to ruin the moment.

"Yeah," I say, nodding my head, hoping she doesn't ask anything more.

"Well then." She grins, widening her legs. "Feel free to practice on me."

My lips part in shock. Is she for real? Or is she going to pull away at the last second and start laughing at me?

A part of me wants to call her bluff, and the other just doesn't give a shit. If this is a prank, she's really committing to it.

Licking my lips, my eyes look down to her waiting pussy. Fuck it. I'm going for it. I've had dreams of this. Of tasting her sweet release on my tongue while I make her moan my name.

"What are you waiting for?" she challenges me, scooting herself closer to the edge. I push the chair toward her until her pussy is practically in my face. I can smell her from here, and my mouth waters.

Leaning forward, I bring my mouth to her lips, letting my tongue slip free to have a taste.

Rylee lets out a breathy moan as her juices hit my tongue. I need more. More of the sounds of her pleasure, more of her sweet pussy.

Gripping her thigh, I hold her down as I swipe my tongue up through her slit. Again and again. Quickly I become addicted, and as soon as I feel confident enough, I go for it.

"Fuck, Colton!" she shouts as I bury my face between her legs. She grabs a handful of my hair, holding my face in place as she grinds against my mouth. "That's it. Damn, that feels so good."

Her praise boosts my confidence. I suck her clit into my mouth and bring two fingers up, teasing her entrance. She's wet, her juices dripping onto my fingers.

"Fuck me with your fingers, Colton. Make me scream."

Holy shit. I'm trying really hard not to come right now.

Looking up, I see Rylee has her head tilted back, lost in the moment. I'm doing this, I'm making her feel good. That's what I want. No more pain, only pleasure, when it comes to me and her.

Slipping my fingers inside, I moan against her core at how tight she is. "God, yes."

For a second, I have no idea what to do. How to move my fingers, but then I remember the few videos I've watched.

I was never really one for watching porn, but after meeting Rylee, I wanted to know a few things, so I didn't look like a fool the next time we did things.

And boy am I glad I did.

Crooking my fingers, I seem to be doing something right as I make a beckoning motion. She lets out another moan, her hips bucking forward. "Right there," she pants.

I keep up the motion as I suck and lap at her clit.

My cock is painfully hard and really uncomfortable. Using my free hand, I rub the heel of my palm over the hard outline of my pants and groan, my eyes rolling back at the little bit of relief.

Something in me snaps, and I start to feast on her pussy like a starved man.

"Oh fuck, yes! God, your mouth!" Rylee screams.

It hits me that we're in school right now. Anyone could walk in on us. But I can't find it in me to care as I chase both hers and my own release.

The girl of my dream's has her pussy in my face right now,

her hand in my hair as she uses me to take her pleasure. Not even God himself could tear me away.

"I'm so close, Colt. Please, please don't stop," she begs me, her breathing coming out in quick, short pants.

I'm close too, as I start to rub over my cock harder and faster.

"Yes, yes, yes!" she shouts, her thighs clamping around my head like a vice grip. "Colton!" she sobs as her pussy latches onto my fingers, her body arching up as her orgasm rips through her.

Her release triggers mine and I let out a long groan, I come in my pants at the same time as Rylee gushes on my fingers and into my mouth.

"Hey man, are you done working or whatever. I thought we could go and grab a bite to—"

Donny's voice has my eyes snapping open.

"Never mind. I see you already have lunch," he says. I'm not sure if he's pissed off or not, his tone not giving too much away.

But Rylee snorts out a laugh.

I slowly pull my fingers from Rylee and lift my head from between her legs.

Looking from a blank-faced Donny, then up to Rylee, I wait for her to freak out or something at being caught. I push the chair back, giving her space. She doesn't though. She grins down at me, looking beautiful as ever with a glow to her skin, her cheeks flushed from her fresh orgasm.

"Thanks for that," she says, hopping off the desk and fixing her skirt. "I really needed that. And for your first time,

I have no tips to give. You eat pussy like a pro." She gives me a wink before giving me a quick peck on my cheek.

I watch her in stunned shock as she bounces her way toward the door. "See you later, boys," she says, giving us both a smug smirk before leaving.

"What the fuck was that?" Donny asks, his head snapping in my direction. "Did you just eat Rylee out on your desk?" he asks as he walks over to me.

I can't seem to find the words, so I nod. My mouth is still wet with her release, my fingers are still coated too. And my pants now have a wet spot. It's safe to say I'm a mess in the best way.

"No fucking fair," he whines. "How do you get to have her more than once, and I still haven't?!"

"No idea," I whisper, looking down at my hand.

"Did you finger fuck her too?" he asks.

"Yes," I say, looking back up at him with a furrowed brow. "So?"

"Give me that," he says, snatching my hand as he bends over and fucking sucks Rylee's release off my fingers. I gape at him in horror.

"Dude!" I shout as I pull my hand from his grip and jump up.

"Look, I needed to taste her again, man! It's been ages. Pity me."

"I don't even know what to say." I sigh, shaking my head.

"Man." He laughs. "You totally came in your pants like a teenage boy, didn't you?"

"Fuck you," I mutter. "Don't act like just a look your way

from Rylee doesn't make your dick hard. Try having your mouth on her as she screams your name."

"Fair." He nods. "I'd totally lose my load too."

"I need to go clean up," I groan, running my clean hand down my face.

"Hey," he says, bending down and picking up Rylee's panties. "Are these hers?"

"Yes," I say, going to take them from him, but he pulls them away. "Donny. She gave them to me."

"Mine," he growls before stuffing them into his pocket and taking off, muttering some nonsense about his precious.

"Donny!" I shout, but he's gone. "Damn it. Fucking weirdo."

I have no idea what just happened or why, but I'm marking this as the second-best day of my life. All I hope for is that this will be a turning point for us. But I know until I open up to her, tell her about my past, she won't even think about trusting me.

I'm going to tell her. I just don't know when a good time will be.

But I do know one thing, the sooner the better.

CHAPTER FIFTEEN

Rylee

What happened with Colton has left my mind a jumbled mess when it comes to my feelings for him.

All I can think about is his mouth on me, and the way he brought me pleasure. I want to tell myself the only reason I enjoyed it so much is because I haven't had sex in months, but that's not it. At least, not the only reason.

I don't want to like him. But I'd be fooling myself if I didn't find myself thinking about the things we've done together. Or my eyes lingering on him whenever we're in the same room.

The way he smiles when he brings me random coffees always makes me want to smile back.

Colton isn't the only one who's been leaving me little gifts though. Donny thinks he's sneaky, but I know he's the one leaving gift bags at my dorm door. So far I've gotten baked goods, candies, clothes, and bath products. Not that I have a bath I'm able to use them in. But I think it's sweet.

Alex had started thinking I had a stalker, so he installed a ring door camera. I don't think Donny has even realized it's there yet. But the grin on his face every time he drops something off is adorable.

As for the other two—Mateo has laid off on the snarky comments and dirty looks, so I'll take that as a win. Lennox has been oddly sweet, too. It's not something I'm used to from him.

He takes the time to see how I'm doing, how school and work is going. I do the polite thing and engage with him. The frustrating thing is, I'm starting to see a new side to these guys that is making it very hard to keep hating them for what they did to me.

They remind me of the men I met in Florida, but that doesn't change anything. I have no plans to forgive them anytime soon. They haven't earned that. But would it be so wrong of me if we... I don't know... became friends?

Life is too short to hold grudges, and if people are capable of showing they can change, am I wrong for wanting to give them another chance?

"Come on!" Alex whines as I add the last of my makeup. "I'm hungry."

"Relax, baby." Serenity laughs. "You're not going to starve to death."

"That's easy for you to say. You have no idea how much I need to eat to stay alive."

"Trust me, I do. I've seen you eat," she says.

"I'm done, I'm done!" I say, tossing my lipstick into my purse. "Don't get your panties in a twist."

His eyes go wide and he looks at Ren. "You told her! I know I lost the bet, but you said you wouldn't tell anyone I'm wearing your panties!"

"What? No, I didn't," Serenity hisses.

"Oh, my God." I snort out a laugh. "Dude, are you really wearing panties? Let me see."

"No." He shakes his head as I stalk toward him, a wicked smile on my face. "Get away from me!"

"Let me see."

"Back, you devil woman!" he shouts, jumping up on his bed.

I dive forward, gripping the bottom of his shorts and pulling them down, revealing pink panties with little yellow duckies on them.

"Oh, my God." I start to lose it, laughing so hard my belly hurts.

"I hate you," he grumbles, pulling his pants back up. "And you!" He points to his girlfriend who's laughing with me. "The betrayal hurts."

"Sorry, baby. You look so cute!" She snorts a laugh.

I'm about to ask what bet he lost to earn him this punishment when someone behind us speaks.

"Uhh, am I interrupting something?" Trevor says, his voice laced with amusement.

"Just these two being bullies," Alex says, jumping off the bed and over to his best friend. "Save me."

Trevor laughs. "Oh, come on. Look at these two sweet faces," he says, looking over at us. Serenity and I give them puppy dog eyes and a pout.

"Don't let their innocent faces fool you. They like to de-pant people!" Alex huffs, giving us a glare.

"What are you doing here?" I say, giving him a smile. "Not that I'm not happy to see you."

"You didn't tell her?" Trevor asks Alex.

"Tell me what?" I ask, tilting my head a little bit.

"I thought we could all go out... you know, on a double date," Alex says, his grin telling me he's not even sorry for leaving me in the dark.

Me and Trevor have been texting a lot since he gave me his number, but I haven't had the chance to see him since Donny's prank. The thing is, I like him. But I also like Colton. Maybe even Donny. The other two I'm still not sure about.

"Don't you think that's something you should have run by me first?" I ask, raising a brow as I place my hands on my hips.

"I can leave," Trevor says, looking between us, his cheeks pinking a little.

"No. Stay. I think it will be fun. We were just going to dinner and a movie. Do you like horror movies?"

"Love them," he says, giving me a grin that makes my belly flutter.

"Perfect."

"YOU SCREAMED LIKE A LITTLE BITCH." Trevor laughs as we walk out of the theater.

"He just popped up out of nowhere!" Alex grumbles. "Way too many jump scares for my liking."

"I loved it," I say with a grin. "Had my heart pumping."

"You screamed too," Alex mutters.

"Yeah, but, like I said, I loved it."

"I did too. It was a good movie," Trevor laughs.

"You're all crazy," Alex grumbles.

"It's okay. I'll always protect you from the big bad monsters," Serenity says, trying not to smile.

"You all suck!" Alex growls, walking a little faster ahead of us.

"Oh, don't be like that," Serenity shouts as she takes off after him.

"Those two are adorable," Trevor says.

"They are. I want that some day," I reply, looking up at him. There were a few times I grabbed his hand during some of the scary parts. He let me squeeze it as tightly as I wanted and never complained.

"You deserve it." With the way he's looking at me, it's like he wants to say he hopes he could be the one to give that to me.

I could see it. I could see myself falling hard for him. But the last time I fell for a guy, I got hurt. Repeatedly.

"So," I say, the moment getting a little too intense for my liking. "Did you get that video of Colton?"

"Ah, yeah," he laughs. "Although, I wasn't the first to share that one. I have to admit, I kind of felt bad for the poor guy."

"Don't worry, his dick isn't that small." I snort out a laugh as I realize I've said too much, giving him a guilty look.

He's a good sport and lets it go. "How pissed was he?" Trevor asks.

"He wasn't." I sigh. "And that's the thing. I'm trying to enjoy my revenge. Enjoy watching them squirm. But none of them have confronted me about the pranks. They know it's me, I haven't done anything to hide that. Still, they say nothing, do nothing. Just take it like they think they deserve it."

"They do deserve it," Trevor points out.

"Yeah, but where's the fun in that?" I sigh dramatically.

He laughs. "So are you done messing with them?"

"No." I snort out a laugh. "If they're going to take it like my little bitches, then I'm more than happy to keep dishing it out."

"That's my girl," he says.

His girl. Why do I like the sound of that?

"Rylee?" Donny's voice has my spine going rod-straight.

"Great," Trevor grumbles. "It's like they're Beetlejuice. Talk about them three times and they show up."

Turning around, I see all four guys. Colton's eyes find

mine, and a wave of heat hits me at the way he's looking at me. He's thinking about what we did.

Donny, poor guy, looks confused. Lennox is watching us with a calculated look, but Mateo... dude, is glaring at Trevor like he wants to rip his head off.

Well, this night is taking an interesting turn.

Tonight has been amazing. Maybe it's sad that just going to a movie has made this the best night I've had in a long time, but I'm here with Rylee. Every time she grabbed my hand during the movie, I had to hold myself back from wrapping my arm around her to hold her tight.

Am I a fool to have fallen so hard for her so fast? Alex thinks I should go for it, to pursue her further, but the reasons why I haven't picked a date for that coffee I asked her out on are standing right in front of us.

Why can't these guys just fuck off and leave her alone? Let her move on and be happy. I get that they're on the same cheer team. They're going to be in each other's lives, but it doesn't need to be more than that.

Yet Donny is sniffing around her like an obsessed puppy, Colton is looking at her like a love-sick fool, Lennox looks like he regrets everything he ever did to her, and Mateo looks seconds away from kicking my ass.

Knowing that I get to them makes me really happy. Like they think I'm a threat.

"What are you doing here?" Mateo asks, his eyes finally leaving me to look at her.

"We just got done seeing a movie," Rylee mutters, crossing her arms.

"You're on a date?" Donny asks. Now the dude looks like we just kicked his dog. He really does have it bad for Rylee.

"Yeah, we were. And we were just about to go out to eat, if you don't mind," I say, finding myself wrapping my arm around her waist. I don't know why I did it, and I hope she doesn't get pissed off, but these guys appeared out of nowhere and act like she owes them an explanation.

To my surprise, Rylee doesn't move, she doesn't even stiffen. If anything, she leans into my touch, making me fucking preen with pride.

I swear Mateo lets out a low growl. I'm not going to lie, the dude terrifies me, but I'm not going to back down. I guess this is me showing everyone I'm throwing my hat in the ring? I don't know what the fuck I'm doing, but I'm going with it.

"Really?" Mateo scoffs. "After you were with Colton the other day? Nice." This time Rylee does stiffen. I don't know what they're talking about. It's none of my business what she does and who she does it with, but I don't like how they're making her feel uncomfortable.

"Man, no," Colton says, shooting his friend a glare.

But my girl has a backbone and she uses it, not needing

anyone to protect her. "Fuck you. You have no right to say anything. I'm single, and if I want to mess around with someone, then go on a date with someone else, I have every right to," she grumbles, then shoots me an apologetic look. "Sorry."

"No need to be," I tell her. "You're right. You're free to see whoever you want. You owe no one an explanation, not even these guys."

"No one asked for your opinion," Donny says, sounding defensive.

"How's your asshole doing?" I ask, raising a brow, a grin taking over my lips.

"Fuck you," he spits.

"Nah, I don't like to put myself in shitty situations." I taunt them. Probably not a smart idea, but these guys are really fucking pissing me off.

"Look. We have somewhere to be," she says to the guys. "I'll see you all tomorrow at practice. And I'll see you at our tutoring session after." She directs the last part to Colton.

She doesn't let them say anything else as she grabs my hand and pulls me away from them, toward the car where Alex and Serenity went.

"Sorry about them," she grumbles.

"Don't be. They're jealous." I laugh.

"I know." She sighs. "I hope they didn't ruin our date."

I pull her to a stop, wrapping my arm around her waist. "So is that what this is? A date?"

"I mean..." She bites her lower lip, and fuck, she looks so sexy. "I'd like it to be?"

"Then it's a date," I say softly, smiling at her as I reach up to brush some of her red locks out of her face. "Can I say something that might totally make or break this night? But I feel like if I don't say it now, I'll miss my chance."

"What's that?" she asks in a whisper.

"I like you, Rylee. You're strong, beautiful, talented. You make me laugh and smile, and you always seem to know what to say to make me feel like I'm wanted when we talk. You didn't deserve all the bullshit you've had to deal with since being here, and I wish more than anything that we met before we did because I would have fought to protect you, Rylee. I would have done whatever I could to make it stop. To take the hits myself if I had to."

"Trevor." Her voice cracking as her eyes water.

"Shh," I say, cupping her cheek. "No crying. I don't wanna make you cry. Only smiles."

"Kiss me," she whispers, surprising the fuck out of me. "Please?"

My heart starts to pound in my chest. She doesn't have to ask me twice. Leaning forward, her eyes flutter shut just before my lips meet hers. They're soft and warm, and the whimper that leaves her puffy pink lips as our mouths lock together has my cock twitching in my pants.

She tastes like cupcake lip gloss, so sweet. Just as I'm about to part her lips with my tongue, our mutual ass of a best friend has to go and fuck it up.

"That's my boy. Get it!" Alex whoops.

Rylee giggles against my mouth and I grin. Our eyes open and my heart fucking bursts at the look she gives me. "I'm gonna kill him." I laugh.

"Not if I kill him first." She smiles.

Tonight is perfect, and not even those assholes from before could ruin it. I'm not sure what this means for Rylee and me, but one thing I know for sure, I'm not backing down. There's something special about this girl and I want to get to know her better. She's worth fighting for and that's what I plan on doing.

CHAPTER SIXTEEN

Rylee

"You have got to be kidding me," I mutter to myself as I read the sign posted on the library door that reads 'Closed until further notice due to plumbing issues'.

I'm supposed to be meeting Colton for one of our tutoring sessions today. With Thanksgiving coming up next week, I want to make sure I'm caught up so that I can enjoy the holiday. I've offered to help the guys volunteering at one of the rec centers, and I really would like to not have to worry about unfinished school work.

Turning to leave, I reach into my pocket to grab my phone to call Colton and tell him, but I see him jogging over to me.

"Hey," he says, sounding a little out of breath. He pushes his glasses up his nose, his cheeks flushed from jogging. "Sorry I'm late, class ran longer than expected."

My cheeks heat at the mention of him and class. His face between my legs, the way his tongue licked me so good.

And now I probably look stupid standing here as I try to discreetly press my thighs together, getting turned on by my memories.

"It's fine. The library is closed anyway," I say, waving my hand toward the notice on the door.

His brows furrow as he reads it. "Well, that's unfortunate." He sighs, looking back at me. "We can still study someplace else if you'd like?"

"Sure," I reply, shrugging. It's not just me wanting to get this work done that has me saying yes, it's that I actually want to spend some time alone with Colton.

I've already decided to stop hating him, and accept the fact that I'm crushing on him again. This time, it's different. Before it was a sweet boy who I knew nothing about yet clicked with right away.

Now it's a man who's seen me at my worst and didn't go running for the hills. Mind you, his friends were the cause of most of my trauma. He's almost there when it comes to redeeming himself in my eyes.

There's just one more thing he needs to do. Well, two. Apologize to me sincerely, and tell me why he did what he did. Why he reacted so recklessly before coming to me and confronting me about what he saw.

"Awesome," he says. The smile he gives me is making my belly flutter. "We could go to the park, maybe sit on a blanket under a tree, or try the coffee shop?"

"Coffee shop would be too loud, and they're doing some landscaping at the park."

"We could go back to the cheer house," he suggests, giving me an unsure look. "You won't have to worry about seeing anyone, we can go to my room." His cheeks heat at his words and I find it adorable. "I mean to study."

"Yeah, I think that would work." I laugh.

"Okay... good," he says with a smile.

As we walk to the cheer house, we talk with ease. Colton is a little more quiet today than he normally is when we get together for tutoring. He usually gets excited about the book he's reading, telling me about it, going into details about the plot and the characters. I adore seeing the way his face lights up when he's talking about something he loves. It's rare to see Colton happy.

"Our room is in the basement," he says as we step into the cheer house. I knew that. I think he's forgotten I've been here before as he starts to give me a mini tour, but I let him.

Colton takes me down to his room and opens the door, letting me enter first.

"Nice room," I say, looking around. It looks like a typical guy room with the dark bedding and posters on the wall. But it's very Colton-like, with it being clean and smelling like freshly washed linen.

"Ah, thanks," he says, stepping inside and closing the

door behind him. "We can sit on the bed if you want? It might be a little more comfortable."

"Sure."

We get situated on the bed and get to work. As time goes by, the work is getting done, but I notice Colton is a little distracted. He keeps looking at his phone when it dings and frowns.

"That's it," I say, slamming the textbook shut. "What's going on?"

"What do you mean?" he asks, blinking at me in confusion.

"Talk to me, Colt. There's something bothering you and I'd like to know what. You can talk to me."

Open up to me, let me in. Let me know how you went from being such a sweet man to cold and closed off.

He looks at me for what feels like forever, chewing on his lower lip before nodding, letting out a sigh that makes him sound like he has the world on his shoulders. "Yeah, okay, I'll tell you. If we're ever going to put things in the past and move on, I need to be open and honest with you about myself."

"Okay," I say, putting the books to one side and sitting up with my legs crossed, giving him my full attention.

"I'm sure by now you know I'm a bit of a control freak."

"A bit?" I tease him, glad that he gives me a hint of a smile.

"Okay, a lot of a control freak. But there are reasons for that." He looks me in the eyes and I can tell things are about to get real, fast. "Rylee, I've never told anyone what I'm about to tell you. The guys know a lot, but there's even some things I haven't told them." He swallows thickly, his face going a little pale. My stomach drops as my heart rate starts to pick up.

"I'm listening," I tell him, my voice soft as I reach for his hand, taking it into mine. He looks like he could use a little strength, and I'm more than willing to give him some of mine.

"I had a sister. Her name was Caitlyn." He gives me a sad smile and I don't miss the fact that he said *had*. Past tense. Already my heart is breaking for him. "We were close. We shared a love for cheer, and a lot of what I know, I learned from her."

He looks down at our hands and he brushes his thumb over the top of mine. "When she was sixteen, she was killed. It was bad. Really fucking bad." His voice cracks. My eyes start to sting, but I hold the tears back as he continues. "I can't speak the details, it's too hard. I feel sick even just thinking of it."

"You don't have to," I whisper. "It's okay."

He nods, looking grateful and continues. "It hit our family hard. My mom started drinking. My dad left us and found a new family with a younger woman. I have other siblings I've never met."

"Wow," I say.

"Yeah," he sighs. "I haven't seen him since he left. It was just me and Mom for a while. But I never felt so alone. Thankfully, I had the guys. They were my best friends, then they became my family. We all have our own fucked up trauma that bonded us together, you know?" I nod, because I can understand that. I'm not that different from them. I have my own messed up past.

"I started spending all my free time with the guys. Then, when it was time to go away to school, I jumped at the chance to be out of that house, away from my mom. Because she stopped being my mom the moment my sister died."

My heart breaks for him. My mother means the world to me. She's my best friend. Just the idea of not having her, of her changing and giving up on me, makes me want to cry. I make a mental note to call her more. We've only talked a few times since the whole kidnapping thing with the guys. Life got so busy, so fast.

"After my dad left, he would still send Mom money. He even gave us the house, but it's not enough for her. I knew she was using some of the money to support her habits, but when I left for school, it got worse. She started calling me, telling me she needs money for food. I'd ask her what she did with the money Dad sent because it should have been enough, but I knew. I also knew she would starve to death, choosing her addiction over living. I couldn't live with the guilt of knowing I could do something about it."

"It's not your job to take care of your parent, Colton," I tell him, hating the tired look in his eyes.

"I know," he says. "But she's my mom, you know? So I sent her whatever money I had left, a little bit at a time. She would call me up a few days later, telling me she needed more. She was blowing the money on drugs. Not having much else to give, still needing my own money to live on, I got a job. School is what I knew best, so I became a tutor. And at a school like this, the pay is well worth it.

"Not being able to trust her to spend the money the right way, I contacted my neighbor. Ever since then, I've sent her the money and she would have food delivered to my mom's house, get it put away, and every now and then, check in on her. She also happened to be my mom's best friend. The whole thing's fucked up."

Tears fall from his eyes and it takes everything in me not to pull him into my arms and hold him tight. I'm breaking right alongside him. He doesn't deserve all this pressure and the burden.

"Colton," I whisper, scooting closer to him until our knees touch. He takes both my hands now, squeezing lightly like he's pulling from my strength with what he's about to say next.

"I hated her, Rylee," he says, his voice cracking as he starts to cry. "I hated her so much. How could she choose drugs over her kid? How could she choose to get high to drown out the pain of losing one kid while the one who was still alive was hurting?" A sob rips from his chest and I start to cry with him. I don't say anything, letting him get everything out.

"There were times I'd wish she'd die. When I was so overworked with school, work, cheer, hers and my own life, all I could think about was having one less thing to worry about. How fucked up is that? I'm a fucking monster."

"No." I sniff, a tear rolling down my cheek. "You're not a monster, Colton. You took on a lot at a young age. You're allowed to feel this way. It doesn't make you a bad person."

"I'm not sure I can agree with you on that." He shakes his head. "Because I got a call a week ago. My mom was taken to the hospital. She was at the store, had a breakdown and hurt herself. They kept her there for a few days, forcing her to detox. She started seeing things, talking to people who weren't there. They kept her longer to run some tests, and fuck, Rylee."

Tears stream down his cheeks now. God, I hate this. I hate seeing him hurt like this. "They think she has early-onset Alzheimer's, and the reason we didn't know was because the drugs and alcohol were masking it. I just assumed she was out of it, high out of her mind, when really she could have been sick all this time. I wanted her dead, and this whole time she couldn't help it."

"Oh, Colton." My heart shatters in my chest as he breaks down, his whole body shaking with sobs. I climb into his lap and wrap my arms around him. He wraps his arms around me, pressing his face into my neck. We stay like this, crying in each other's arms.

I just hold him as long as he needs me to. When our bodies are still and the crying calms, Colton moves back just enough for me to see his face. His glasses are wet and foggy, his eyes red-rimmed and swollen around the edges.

"Cheer and my school life is the only thing I feel like I have any real control over. I became blinded by the need for that control that I didn't even see it was causing me more harm than good. I did you wrong by not confronting you that day. By hearing what I did and letting my mind see it as the truth. I'd already fallen so hard and fast that I didn't want to risk you confirming it yourself and have it hurt so much more.

"We fucked up, Rylee. I fucked up, and I hate myself for

it. The idea of any pain coming to you makes me sick, but knowing we caused some of it, I can't even look at myself in the mirror sometimes. I can't speak for the others, they need to come to you on their own. But I'm sorry, so fucking sorry that I hurt you. I'll do anything to earn your trust, to earn your forgiveness. You mean so much to me, Rylee." He takes his glasses off, tossing them to the side before wiping at his face.

Hearing him finally own up to his mistakes, knowing why he did the things he did, I can finally forgive him. As soon as I think the words, it's like one of the many weights are lifted off my shoulders.

Grabbing the back of his head, I bring my forehead to his. "I forgive you, Colton," I whisper, truly meaning the words. I feel something for him, something strong that goes beyond friendship or teammates.

A choked sob leaves his throat. "You do?" he asks in disbelief.

"I do." I nod.

"I love you," he says, and I suck in a gasp, eyes widening at his confession. "You don't have to return the feeling or say anything. I just wanted you to know how much you mean to me. You're the light in the darkness that clouds my life. The rainbow peeking through. Just having you in my life as a friend is more than I could ever ask for."

"Colton," I whisper, my voice wobbling. I'm not sure if I could say what I feel for him is love, but I know that's what it could turn into. That scares me because the last time I allowed myself to feel something for him and the others, they crushed my heart into dust.

It's going to take a while for me to truly feel like Colton won't do it again, but I can't let the fear keep me from living.

That's why I do what I do next.

"Rylee." He says my name like a desperate plea. Moving back enough to look into his eyes, my heart starts to thud in my chest like a drum at the intense amount of emotions swimming in his stunning blue eyes.

My lips find his and everything snowballs from there in the best way possible.

Colton groans as he moves his lips against mine with a hungry need. I lick the seam of his lips, asking them to part. He opens for me, allowing me to slip my tongue past his lips and over his.

Falling back onto the bed, he takes me with him so that my body is draped over his. One hand glides up my back into my hair, his fingers tangling in the long strands as he cradles the back of my head, holding me to him. The other grips my ass, urging me to grind against him. He's so fucking hard. My body flushes with the need for him to be inside me.

I whimper when my swollen clit rubs against the rigid outline of his cock. "Fuck," I hiss, moving faster, chasing the burning pleasure that's growing inside me.

I want him, need him. Is it fucked up to have sex with him when we're both in such vulnerable states?

"We should stop," I say, panting against his lips.

"You don't want this?" he asks, hurt lacing his question.

"I do. I really do, Colton. But I don't want to take advantage of you." I close my eyes, my whole body feeling like it's being pumped full of electricity.

"You're not. I want this. I've wanted this for so long,

Rylee." He lets out a little growl that has my pussy weeping as he leans up and smashes his lips to mine. Wrapping his arm around my waist, he holds me to his body as he flips us so that he's on top now.

Thrusting his cock against my clit, I moan, my eyes rolling back. "You're so sexy when you cry out for me, Rylee." This is a different Colton than I'm used to. Where's the sweet, shy boy? Doesn't matter right now because the way he's looking at me, like he wants to devour me in any way he can, has me aching for him. "I wanna hear you scream, sweet girl."

"Fuck me," I breathe out.

"With pleasure." He grins as he climbs off the bed. I lay there and watch him strip for a moment, admiring the sight of his body. He's lean but toned, his muscles filled out nicely. He's gorgeous.

Holy shit, I'm about to have sex with Colton. And I'm fully clothed. *That just won't do.* I start to undress too, and when I'm done, I find Colton standing there, a primal look in his eyes as he strokes his cock. Fuck, I forgot how big he is, and the fact that he has a pierced dick.

"Like what you see?" I ask, letting my thighs fall open, revealing my wet core to him.

His confidence starts to dissolve a little as he swallows hard, a nervous look taking over as the haze of the moment starts to clear.

"Colton," I say, holding out my hand. "Come here. Come make love to me."

He brightens up, a happy smile taking over his lips as he

takes my hand. He moves his body over mine and I find myself getting nervous. But excited too.

"Hi," he says, looking down at me, brushing the hair from my forehead.

"Hi," I say back, smiling up at him as my finger runs lazily up and down his arm.

"I don't deserve you. But I plan on spending every day showing you how lucky I am to have you in my life," he says with a sincere tone.

"Okay," I reply softly. He kisses me again, this time it's slow and sweet. The kind you feel slowly taking over your body, filling you from head to toe with the warm and fuzzies.

Without breaking the kiss, he adjusts himself, bringing his cock to my entrance. "I need you," he says with so much pain that all I want to do is take it from him.

"Then take me." Our eyes flick between each other before Colton bites his lower lip and presses forward.

It's a struggle to keep my eyes open as he inches his way into me, the pure shock and bliss on Colton's face is worth it.

It feels so good, his Jacob's ladder rubbing against my sensitive inner walls. I whimper in pleasure, a little 'oh' slipping from my lips as he presses himself fully inside me.

"Fuck, you feel so good." He groans, his breathing already starting to come in fast pants.

"So do you," I breathe, lifting my hips. "I need you to move, please."

He nods, bracing his weight on his arms to hold himself above me. Slowly, he pulls all the way out before thrusting back in. "Rylee," he groans.

"Colton."

He does it again a few more times and the pleasure starts to build. I can see when the control starts to break on Colton's face, like he can't hold himself back any longer, and he picks up the speed.

"Oh, God," I moan as he starts to fuck me, really fuck me. The grunts he makes and the determined look on his face just makes me wetter.

My hands slide up his thighs as my legs wrap around his waist. Bringing his lips back to mine, I let my hands roam over his body, loving the feeling of him under my touch.

I don't think Colton has had sex very much. I can feel the uncertainty in the way he moves—but I can see the need to get it right as he starts to get into a rhythm.

Sex with Colton can't be compared to anyone else I've been with before. It's special and meaningful. The way he makes my body come alive. He and the others have been the only ones to make me feel that way.

"This is amazing," he says, his voice cracking, kissing me again. "Holy shit. Fuck, this feels so good. I can't believe we're really doing this. You're gripping me so tight."

He adjusts his position, moving to sit back on his knees and I cry out as his cock hits my sweet spot in this new angle. He pumps into me and my eyes roll back. I dig my nails into his thighs, earning a hissed groan.

"Colton, fuck yes, yes right there," I sob as the pleasure starts to build.

"Oh, fuck," he growls. "At the risk of sounding like a loser, I don't know how much longer I can last. I want you to come first, please," he pleads, as he brings his thumb to my clit.

He presses down and my body jerks at the lighting bolt of pleasure that hits me.

"Yes, yes like that." I encourage him to keep rubbing. "So good," I whine, my hips lifting into his touch.

My breasts bounce every time he thrusts into me, a layer of sweat coating both of our bodies.

His lower lip is trapped between his teeth as he fucks into me and his thumb works me over. My hands find my breasts and I pinch and pull at them, loving the little bite of pain.

"So fucking hot." He grunts.

"I'm close," I pant out. His eyes find mine and I can tell he is too.

He's struggling to keep going.

"Eyes on me," I say, grabbing his free hand and lacing my fingers with his. He nods, picking up speed, working his thumb faster, firmer.

My orgasm starts to build rapidly, the pressure ready to pop. My lips part and my eyes widen. Colton gives me a look that mirrors mine and we both come, falling over the edge together. I scream, crying out his name as my spine arches off the bed, eyes rolling back. I grind against his thumb, using it to draw out my climax.

Colton lets out a strangled groan as he comes, his cock jerking inside me as he fills me with thick ropes of cum. For a moment, I worry about the fact that we didn't wear a condom, but then I remember I'm on birth control. I don't think Colton is one to sleep around, but that's going to be something we have to talk about.

For now, I relax into the bed, enjoying the afterglow as he

collapses on top of me. "That was... Holy shit, that was amazing," he says, sounding out of breath. He kisses my neck before tucking his face into it.

"I'm gonna have to agree." I laugh.

"I love you," he whispers. "I love you so much." I want to say it back, but I can't. So I hug him closer to me and play with the strands of hair at the back of his neck.

We lay like this for a little while, just enjoying being in each other's arms. Eventually, he rolls us, bringing me out on top. We don't talk, and instead we end up falling asleep in a messy, sleepy heap.

Right now, I just want to enjoy being in Colton's arms. Reality can wait a little longer.

"WHERE ARE YOU GOING?" Colton's sleepy voice has me pausing.

"Hey," I say softly, leaning over to place a kiss on his lips. "I hate to run out like this, but Alex blew up my phone. Serenity is in the ER with food poisoning. She's doing better, but I gotta go see her."

"Oh," he says, blinking, looking a little more awake. "I can drive you."

"That's okay. Alex is coming back for a few of Ren's things. I'm going to go meet him."

"Okay," he says, sitting up. I finish putting my clothes on and slip on my shoes. "Rylee?"

"Yeah?" I ask.

"Are we okay?" he asks, a look of fear taking over his sleepy face.

"We are good," I tell him, giving him a smile. "More than good. I want to talk more about this," I say, pointing between me and him. "I don't regret it."

"Good." He lets out a breath. "It would kill me if you did. I'd never want to guilt you into anything."

"Trust me, I wanted it. And very, very much enjoyed it." I laugh, packing up my books.

"It was amazing for my second time," he says, flopping back onto the bed with a grin on his face.

How he phrased it has me pausing. "You mean, the second time between you and me, right?"

His cheeks pinken. "Ahh. This was not how I wanted to tell you."

Holy shit. Holy fucking shit. That time at the hotel, that wasn't just our first time, it was his first time... ever. I took this sweet boy's virginity?

My phone rings, snapping me out of the mini spiral I was about to go on. "Shit, I gotta go. We will talk more about this now too," I say, grabbing my bag and flinging it over my shoulder. I start to rush out, but come to a halt, spin around, run back over to him and place a hard, fast kiss on his lips. "Bye. Thanks for the orgasm," I say before rushing back out the door.

I swing it open and crash into someone. "Whoa there."

With a horrified look, my eyes flick up to Donny, then over to Len, then Teo. Fuck, this is awkward. Saying nothing, I step past them and get the fuck out of there. If there was ever a worst walk of shame, it would be this one. Although there's nothing that I am ashamed of. I loved every moment of it, and I find myself wanting more.

A virgin. I'm a little shocked, but also, this might be fun. I get to teach my nerdy little virgin boy all the firsts.

As I jump into the shower, washing away the remnants of our sex session, I remember everything Colton told me. My poor, broken boy.

Maybe that's why we clicked so fast when we first met. My darkness called to his. To all of theirs.

CHAPTER SEVENTEEN

Mateo

"Can someone please fucking tell me what's going on here?" I snap, and Donny rolls his eyes then crosses his arms against his chest.

"Yeah, and tell me why I'm the only one not getting any action in this stupid house," he whines with a pout. I turn to face him and give him a glare.

"Seriously, that's what you have to say? How about asking why the hell Rylee is screwing Colton, but still treating us all like we're the bane of her existence?"

"Um, well, that's just you, baby," Len chimes in, not helping at all.

Colton glances at his body hidden beneath the blanket and his cheeks are pink. "Can I at least get dressed?" he asks, and I shoot him a glare now.

"Fine, but we need to talk after," I say, then march out to the living room and take a seat. I can smell her. This whole place smells like strawberries and sex, and I'll admit, I'm hard as stone right now, but that doesn't matter. We have been trying to make things up to Rylee for weeks now and she's still not giving us any clue as to if it's working or not.

I'm ready to just cut our losses at this point. We're not the same people we were in Florida. Too much damage has been done, and if she's just going to string the guys along and break their hearts, I won't allow it.

Donny plops down beside me and pulls out his phone, pouting. "I shit myself at practice. It was recorded and put all over social media. People laugh at me now, and I can't even get Rylee to kiss me. I never yelled or reacted to the prank. So, why is she still being mean to me?" he whines, and I roll my eyes and cross my arms.

"Have you actually apologized to her?" I ask, because I don't think any of us have, besides the stuff we said at the cabin. *Not that I can say much, as I haven't tried to apologize either.* He thinks for a minute and then opens up his Amazon app and starts adding things to his cart.

"You can't buy her forgiveness, Donny," I grumble and then shut up. He's not paying any attention to me. Lennox swings by the kitchen and grabs some snacks and drinks, dumping them all over the coffee table. He's been doing so well by not drinking, and I'm proud of him.

"When did you want to go to your house and get your stuff?" I ask him. I've been reminding him for days, but he always changes the subject.

"Maybe after Thanksgiving. I don't want to risk running into my dad, and he's always busy with football after the holiday." I nod and drop it for now. Colton shuffles in from the hall and I can tell he showered. Not that it matters because with no windows in this basement, I can still smell her.

"So... how was it? Tell me everything," Donny starts and I groan, slapping him on the back of the head.

"Please don't share. It's different when we are all in the room together, but I think, when we have separate time with Rylee, it should stay private... special," Lennox mumbles and I raise an eyebrow at him. Is he planning to have one-on-one time with Rylee?

I guess I never thought of it before now. We have always shared. Am I going to want alone time too? Honestly, probably not. We'd more than likely kill each other.

"It's Rylee, so of course it was amazing. But, yeah." Colt clears his throat, his ears turning pink. "I'd like that," he mumbles then takes a seat on the coffee table. "For what it's worth, I didn't plan it. The library was closed so we came back here for tutoring and I found myself opening up to Rylee about everything," he says and Donny sits up, still rubbing his head. I let out a huff of annoyance. I barely tapped him.

"You told her everything? Even Caitlin? What did she say? Is that how you got to bang her? By opening up... I'm not sure I could do that. If Rylee knew... She'd probably be disgusted," Donny grumbles.

Ah, fuck. I pull him into a tight hug and he sits there frozen for a few minutes, trapped in his nightmarish past.

"I don't know if that's why, Donny. I think it's more that I apologized and asked for her forgiveness. We can only buy her so many things, Don. Rylee isn't materialistic. She doesn't want to be treated like a princess, she just wants to have someone love her. Like we all do. I think we have more in common with her than we ever thought," Colton says, then sighs. He looks really happy, and like some of his stress is gone. I guess if Rylee is capable of doing that for him, then maybe she's not a bad idea after all.

We could use some cheering up in our lives. You'd never know it since we're cheerleaders, but we hide a lot of shit, masked behind our smiles. Some things that would haunt people. Is Rylee really the one that could handle the darkness that shadows us?

I drop off another little surprise at Rylee's door then head to class. We have an exciting lecture today about forming our own companies, and I just bought myself a new pen. It's black with red sparkles, plus it matches the one I just gave to Rylee. So, we're twinning.

I have a huge smile on my face when I leave the court-yard and head to Camden Hall. I still don't know what I want my fake company to be, but this is the most fun we've had in class in a long time.

I pass Adams Hall and almost run face first into the guy that's ruining my life; Trevor Haynes. He's not paying atten-tion, walking while scrolling on his phone. If I were to just knock him down, accidentally of course, it would totally be his fault.

Damnit. I hesitated too long and missed my chance, but maybe it was a sign. Rylee seems to like this douchenozzle. He looks up and it takes him a minute to realize it's me as his grin turns to a scowl.

What the fuck does he have to be angry about? I'm not the one coming into his life and stepping on his toes, trying to steal the girl that controls my heart and dick.

"Sup?" I grunt like an asshole, and he puts his phone away with a shrug before standing up tall.

We're about the same height and weight, but I'm sure I could take him down if this were to get physical.

"Class. You?" he replies and I nod. His arms are crossed and his shaggy black hair is in that perfect 'I don't give a fuck' style. I can admit he's good looking. That only makes me hate him more.

"Yes, business," I say with a puffed up chest. I don't know what he's majoring in, but I'm going to be some big time CEO and give Rylee whatever her little heart desires. I will spoil her until she bleeds gold.

Someone walks by us and I recognize him from my class. Shit! I'm going to be late if I don't stop this weird as fuck chat with Trevor.

"Yeah, well, I have to go. Maybe keep your eyes off your phone and not cause a pile up like you do on the field," I grunt then walk away, shaking my head.

What the fuck did I even just say? Rylee has my head all twisted, and I don't like that some new guy is trying to take her from us when I've been trying so hard for my second chance.

I LEAVE the locker room and say goodbye to Teo as I ponder what to do for my assignment. Class was even better than I expected, and I get to create any company I want and I even have a fake budget. Maybe Colt can help me with the numbers. I think I want to run something for kids.

Maybe a community center like the one we went to, but mine will have private tutors, coaches, and opportunities for kids who just need a little help. Whether it's school related or family. I want them to have a safe place, but before I can do that, I need to create a company that will make me billions... I have some time to come up with a few possible choices.

Rylee brushes by me as she talks to Serenity and I bite my lip. Her strawberry scent makes my mouth water and I'm dying for a bite. I have some laundry to do later, but right now, I'm getting hard and I need some fucking relief.

When I get back to the house, I toss my bag on my bed and listen to see if anyone else is home. I don't hear anything as I make my way into Colt's room. I know I need a new hiding space, but at the moment, this is perfect. No one would think to check here. I open his door, then quickly close it and drop to my knees on the side of his bed.

I pull out the bags he keeps packed for emergencies and grab the small Ziploc I have in a side pocket. I'm almost in the clear, and I can't help but to smile at the thought of taking a hot bubble bath with some candles and my preciouses.

A blast of AC hits my back and I know I'm busted when Colt snaps, "Donny, what the hell are you doing? Why are you in my room? What's that in your hand? If you're planning another prank, today is not the day, man."

He seems tired, and maybe he needs some relief too. I contemplate dropping the Ziploc and claiming I was looking for something, but maybe Colt needs this too.

I mean, I have enough to share.

I climb to my feet with a huge smile on my face and hold the bag to my chest. He looks confused for a minute then shakes his head, frowning. "Please tell me that isn't what I think it is, Donny!" I don't reply and he groans, taking his glasses off and pinching the bridge of his nose. I don't see why he's so frustrated.

"Here, I'll share," I say, holding the bag out, but not letting it go. He doesn't move to take it as he puts his glasses back on and shakes his head.

"You've gone too far this time, Don." He doesn't let me explain, just turns toward the hall and stomps away, shouting. "Family meeting, right the fuck now."

I groan and consider bolting for a few hours so they get a chance to calm down. I mean, it's not like I did something horrible. Maybe a little stalkerish, but they're our girl's.

I tip-toe toward the stairs, avoiding the living room, when a hand grabs my shoulder, spinning me around. Mateo looks pissed and his pants are unbuttoned with his hair a mess.

Oh, fuck! Him and Len must have been playing. They have seemed closer lately, which is good. Now we just need our girl to join our family and everything will be peachy.

"What is this about?" he grunts, pulling me toward the couch and sitting next to me so I can't move.

I still have the bag in my hands and I hold it tight to my chest so no one can take it. It's taken me weeks to get the perfect collection. I have naughty, sweet, clean, and ripe.

They will have to pry these from my cold, dead hands.

"I think you are all overreacting. I mean, it's not like I raided the laundry room. They are Rylee's. I've been doing her laundry for over a month now. I say it's my payment, especially since I have to wash Alex's crusty shit too."

Len sits on the coffee table and looks at me with disgust. "I never saw myself saying this to you, Don, ever, but hand them over. We need to dispose of them. Get rid of the evidence before Rylee finds out and we all take shit for your stupidity."

Colt enters the room with rubber gloves on his hands and

an open garbage bag. Is he crazy? We are not throwing these away!

Mateo grabs my wrist and tries to help Len. I'm stunned that Teo even cares. Out of all of us, he hasn't seemed very keen to make amends with Rylee. All they do is argue, and he's not putting his all into making things right.

"No, no!" I shout, twisting my body as best I can as I keep the panties in a death grip. "It's my precious," I cry and Len slaps me across the face, then freezes and blinks at me, stunned at what he just did.

I take their moment of shock as a gift from God and throw myself off the back of the couch, ignoring the sting on my cheek, and rush past a stunned Colt. I need to hide these somewhere they will never find them.

I shove the bag into my shorts, ignoring the large bulge and race out the front door.

Footsteps sound behind me, but they are heavy and I know I'm faster than Mateo. They can try to catch me but, like the gingerbread man, I'm not going to make it easy.

I chase Donny until he gets in between a large group of students. They seem to be having some type of rally in the courtyard. I look for his messy blonde hair and shirtless body, but he seems to have vanished into thin air.

But I'll be waiting for him whenever he decides to come back home. What the fuck was he thinking? Her panties? Seriously? Not only is it a crazy stalker thing to do, but Rylee is going to castrate us all if she finds out.

I'm surprised she hasn't already accused us of stealing her underwear. He's been doing her laundry for a few weeks now, and from the small glimpse I saw of that Ziploc, he has to have at least twenty pairs.

I shake my head and groan with frustration. I love Donny, I do, but sometimes I feel like he just doesn't think about shit before he does it. Lennox catches up to me and gives me my phone.

"Your mom has been calling non-stop. She wouldn't tell me what's wrong, but she seems upset," he says. I rub my eyes and turn back toward the house. I think I know what this is about, and if I'm going to have to go kick someone's ass, I need shoes.

We reach the porch stairs and I pause. Someone is snickering in the bushes, and they are not being sneaky. I nod to Lennox and he rolls his eyes, but he's smiling.

"Go grab my shoes will ya, and Colt," I say quietly, and he nods before jogging up the steps and going inside. I wait. I don't make a sound. It doesn't take long, and I'm almost disappointed. Donny crawls out of the bush on his hands and knees, trying to sneak around the corner of the house.

I bend over and snatch him up by the back of his throat. He makes a gagging sound as I choke him and raise him to his feet.

"Fuck, Teo, man. You scared me." He pants, gasping for breath, and I bring him around until we are nose to nose.

Lennox and Colt meet me at the side of the house, and Len gives me my shoes. "Don't let him move," I growl, ordering one of them to grab Donny.

"You guys are overreacting. This isn't a big deal," he whines, and I'm about to lose it on him, but I won't. I only fight guys in the ring.

"Shut up!" I snap and he gulps. I tie my laces, then stand and grab Donny by the ear.

"What are we going to do with him?" Colt asks and I give him a smile.

"We're not going to do anything except bring him to Rylee and let her come up with his punishment," I say as I tug him toward the dorms. Lennox and Colt trail behind me, and we ignore Donny yelping and moaning.

"Shut up! You did this," I growl and he whimpers, pleading for us not to do this.

"You act as if we're about to hang you, or tie you to a burning post," I snark and he groans.

"I'm never going to get laid. Never ever. My dick is going to fall off."

I snort and shake my head. God, he can be so dramatic at times. Lennox holds the main door open for us and we head toward Rylee's dorm room.

I bang on Rylee's door and wait for her to answer.

"You guys don't really need to do this. I can just wash them up lickity-split and add them to her next load. She won't ever need to know. Seriously, please," Donny pleads with us, but I roll my eyes and Colt looks nervous.

"You should have thought of that before you stole twenty, Donny! Twenty fucking pairs. I just..." Len trails off shaking his head. I knock again and Donny takes a deep breath.

"It wasn't twenty. I only have fourteen. That's it!"

"That's not any better. I think you have a problem," Colt starts as I knock again. Donny fights for me to let his ear go, and I'm questioning my decision not to deck him.

"She must not be home. See, it's a sign," Donny starts to say when the door swings open.

"Um, hey, guys," Rylee says, looking confused at all four of us fighting outside her dorm room. She's changed into pajamas and has her hair tossed up into a messy bun. "What's up?" she asks as I shove past her and toss Donny into the room.

He lands on his knees, and the bulge in his shorts is huge. I know it's the Ziploc but Rylee doesn't. Her eyes go wide and she glances at all of us in shock.

"What's going on? Why are you all here at my door?" she asks and Donny stays silent. Len steps forward.

"Tell Rylee what you did, Don," he orders, and seeing how assertive he's being is turning me on. Now I'm about to have a huge bulge.

"I didn't do anything. Nothing at all. Hi, Rylee, you look pretty." He blinks up at her with a flirty smile and I growl.

"I was just minding my business. Taking a stroll on this fall day, listening to the birds chirp, when you guys grabbed me and dragged me here by my ear." He glances at Rylee and pouts. "It really hurts, Cherry," he whimpers all pathetically, and I don't have time for this shit.

"You were hiding in the damn bushes, crawling on all

fours, trying to sneak away," I grunt with a laugh, and Lennox stands next to me, with his finger out, pointing.

"You tell her right now or I will, Donny. I am not going down for this shit!" Lennox snaps and Donny actually looks scared.

"Oh, that." He giggles nervously, looking from us then back to Rylee. "You're going to laugh," he says, then grabs the band to his shorts and sticks his hand inside.

"Woah, wait. Donny, what the hell are you doing?" Rylee squeals as Donny pulls the Ziploc full of her underwear out.

Her emerald eyes widen and her mouth purses as she sucks in a breath. "Um, please tell me that's not what I think it is?" she says, and she looks a little sick. "You're kidding, right?" She ignores Donny as he grabs her ankle and starts to apologize, looking at us.

I step away and hold my hands up. "Do not look at me. This is all him."

"Does he do this a lot? Is this like a kink of his?" she asks Colt and he shakes his head.

"I'm not some kind of pervert," Donny wails from the floor and we all turn to look at him.

"You have a bag of my dirty panties, Donny! That's the definition of a pervert," Rylee says, exasperatedly, then kicks him off her.

"Stand up," Len says and pulls him to his feet. "Start talking."

He faces Rylee and his cheeks are all red as he rubs the back of his neck with one hand. "I've only ever stolen your panties. You're the only girl to make me wild and crazy enough to do something stupid like this. I can't come unless it's to thoughts of you. No one else since Florida can get me hard. You broke my cock, Rylee," he mutters, and now he won't look at anyone.

I'm starting to feel like this should be a private moment when he drops to his knees again and buries his face into Rylee's stomach, growling. She runs her fingers through his hair, looking at him as she thinks for a moment before glancing over at Lennox.

"Is it wrong that in some weird, fucked up way, it's kind of sweet?" she says quietly and I laugh. Damn, we found the one girl insane enough to deal with our crazy. She grips Donny's hair and tugs, making him look up at her.

"But it needs to stop. And you are taking me lingerie shopping. Those are going in the trash," she says, pointing to the baggie that's now on the floor. "I thought the machine was eating my damn underwear, and this whole time, you were taking them. Do you know how much money I've had to spend on new ones? This shit isn't cheap, Donny." Donny looks like he might actually cry.

"I'll pay you back for all of them, on top of replacing the ones we have to toss," he says, looking up at her with puppy dog eyes.

Fucker is lucky he gets to see another day. I thought she would lose her shit on him, for sure. I mean, what he did would be seen as really fucking creepy to most woman. Maybe she's not as bad as I thought.

CHAPTER EIGHTEEN

Mateo

I leave Donny with Colt and Lennox to deal with the aftermath of that shit-show, then take Lennox's truck and head toward home. I don't know why my mom is there. She's supposed to still be hiding at her friend's place. I really need to get her and Nando out of LA, somewhere my uncle will never find them.

My sister doesn't seem to care anymore and is permanently staying with her boyfriend. I should argue that she's only seventeen, but if he can keep her safe while I'm not around, then I guess I will learn to live with it.

I pull up to the house and it's quiet. The neighbors are all inside, and I don't even hear anyone yelling. This is weird. Maybe I should have had the guys come with me. I park in the driveway and climb out.

Tingles run down my spine, and I feel as if I'm about to be ambushed or something. Today has been fucked up enough, I don't need to deal with more shit. I watch my surroundings as I unlock the front door and walk inside.

It's not that late, just past eight at night. My mom is sitting on the couch, reading a book, and Nando is passed out beside her.

"He tried to stay up to see you, but he fell asleep about twenty minutes ago," she says quietly.

"Yeah, I didn't expect things to take so long. We had to deal with some of Donny's antics," I grumble, and walk over to my mom and place a kiss on her head, then lean down and ruffle Nando's hair.

A snore slips through his lips and I smile.

"You look tired yourself," my mom says and I laugh, shaking my head.

"Yeah, that's an understatement these days. With classes, practice, and girl drama, I don't get much sleep." I take a seat in the chair facing my ma and wait for her to catch on.

"Did you ever find out why that girl backstabbed you? The one you called and told me about when you boys were on vacation?" I groan and rub my eyes, then lean back in the chair and look up at the ceiling.

"Yeah, turns out it's all one giant misunderstanding... Well, according to her it is. Not sure if I believe it, but the guys do, and they have been trying to make things up to her," I grumble.

"If she's worth it, like I suspect she might be, I think you need to try a little harder, baby. I know it's hard for you to trust people, Teo. It's the same for me. But if your best friends—your family—believe her, and want to make amends... I think she must be a good person, and I'd love to meet her. When you get your head out of your ass, *culo terco*," she says and I snort.

I know she's right, and the guys are starting to get pissed at my lack of effort, but is this all really worth it? One girl and four guys. Well, maybe five, if I have to go off that new one sniffing around her. Plus, would she accept Len and me?

I get lost in my thoughts and Nando wakes up. My mom is back to reading her book, I think she knew I needed a minute.

"Teo!" Nando shouts with excitement and sits up on the couch with a big smile. "Did you come to read me a story?" he asks and I nod. No, I didn't come just for that, but since I'm here, there's no way I'm missing out on some brother time.

"Go brush your teeth and pick out a book, I'll be there soon." Nando rushes from the couch and we hear the pitter-patter of his bare feet running down the hall.

"So, are you going to tell me why you're back here and needed to see me?" I ask my mom, and she won't look me in the eyes.

"Your uncle found us. He threatened to take Nando from me if I didn't return. He's been more erratic lately and I wanted to warn you, but I don't know if he's tapped our phones. I know I'm being paranoid, but you can never be too careful with that man. Just watch your back, and if something was to ever happen to me..." She trails off and my hands fist with rage and my eyes blur.

"I won't let anything happen to you ever, Ma," I growl and she leans forward to pat my hand and places her palm on my cheek.

"I know you won't, mijo, but if something does, I've marked you, Lennox, Adonis, and Colton as Nando's next of kin. I'm not so worried about your sister, but Nando is still young, and he idolizes you boys. I know you will take good care of him." Her voice becomes choked with emotion, and I stand from the chair and scoop her into my arms, holding her tight as she shakes with her sobs.

"I'll kill him," I growl, and she pulls away to look into my eyes.

"No, that's what he wants. He wants you to do something reckless and throw your life away. Don't let him win, baby. He will get his just desserts, eventually. You know what they say about karma."

IT'S LATE when I get back to the cheer house, and I quickly change into some swim trunks. After reading Nando his fourth book and he fell asleep, I kissed my ma goodbye, then went off to find that asshole, Angelo.

He wasn't hard to find, since he's staking out the house. I

was able to get the jump on him, but he got a few rib shots in. I know I can't miss any more practice, so a soak in the hot tub it is.

I should wake Len and see if he wants to join me, but he looks so peaceful. I grab a towel and sneak back out into the hall. Colt is sitting on the couch with his laptop and I give him a nod.

"Everything good?" he asks and I shrug, because truthfully? No, everything is total shit, but he doesn't need my drama on his plate. He has enough to deal with.

Walking toward the athletic department, I use my twenty-four hour pass to get in. I bypass the weight room and stride into the pool area. The lights are already on and the tub is roaring with steam and jets.

I don't know who is also in here, but as long as it's not Missi, I don't care. She has been giving Lennox and I evil glares every chance she gets, and I know she's planning something sinister, but that's an issue to deal with another day.

I drop my shit on the floor, then step into the water. Fuck, it's hot. But after I get the water above my dick, and then drop in quickly until it's over my nipples, it's not so bad. I reach for my phone and turn some music on low, then lean back and rest my eyes.

The door slamming has me peeking my eyes open. I groan as her long, tanned legs come into view and her fiery-red hair. Why me?

She shuffles closer to where I am and points to the water. "Can I join?" she asks, glancing around hesitantly and I shrug, then wave my hand to the other side of me before I close my eyes again.

She's quiet until one of my favorite songs starts to play, and she makes it known it's one of her favorites too.

"Turn it up," she says and I roll my eyes but listen. It's a good song. I watch her as she bobs her head along to the music. She looks relaxed, and not like she's about to take a chunk out of my ass.

"So, why are you here so late?" I ask, and she blinks her green eyes at me as she runs her hand through the water.

"I come here some nights when Ren and Alex need the room. Sometimes I use the pool, but after practice and work, I like to use the jets and relax."

I nod, because I can understand that. "I should scold you about being here alone at night, especially in a place where you could drown, but I won't. I'm too tired to keep fighting," I grumble and Rylee snorts.

"I know how to swim, Teo. I grew up on the ocean, remember?"

"That's not what I meant and you know it. Missi may seem to have calmed down, but I know it's just the calm before her storm. Watch your back, Rylee."

She's quiet for a minute, then moves a little closer to me. I don't know what her game is, but I won't comment on it.

"Do you really care about what Missi does to me, Teo, or is it only because your friends would miss me?" she asks and I suck in a breath.

"We may have our shit to deal with, Rylee, but I wouldn't ever want you hurt," I grumble as she slides even closer. I can see her green eyes more clearly now, and the small freckles on her nose.

She laughs and licks her lip. "Could have fooled me, Teo. Out of all the guys, you have been the worst. Which is a shame..." She trails off and looks at my naked chest. "I was so excited to find out I was coming here, but when I saw you four, I thought maybe we could have..."

I sit up. "Could have what, Rylee?" She shakes her head and sighs.

"It doesn't matter now." She watches me, waiting for something. My dick starts to rise and I curse it, hoping Rylee doesn't notice.

"I just thought maybe we would have a repeat of that week," she says softly, placing her hand on my thigh. My body tenses and I know she's seen how hard I am for her. Leaning closer so I can feel her breath on my neck, she speaks again. "I think about it sometimes, you know. Even when you were all being complete asses to me, I would visualize that night. The way you and Lennox shared me. How you felt against my tongue as I took your cock deep into my throat... Do you miss that, Teo? Me on my knees for you. Submitting to you."

She angles her body toward mine, shoving her tits closer to my face. Fuck, she's making it hard to think right now.

Looking into her emerald eyes filled with heat, I nod. I don't know what kind of trance she has me in, but I do think about that night.

"If you think about us, then why are you playing hard to get?" I ask, my voice a low rumble, as I bring my hand to the back of her neck and pull her lips to mine, close enough she can feel my breath as I speak.

She slowly inches her hand up my thigh. The closer she gets to my cock, the harder I am. I wonder if I were to reach down and check, would she be as turned on for me as I am for her.

"You deserve a little torture for all you've done." She purrs and I push back a little, looking into her green eyes again.

"Will you ever forgive us? Will you ever consider giving us a second chance, or are you just playing us?" I have to ask, because if this is just a game, then she needs to let us go. We aren't normal guys. We have been damaged too many times.

"I don't know. I guess what I can't get over is why no one just confronted me. We could have been together all these months, but no one asked." She shakes her head and her hand finds my cock. She cups me over the shorts, giving it a squeeze and making me groan, my eyes rolling back.

"You're such a tease," I growl and she gives me a smirk. I know I'm going to regret this as she slides her hand inside my shorts, pulling my length free. We still have a lot to discuss, but with her hand wrapped around my dick, my brain isn't really working.

I want to taste her, to see if she's just as sweet as I remember. I rest my forehead to hers, catching my breath. "We have been burned so many times. The thought of you being just like all the other girls hurts more than I thought was possible for all of us." She rolls her eyes and my hands twitch to smack her ass.

"Right there was your mistake. You should have just

talked to me, then we could have been doing this all along."
Rylee tightens her fist around my cock, stroking me firmly
but slowly.

Her breasts are barely being held within the bikini top
she's wearing. I grip one side and give it a tug to get to her
nipple. She moans, her eyes flashing with needy hunger.

"Fuck, do you have any idea what you do to me?" I ask,
but I'm too far gone to even think of what I'm saying.

"No," she says, blinking up at me. "Why don't you
tell me?"

"Most days I want to throw you over my knee and smack
that ass you like to taunt us with, before railing you with my
cock, and making the others watch you scream as your juices
run down my balls."

She makes a little whimper. My eyes close as I let my
head fall back. "Fuck, don't stop, baby," I growl. I forgot
what it felt like to have her hands on me. The smell of her
skin, her hot breath against my lips.

After I get off, I'm going to slip off these tiny bikini
bottoms and bury my face in between her thighs and return
the favor. Lick all her cream until she's exploding on my
tongue. I forgot how addictive Rylee is.

Her soft moans, her taste. I know I should stop this.
Things between us are still complicated, but when she shatters, cumming on my lap, I'll be done for. I grip the back of
her neck and pull her lips to mine.

I'm close, but I'm not finishing until her tight pussy is
clenching my cock.

Just as I'm about to explode all over her hand, she freezes
and pulls away from me. Lifting my head up to look at her, to

ask her why she stopped, I find her standing up and backing away. A cocky grin takes over her face.

"Well, this was fun and all, but I gotta run. Sorry about that," she says, looking down at my thick, aching cock.

"Rylee, come the fuck back." I groan as she runs for the door, stealing my towel on the way without looking back at me. "Fuck," I roar, slamming my fists into the water, making a huge splash. Why the hell did I let my dick take control and not my head? I should have known shit was too good to be true.

Now I'm all alone, rock hard, with bruised balls.

Ugh, that little bitch. I want to wrap my hands around her throat and squeeze her pretty neck. I can still smell her scent and it's not calming me down. My dick throbs and my balls continue to ache.

I shove my erection back into my shorts, climb out of the water, grab my phone, and head home. The water drips off my skin and I don't care. I storm out of the gym and walk back to the cheer house.

The air is cold when it touches my heated flesh, but my rage keeps me warm. I slam into the apartment and head straight for Lennox's room. This is all his fault. Him and the others. They wanted to make shit right with her. Try to get her back. Well, fuck that shit. She is a little cock tease and I'm done.

"Get up and on your knees," I order Len when he wakes up. He blinks a few times as I've turned on the light.

Yeah, I'm being a massive dick right now, but it's all of their damn faults. I rip my trunks off and throw them in the corner. They land in a plop, but I don't fucking care. All the blood in my brain is currently in my dick, and I just need the ache to go away.

I grip my cock and ignore Len asking me what happened. No, he doesn't get to question me right now.

"I'm serious, Len, or I will climb onto the bed and straddle your neck," I growl and watch as he gulps, throws the blankets off and gets onto his knees like a good boy. He grips me tight and sucks the tip, but I can't deal with foreplay.

"Make me cum," I grunt and he takes me deeper, reaching up to play with my balls. I groan loudly, but I don't give a fuck. He bobs faster but it's not working, I need more. Rylee has me so highly-strung.

"Get on the bed and grab your ankles," I command, and he stands, wiping his mouth with the back of his hand. His brown hair is a mess and his eyes are watering. I watch as he strips quickly and gets on the mattress.

I reach into the bedside drawer for a condom and some lube. He takes the condom from my hand and throws it on the floor. "I want to feel you raw," he groans as I coat his tight little hole with some of the oil, before lubing up my finger and pressing it in gently.

"Fuck," I grunt, as his ass sucks my finger in. "Can't wait to feel this tight little hole swallowing my cock." I praise him and he grabs my arm, pulling me on top of him. "Grab your ankles, baby." He bends for me perfectly as I rub my cock against his, getting it slick.

"I don't know why you're acting crazed, but if you don't stick that fat dick inside me, I'm going to flip us and take your ass," he growls and my cock leaks. Shit, I love it when he's vocal.

I grip my dick and press it against him, but he's not wanting me to go slow. Taking his foot, he places it onto my shoulder and lifts himself just enough to impale himself on my dick.

"Fuckkk." He whimpers and my balls draw up. I'm on the edge, and I need to get him off before I bust.

I mean, it's only fair. I did wake him up. "Fuck yourself on my cock, baby," I grumble, then grip his dick and jack him off. It doesn't take long until sweat coats us and he's shaking. I know we're being loud as hell, and I didn't even shut the door.

"Not yet, Lennox," I growl and he gives me a glare. This is the second time I've edged him, and I know I'm pissing him off, but I need more. I grip his throat and pull his lips to mine as I fuck him deeper into the mattress. Hot, sticky cum coats my abs and I explode as his ass grips me so tight, I might pass out.

I know we need to talk, and definitely shower, but for once, I'm content, and I don't want to move.

"Damn, that was one hell of a show," Donny grumbles from the door. I glance his way and he looks pissed off. "Everyone in this fucking house is getting laid, and I can't even jerk off with some panties," he grumbles before slamming our door, and I laugh.

Lennox chuckles under me, then groans as I slip out of him and roll to lie beside him.

"So, are we going to talk about what happened just now?" he asks, and I sigh.

"Rylee joined me in the hot tub and things got heated, but just as I was about to come, she bolted like the little cock tease she is," I groan and cover my eyes with my arm.

Lennox pulls it off and wraps it around his neck, resting his head on my chest. "I'm not sure what to say to that, except it's about fucking time." I shove him off me and glare at him.

"This is not funny. I thought she was going to permanently bruise my balls. Why the fuck are you laughing?" Lennox sits up and his green eyes are gleaming. He's almost in tears.

"Teo, that was obviously your prank. And the fact that she even tried to get you back means that she doesn't hate you as much as we thought, and that's good news."

"Yeah, breaking my balls is the best prank ever," I grumble as I climb off the bed and over to the shower.

Today has been wild, and I'm ready for it to end.

CHAPTER NINETEEN

Rylee

I f you asked me what was going on inside my head, I don't think I could give you a good answer because I have no fucking clue.

After Colton opened up, putting his heart on his sleeve for me to see, everything has changed between us. We didn't have sex; no, we made love. The whole experience was amazing, but it also freaked me out. So many emotions to feel at once.

When he told me he loved me, I felt it. He wasn't lying. And when he pretty much told me I took his virginity, I almost freaked the fuck out. That's big, really big. And the fact that he gave something so important of himself to me, it means a lot.

Tomorrow is going to be a busy day with Thanksgiving and everything the guys and I have to do, but I can't shut my mind off.

In the past week, I've gone on a date with Trevor, fucked Colton, and nearly jerked off Mateo. My mind is a mess, and I feel like a horrible person because I like more than one guy. If it was just the guys, I know it wouldn't have been an issue. They were willing to share me from the start.

But I have no idea what Trevor will think. All I know is that I have to be honest with him. I hate being lied to, and would hate to be strung along.

"Hey," Trevor says, giving me a half grin as he joins me at the table. I asked him to meet me at the coffee shop to talk before things go any further.

"Hey," I say, trying to mean the smile I give back to him. My belly is a mess of nerves. I like Trevor. I really like him. He's only ever been nice to me, and he understands the hurt the guys put me through. I have hopes that he wouldn't do that to me too. But I'm not sure if he's going to like what I have to say.

"When you said you wanted to meet, I'm not going to lie, I was happy to get to see you again. But given the look on your face, I'm not too sure now." He gives me a nervous laugh, running a hand through his raven locks to get some out of his face.

"I have no idea where to begin," I say, shifting in my seat.

"Please don't tell me this is where you're dumping me?" he asks with a grin, but I see the sadness in his eyes.

"No dumping on my end." I huff out a laugh. "But I'm not too sure if you're going to want to be with me after this conversation."

"Okay..." he says slowly, tilting his head to the side.

"As you know, my past with the guys has been... complicated, to say the least." He nods. "After Halloween, I found out the truth of why the guys treated me the way they did. And I'm not making any excuses for them, because the whole thing was fucked up, but it just made everything even more of a tangled mess. They've been trying to show me how much they're sorry, and that they're changing."

"Don't tell me you're just going to let them get away with it?" he asks, eyes widening.

"No." I shake my head. "They still have a long way to go. Some more than others."

"Colton," he says. "He seems to be the one out of their group with the most promise." He sighs, leaning back in his chair, seeming to know what I'm going to say on some level.

"I'm not going to lie, I like him. A lot. Things have escalated in our friendship to something more. I'm not sure what we are right now, but ..." I look out the window, trying to hold back the tears.

"You want to see where it goes." He answers for me.

"I know it's stupid. That he hurt me, but I can't shut off how I feel," I say, my eyes meeting his.

"And what about the others?" he asks.

"Donny is trying. Really fucking trying." I laugh. When I found out he was the one who took my fucking underwear, I was pissed because replacing them cost me most of my damn paycheck. But, it's Donny. He tends to be endearing in really weird, Donny-like ways.

Also, call me fucked up, but the idea of me being the only one to make his cock hard, and that he uses my scent to jack off too, is kinda hot. I'm going to hell, I know.

"Lennox and Mateo are still in a gray area," I say, gnawing on my lower lip. I'm not going to mention the hand job I gave Mateo. That was mostly meant to be his prank, and I have the satisfaction of knowing that I was able to be the one to make him lose control.

"What does that mean for us?" he asks. "I meant what I said before Rylee. I like you a lot."

"I like you, too. That's why all of this has me freaking out. I don't want to hurt you. But I don't think I can choose right now. Or at all," I say, tears forming in my eyes.

Maybe it's selfish of me to want more than one person. Maybe I should let the guys go and see where things lead with Trevor. He's a good guy, and hasn't hurt me. Start off fresh.

But I can't just choose to forget about the guys. It's not that easy.

"Then don't," Trevor says, shocking the shit out of me.

"What?" I ask, blinking at him with confusion filling my mind.

"Don't choose. The guys are okay with sharing you with each other, and while I might never like the guys, I can learn to coexist, if being with them is what you choose. As long as I'm a part of the equation, that's all I care about," he says, grabbing my hand with a smile and bringing it up to his lips.

"You mean a lot to me, Rylee, and I want to get to know you better." He brushes his lips across my knuckles and I shudder in pleasure. Fuck me, the way he's looking at me, it's making it hard to sit still.

"I don't think they deserve you. But I don't have a say over your life. If you choose to be with them, I'll support your decision. But I'm not going anywhere, not unless you want me gone. I'm not afraid of them."

"Are you real?" I ask in a soft whisper. His chuckle warms my heart, and this time, I want to cry happy tears. "No, really. Is this some kind of prank?"

"I'd never do that to you, Rylee. I'd never hurt you," he says, his tone so sincere. He stands up, never letting go of my hand, and makes his way to my side of the table. He towers above me, forcing me to look up at him. "I'm here to stay, as long as you'll have me. With or without them in your life. Give me a chance to show you that I can make you happy."

"Okay," I say softly.

He smiles, leaning down so that we're less than an inch apart. "I need to get going, stupid football," he grumbles. "Come watch me play sometime, Red. I'd love to see you in my jersey." And then he kisses me. It's soft and sweet, but has me moaning as my belly fills with heat. "I'll text you later, pretty girl," he says, pecking my lips once more before he steps away, leaving me stunned.

He heads toward the door just as Colton walks in, and Trevor steps in front of him. Trevor towers over Colton by a few inches, making him have to look up at him. Poor Colt looks so confused, and maybe a little frightened.

"I don't care what you have with Rylee, but I'm going to

make this known right now, I'm not going anywhere. So get used to seeing my pretty mug," Trevor growls before stepping around him and leaving the shop.

"What the..." Colton says, eyes wide in bewilderment. He looks around, still frazzled before seeing me.

I grin, giving him a little wave.

Holy shit. Did that just happen? Should I pinch myself and make sure I'm not dreaming?

Just to be sure, I do and it hurts. I'm still sitting here watching a shocked Colton. Well, fuck me. Maybe my life might be looking up for once.

"Cutting it close, T," Alex says, standing there stark-naked with his fucking cock out.

We're in the guys' locker room. I'm not a stranger to naked guys, but Alex just stands there like we're having a conversation on the street.

"Sorry, man," I say, going over to my locker. Opening it up, I start to stick my things in and undress to change into my practice gear. "Was at the coffee shop with Rylee."

"Oh, really?" he says, perking up. "How are things going between you two?"

"Since the date a few days ago, we've been texting a lot,"

I say, unable to keep the smile off my face when I think about her.

"Sexting too?" He grins, wiggling his eyebrows.

"No, you asshole." I laugh. "Nothing like that. Mostly just playing twenty questions, talking about random things we like."

"You're no fun," he says, tossing a dirty sock at me. I dodge it and cringe.

"Get dressed, please. No one wants to see that thing," I say, waving toward his dick.

"My girlfriend does," he says with a chuckle but starts to get dressed.

"Not your girlfriend."

"You're not hot enough," he says, nudging me with his elbow. "Too much dick for my liking, no offense."

"Don't worry, none taken. I got myself someone way better."

"So what were you two talking about? Were you on like a coffee date or something?"

"No," I sigh, shoving my clothes into my locker. "She wanted to talk."

"Did she dump you?" he says with caution.

"We're not really dating, so it wouldn't count as dumping, but no. I don't want to talk about her personal life. I don't have the right."

"Come on, man. She's my best friend. You know she's going to end up telling me. She always does." Alex sighs.

"Nope. Sorry, ask her. But, what I can say is that I told her that no matter what happens with her and the guys, I'm not going anywhere. I will fight to be in her life. She deserves the world, and I'd like to be the one who gives it to her."

"Damn, man, you have it bad." He laughs. He's not wrong. She's all I can think about, and I hate that I can't see her more often because of her work, cheer, and school.

"I'm not even ashamed." I shrug.

"Good. Don't be. Rylee is amazing, and I'm glad she has someone like you on her side."

"She has you and Ren too," I point out.

"Yes, but it's different. We're her best friends. You could be something more to her. Something those guys were too much of a pussy to be."

We get dressed and head out to the field. The whole time, I can't get Rylee off my mind. I plan on stepping it up, asking her out more.

I'm not going to sit by while those fools steal her out from under my nose, because I know they're going to try. Something tells me, they're not going to be too happy about me joining for a chance to win her heart. Sucks to be them, because no matter what they do, they won't get rid of me.

CHAPTER TWENTY

Rylee

"I miss you too, Mom," I tell my mother as I stand outside the rec center, about to head inside to volunteer with the dinner we're putting on for the community.

"I can't wait to see you at Christmas, my sweet girl. It's not the same around here without you," she says, sounding sad, and it breaks my heart. I wish I could be home with her for this holiday, but I don't have the money to fly back for both, and Christmas is the more important of the two holidays for my mom and I.

"Only one more month, then you get me for two weeks," I remind her brightly, trying to lighten the mood.

"Two weeks isn't enough. Why does summer have to be so far away?" She sighs.

"Trust me, time will fly by before you know it."

"I hope so. Happy Thanksgiving, Rylee. I love you."

"Happy Thanksgiving. I love you, too."

After we hang up, I head inside.

The place is alive with chatter and cheer. Kids run around laughing as parents stand and talk to each other.

The smell of turkey fills the building, making me excited for the meal we're going to be having tonight.

My job is to set the tables and help serve, because the guys insisted they make the food, with the help of Mateo's mom. Apparently this is something they do every year, and it means something to them. I find it endearing that they hold something so important close to them.

"Hey," Colton says, stopping before me with a box. He gives me a shy smile, his cheeks flushing with pink. It's only been a few days since we had sex, but I haven't stopped thinking about it. About him.

"Hi." I grin, loving how adorable he is.

"Ah, do you mind putting these out on the table over there?" he asks, pointing to one of the set ups along the far wall.

"Of course," I tell him, leaning up on my tip-toes to kiss his cheek. I giggle at the shocked look on his face as I take the boxes from his arms, and my heart flutters at how he touches his fingers to where my lips touched.

It's nice not to feel so depressed, not to feel like the

world is crumbling down around me all the time. I'm not stupid enough to think all my problems have come to an end. There's still Missi out there lurking in the shadows, and I know she won't just sit back and accept the fact the guys spoiled her fucked up little plan. I just have no idea what she has planned or when she plans on doing it.

You would think I'd live and learn when it comes to matters of my heart, and while I'm not so quick to open myself up and give pieces of myself freely, I can't hide from what's right in front of my face.

Colton is a good guy who made some wrong moves. He's a troubled soul, and I just don't have it in me to hold that against him. And Trevor, I have to ask myself if he's too good to be true. A part of me wants to overthink everything until I've convinced myself that he's going to hurt me, so that I self-sabotage this before it even starts.

But Alex had a talk with me last night, and was really adamant that he doesn't think Trevor would ever hurt me. I'm really going to try to believe that and not let my past haunt me. Not that anyone can blame me if I do. My dating history isn't exactly the best.

Taking the box over to the table, I take out the contents. Paper plates, cups, and plastic cutlery. Once I'm done setting everything up, I go back to the kitchen and see if there's anything the guys need my help with.

When I step inside, I pause and smile. Donny is dancing around the room to Christmas music, stopping to twerk against Mateo as he passes. Mateo pushes Donny off him with a laugh. Donny keeps singing *I Wanna Wish You A Merry Christmas* as he takes a pie and places it in the oven.

"A little early for Christmas music, isn't it?" I ask, my question laced with amusement.

"It's never too early for Christmas, baby!" Donny whoops as he dances over to me, scooping me into his arms and spinning me around the room. I laugh, a wave of joy filling me, as he sings his little heart out to me.

"Come on," Mateo says. "The main course is done and ready to be served. Just make sure to keep an eye on the desserts so they don't burn."

"I'll help," I say, grabbing a few dishes off the counter.

"Thanks," Mateo grunts, holding my eyes for a moment. I still can't believe that I jerked him off. It was so hot. The way his face contorted in pleasure, how his cock pulsed in my hand as I stroked him. The sexy grunts and groans had me undoubtedly wet. Good thing I was in the water, otherwise it would have been hard to hide.

Just thinking of it has me wanting to rub my thighs together. His gaze darkens, almost as if he's thinking about it too. Fuck.

Turning around on my heels, I take out the massive bowl of mashed potatoes.

Once all the food is out, the kids line up to get their food first. With each person the guys serve, they beam with the thanks they get in return. They truly enjoy seeing the joy on these people's faces.

I'm not sure what each of the guys' financial situations are, but I know at least Donny and Lennox are well-off. And from what Colton tells me, he's struggling. And the way that Mateo seems to be at home with everyone here, I feel like this might be his home, where he came from.

There's so much about these guys I don't know, but I'd really like to find out more. Maybe it will help me better understand each of them. I know that Colton opening up helped a lot with him, and there's something big that Donny is holding back. A part of me knows the other two have different stories to tell, but none are any less fucked up than the other.

After everyone else had been served, only then did we take our food.

"Sit with us?" Colton asks as I walk past where he and the guys sat down.

"Sure," I say, giving him a small smile. I take a seat in between him and Donny, Mateo and Lennox on the other side of the table facing us.

Donny continues whatever conversation he was having with Mateo as I start to dig into my meal. But it comes to a complete stop when I take a bite of the mashed potatoes, the creamy goodness making my taste buds burst, and I let out a moan of delight.

Four sets of eyes turn to me with various levels of hunger, but not for the food in front of them.

"Sorry," I say, swallowing. "But these," I point my fork at the potatoes, "are fucking fire."

"Thank you," Mateo mutters. "It's my abuela's recipe."

As dinner continues, I find myself oddly at peace sitting here with these guys. It's a little awkward, but... nice? Taking the time to look around, I see everyone's happy, smiling faces. So many people who otherwise would be sitting at home on this holiday, eating the same meal they would any other day, if they're even lucky enough to eat at all. And knowing the guys are the reason for this whole event, it earns them a bit of respect in my book.

"Can we go outside and play?" a little boy asks the guys.

"Did you eat all your food?" Mateo asks, and the kid nods.

"So did the others." The little boy points to the table of kids. All of their plates look to be licked clean.

"Does anyone want seconds?" Lennox asks.

The kids look at each other like they want to say yes.

"How about we take a break to let your stomach digest what you already ate, and if you're still hungry, you can come inside for seconds?" Colton says.

All the kids' faces light up, and they nod their agreement. They all get up and race outside.

"I'm done," Mateo says, grabbing his empty plate. "I'm gonna head outside and shoot some hoops with a few of the kids."

"Me too," Lennox says, following suit.

"I'll clean up around here and meet you guys outside," Colton says.

"I'll help," Donny offers.

"You need me to do anything?" I ask.

"Maybe help keep an eye on the little ones, so their parents can have a little bit of a longer break?" Lennox suggests.

"Sure," I say with a smile. "I love kids."

Everyone leaves to do their own thing and I head outside to the playground.

The kids are running around, laughing and shouting. I

decide to just walk around and observe, making sure everything is good with the kids.

I'm walking for about five minutes when I hear some kids laughing, only it's not in a fun and joyful way. This sounds a little too cruel and menacing for kids this age. I know a bully laugh when I hear one. Sad thing is, these kids look no older than ten. Too young to be acting like this, not that it's right at any age.

My eyes land on a couple of boys over by the tree. Three of the little boys are standing and laughing at another one sitting on the ground. Poor thing looks like he's about to cry.

"What's going on over here?" I ask the boys. They all stop and look at me.

"Nothing," one of them says, knowing he got caught.

"Why are you laughing at him? That's not very nice," I say, trying not to get caught up with the stink eye one of the boys is giving me.

"He's watching cheerleading videos." One of them laughs.

"Yeah. Cheer is for girls." Another snickers, making the other two laugh.

"Why would you think that?" I ask, raising a brow.

"Because it is. Boys don't cheer," the little ring leader says.

"Yes they do!" the sweet boy on the ground says, his shaggy blond hair covering one of his eyes. He almost reminds me of a young Donny. "See!" he says, showing the video he was watching. The boys don't look but I do and I grin.

"Well." I laugh. "That video you're laughing at him for

watching, it just so happens to be the routine that got the cheer squad that I'm on the gold in Worlds."

"So," the snotty little brat ring leader says. Okay, so I like kids, but not so much these ones. I think their parents need to have a good talk with them.

"So, the guys on that team just so happen to be right over there," I say, pointing to the basketball court. My eyes widen when I see that none of them are wearing shirts. *Not the time to be ogling hot guys, Rylee.*

Donny looks over at me, seeing me pointing. He stops and gets the guy's attention. They all stop playing and jog over to us.

"Everything good over here?" Mateo asks, running a hand through his sweaty hair. Is it weird that I want to lick the sweat dripping off his nose? Okay, yeah, maybe a little.

"These boys here were telling that little guy that boys don't cheer."

Donny's brows shoot up. "Really? Josh, Peter, and Rex, did you tell Tyler that?"

"It's true," Rex, the one I deemed the leader of the snot pack, says.

"It most definitely is not." Colton snorts.

"Wanna show these boys wrong?" Mateo grins.

I stand by and watch as the guys start to show off, throwing out all their best solo moves. The three bullies look mad that they were wrong and storm off, but Tyler watches in amazement.

"That is so cool! How did you do that?" he asks the guys when they come back over, panting, a little bit out of breath.

"We can teach you, if you want," Donny says, and Tyler's face lights up.

"Really?"

"Yeah, man. We started learning around your age. Start now and maybe you can join the Black Widows' team when you get to be our age."

"That would be amazing."

The guys spend the next hour showing Tyler some basic moves, and by the end of it, he can do a few of them by himself.

As I watch how they are with him, I see one of the many sides these guys have been hiding from me.

Is it really hiding though? It's not like we had a chance to get to know each other much.

I'm not sure I like how they seem to be melting the layers of the walls I put up around my heart. I want to hate them a little bit longer, or at the very least dislike them. But they don't seem to be making it very easy for me.

"Hey," a familiar voice, that sends my heart into a fit of flutters for a whole new reason, says.

"Oh shit!" I say, looking up at Trevor. "Is it seven already?"

Taking his outstretched hand, I let him pull me to my feet.

"Not quite, but I had supper with my family, and it was nothing but old, boring people over there." He laughs. "I thought I'd come a little early and see you."

Biting my lower lip, I smile.

"Oh, I almost forgot something," he says.

"What?" I ask, blinking at him in confusion.

"This." He grins, wrapping one arm around my waist, pulling me flush against his body. Using his other hand, he cradles my head as he kisses me deeply. I fucking swoon, melting into a puddle of goo as I whimper against his lips.

"You have got to be fucking kidding me," Mateo growls from behind me.

We break our kiss and turn our attention to the guys.

"What is he doing here?" Donny asks, glaring at Trevor.

"We have plans after," I tell them.

"Guys," Colton sighs, shaking his head. "I already told you."

"Told them what?" Trevor asks him, his arm still wrapped around me. I feel safe in his arms, and I kind of love it.

"That you're seeing Rylee too, and are not going anywhere."

"We'll see about that." Mateo snorts. My blood boils, my good mood now gone.

"No, we won't see. Colton is right. I'm not going to deny the fact that we all have something here. Some relationships are at different levels than others, but the fact is, I like Colton. I want to see where things go with him. But I also like Trevor. He's been nothing but nice and kind to me, unlike you guys. Don't ask me to choose, because if you do, who do you think will win? The man who's treated me with nothing but kindness and respect, or the guys who caused me nothing but pain for months?"

"Stop holding that over our heads!" Mateo growls.

"Then stop coming into my life, acting like you have a say in anything!" I shout. "Because you don't. And if you ever want a chance at my full forgiveness, this isn't the way to go about it."

"I'm okay with sharing, I told Rylee that. I know you all don't like me, but I'm not going anywhere," Trevor says, tightening his hold on me and pressing a kiss to the top of my head. I don't feel like he's doing it to get a rise out of the guys, but he does get a snarl from Mateo.

"I'm okay with that," Colton says. "We have no right to ask you for anything. I'm just lucky enough to have you in my life. I won't take it for granted."

"Thank you," I say, giving him a smile.

"Suck up," Donny mutters under his breath.

"So you're not willing to share?" I ask him. We're not in the same place that Colton and I are, but I know at some point we could be, if things keep going the way they are.

"I didn't say that. I don't mind sharing with them," he says, meaning his friends.

"Well, you're gonna have to include Trevor in that, because I'm not asking him to go anywhere."

"Not that I'd go, at least not willingly," Trevor says, and fuck, my heart bursts. *Don't cry, Rylee. This is how men are supposed to treat you. These assholes are still learning. Maybe Trevor can give them pointers?*

"Not happening," Mateo snaps before turning around and storming off. I'd be lying if I said I wasn't a little disappointed, but this is Mateo. I didn't expect anything else.

"I'll talk to him. He'll come around," Lennox says, then looks at Trevor. "I don't have an issue with you. Just make sure you don't fuck up, not like we did."

"Trust me, I won't," Trevor vows.

"Bye, Rylee," Lennox says before taking off after Mateo.

"We should get going, the movie is at eight," Trevor says.

"Right," I say. I'm trying really hard not to let them bring my mood down, but for guys who seem to be trying to win my trust back, they keep pushing their luck. Colton isn't included in that.

Donny continues to stand there and glare at Trevor, but Colton steps up to me, not caring that I'm in Trevor's arms. "I hope you have a good night, Rylee. Thank you for coming and helping out today. It means a lot to us."

"I'm glad to help. I had fun," I tell him, giving him a small smile.

He returns it before leaning in and placing a soft kiss on my lips, making my belly flutter with butterflies. "Goodnight, Rylee."

"Night, Colt," I reply softly.

Donny mutters a goodbye, looking like a sad puppy, like he wanted to kiss me too, before leaving toward the rec center.

"He's a smooth one," Trevor says, making me laugh.

"Colton is a good guy," I tell him as we head toward his car.

"He better be. Don't think I won't tie him, or any one of them, to the Blocking and Tackling Dummies and have some fun with them during practice."

That makes me snort out a laugh. "You're too much."

"No," he says, grabbing me by the hips and carefully pushing me up against his car, pinning me in place. "Nothing is ever too much when it comes to you, Rylee. I'm on your side. Always."

Fuck, don't cry before a date. I try not to squeeze my eyes shut to hold back the tears as they sting.

"Okay," I whisper, my heart pounding in my chest as he looms over me like a dark, sexy knight in shining armor.

"It's not okay. But I'll make sure to remind you everyday just how amazing you are, Rylee." He kisses me and my body almost explodes. "You're amazing, Rylee," he whispers against my lips. He kisses me like he means everything he's saying, and my heart just might start believing him. "We better stop," he says, pulling back, leaving us both panting. "Or we will never leave this parking lot."

"I don't mind, not if we can do more of that," I say with a playful smile.

"You're a naughty one, cupcake." The nickname makes me grin harder.

"Only always."

One of the things I like about Trevor is that he seems to be able to pull me out of a mood. My life seems to be a little less dark with him around. I hope it starts to shine brighter soon. We'll see.

CHAPTER TWENTY-ONE

Lennox

I leave practice early and head over to the parking lot. It's my turn to get something nice for Rylee. I was thinking of chocolates, but I have a sneaky suspicion that any time we get her a treat, Alex has been eating them, so no more snacks.

I ignore the group of students standing by my truck and press the keyfob to unlock the doors. I don't have much time today. Donny asked to have a family night. I think he's feeling a little lonely.

I had suggested we should all go back to Dave and

Busters, maybe invite Rylee with us, but he said no. He just wants to order some food and watch some movies. I hope he's not getting depressed. We have a small competition soon so we can qualify for regionals, and with the holiday coming up, Donny always gets in his moods.

His last therapist said it was seasonal depression. I'll have to check out some stores, see if I can find something to cheer him up, too.

I pull out of the parking lot and take the scenic route to the mall. Maybe we should take a trip out to the beach. I haven't surfed in a while, and that's one way to cheer everyone up. We can invite Rylee and her friends too.

When I reach the little outlet mall we have by campus, I want to turn right around and leave. It's fucking chaos. How did I forget today is Black Friday? I circle the parking lots three times until finally someone's leaving and I swoop in, taking their spot.

Someone honks and flips me off, but I had my blinker on and they just showed up. "Asshole," she screams at me and I laugh. Sucks to suck. I wait until she leaves, then turn the engine off and climb out.

The sun is starting to set, and I know Donny will be pissed if I'm late, so I need to just get in and get out. I have four things I want to buy. I can do this. Colton asked if he could come too, but between him and Mateo, they could spend hours here just browsing.

The first store is a bust. The shelves look like they have been picked clean. I don't want to go to the huge mall down on the strip. I might have to resort to Amazon delivery for Mateo's Christmas present.

I pass a woman screaming at her three-year-old, and my heart races as it reminds me of being scolded as a kid. I'm waiting for her to slap him, or grab his arm and give it a tight squeeze, but she surprises me, dropping down so her son can give her a hug.

She shushes him and apologizes for getting mad, and I know I want to be like her if I ever have a kid. I won't be like my parents. I will try to keep my temper under control and be patient.

I wonder what kind of mom Rylee will be. Not that we're ready for any of that, but I think we could make an amazing family. I'm smiling as I enter the next store, thinking about our possible future, and I don't realize I just stepped into a honey trap.

"Oh, Lenny, what are you doing here?" Missi says as she steps away from some lingerie display. Ursula and Fatima are laughing about something. I internally groan and keep walking, ignoring her. "Okay, I'll catch you later, baby," she shouts, playing like I'm not blowing her off in front of her friends.

Why do they have to be here? I've been lucky enough to avoid Missi lately. I think she's been staying with her dad. I check my phone, and sure enough, Donny has sent me two messages reminding me about later. I shake my head and laugh. He's like a little kid, I swear.

But I wouldn't change him. He brings laughter and crazy into our lives.

I leave the next store, after buying three different flavors of gourmet popcorn for Donny's movie night. I also grabbed a huge fuzzy blanket for the floor. I pass a bar and my feet try to stop.

Just one drink while I'm here by myself would be okay. No one would even know, but I made Teo a promise and I plan to keep it. I don't really miss drinking. I just miss how it helped calm the thoughts that like to race through my head. The memories I want to forget.

I swing by the food court and order a banana chocolate chip smoothie, then walk over to the place where I can get Rylee some flowers, and a vase. I've always liked buying girls flowers.

Doesn't even need to be something extravagant. Just a small token to remind them that I am thinking about them. I wonder if Teo would like flowers? Would that be weird?

I browse the shelves until I find what I'm looking for. I did a lot of research the other night about what kind of flowers to buy and what their meanings were. I want to give Rylee something she will love, but I also can't seem to pull myself away from the long-stem red roses. They remind me of her and her flowing dark-red hair.

Damn, I'm whipped. I never thought I'd see the day where I had to work hard for a girl to want me back, but she's worth it. Just those few days together on vacation proved how perfect she is for me... for us.

I feel sick every time I think about what we put her through. In the beginning, it was all revenge for a stupid fucking miscommunication, but then Missi got pissy and went total David McCall, that character from the nineties movie, *Fear*.

I still don't see why she's so obsessed with me. It's not

like I'm anything special. Yeah, I get it, my family's rich. But there are a lot more rich guys out there that she could leech onto.

"Have you found everything you were looking for?" an older woman asks me as I'm trying to choose a vase. The crystal ones are really nice, but it doesn't scream Rylee. I know Donny keeps trying to buy her love and forgiveness, but I don't think she cares about that sort of thing.

Another clue that we really fucked up everything. Rylee is the furthest thing from a golddigger. She works hard and never complains. I let my past cloud my judgment, and I ruined one of the best things I ever had. Even if it was just for a short amount of time.

I know I have Mateo now, but that doesn't change anything. I am in love with Rylee Moore. We all are. Even Teo, who wants to continue to fight his feelings.

I grab a cheaper vase with blue butterflies on it. It's nothing special, but I think she will love it. I also grab Teo a white orchid. It has its own little pot, and I think it would be easy to take care of.

I'm about to check out and the nice lady, who I learned is named Angus, is wrapping the roses up so I can deliver them to Rylee, when Missi stomps in. Her face is flushed and she looks mad.

Her friends wait outside, and I'm thankful. There has been enough talk and gossip amongst the team lately. Thankfully, Missi has been behaving, but I know it's only a matter of time until she tries something again.

Colton and I have been talking about how we could get

her off the team, but with her dad being the dean of the college, it's going to take something major.

"Oh, Lenny, you know I'd take you back, baby. You don't need to get me flowers," she coos, then glances at the bouquet of red roses and frowns. "What the hell are those? You know I'm allergic to roses, baby," she whines and I snort.

"Missi, what do you want?"

She gives me a flirtatious smile, but all it does is remind me of a shark and how evil she truly is. "I want what I've always wanted, Lennox—you."

"Yeah, that's not going to happen," I say with a laugh. "Did you forget that I ended things?"

She waves her hand, and her diamond tennis bracelet sparkles. I remember buying it for her after my father insisted that I had to butter her up, because she wasn't happy that I was ignoring her during our Florida vacation.

We weren't even together then. We've never been serious. It's all been for show, but I think she forgot that at some point and started to visualize our future, making her even more unhinged and psychotic.

I wonder how she would react if she knew that me and Mateo were together.

"I talked to your mom the other day and she agrees with me. All this is just a little temper tantrum. You'll come back to me. I have no doubt we're meant to be, Lennox. I've known for years," she says, batting her eyelashes, and trying to have Angus exchange the roses.

I grip her arm, give Angus a smile, then lead Missi over to the large arrangement of roses.

Missi sneezes and I roll my eyes. "I don't know how you

know this, since we've never even properly been together. It was all fake. A ruse put on so we could keep our families off our backs. You're the one who decided you wanted more without discussing it with me," I snap and she rolls her eyes.

"I had to get you to fall for me somehow. And it was working, until that little bitch showed up. You should have never interfered with my plans, Lennox! She would have been gone by now, and everything would have been perfect. You wouldn't have had any distractions," she says, and I throw my head back laughing.

"Wrong again, Missi. Maybe, if you pulled your head out of that Prada bag, you would have seen the truth right in front of you. Rylee wasn't the issue."

"You know, Lenny, I was really hoping we could just have a nice conversation and you would buy me some lilies, but I guess it's going to resort to this," she mutters as she pulls her phone out of her purse.

"Oh no, don't stop on my account, Missi. Please continue to enlighten me," I say with a sneer and she smirks.

"No, I don't think I will just yet. I'll see you later, baby," she says, then tries to kiss me, but I turn my head.

Once she's gone, I return to the counter to pay and Angus gives me a free box of chocolate. "That girl seems crazy, son. I would end that relationship quickly," she mutters and I laugh.

"She's my ex. I've moved on to much bigger and better things."

"Well, whoever she is, she's a lucky girl." I give her a smile and hand over my card, then wait and sign the receipt.

"I'm the lucky one."

I LEAVE the mall and get stuck in traffic. I was hoping to go see Rylee, maybe even chat, instead of just leaving the flowers at her door. I feel like she spends more time with Colton, and even Donny, than me.

I know Mateo is not ready, but I think he's slowly coming around. He just has to see that what we experienced on vacation could be an everyday thing. Even with that troll, Trevor, hanging around, I could see us being happy.

I wonder if she would go out on a date, just the two of us. I'd really like to get to know her better, while I'm sober too. I also think her and Mateo need to spend some one-on-one time together. I know Colton has something up his sleeve, and Teo might just murder us all in our sleep for it, but he needs this.

He's too strong-headed. I know it's because he has always had to be the adult—the one to make hard decisions and take care of his family—but he's not alone anymore. He has us, and Rylee, if he would just let her in.

I know he's been having a lot of trouble with his uncle lately, and he's worried about his mom and Nando. We all have our own issues, but we're a family, and we need to work together, or this relationship isn't going to work.

I finally arrive on campus, forty-five minutes after I had planned to be home. Donny is blowing up my phone, and I know he's just being impatient, but it's starting to annoy me.

They could have ordered the food already and started a movie. It's not like we haven't seen the same thing over and over again.

I park in the student lot and exit my truck. Grabbing the bags, I head over toward Rylee's dorm. I hope Alex isn't there. I just want to give her the flowers and then go home. When I reach her dorm, I hear someone laughing and I peek over my shoulder.

Rylee is headed this way, walking up the path with Serenity. Nice, I don't even have to go knock on her door now. I can just give them to her here. When she sees me she smiles, and Serenity keeps on walking inside.

"Hey, what's up?" she asks me, and I like that it's no longer tense and strained between us.

"I was at the mall, saw these and thought of you," I say as I hand her the flowers. She gives me a beaming grin and her green eyes sparkle.

"Thanks, Lennox. That was sweet of you," she says as she runs her fingers through her long red hair.

"I also bought you a vase. I wasn't sure if you had one," I mumble and hand her the gift bag that Angus put together for me.

"Did you want to come inside? Alex is still at practice." She gives me a look, and I wish more than anything I could.

"No, I have plans. The guys and I are supposed to have dinner and a movie night. But, maybe next weekend, I could take you out, just us?"

She ponders for a few minutes and my hands start to sweat. I have never wanted a girl to go out with me as badly as I want Rylee.

"Yeah, I think we could do that. Is Mateo coming too?" I shake my head.

"I was thinking, maybe after finals are over, we could all go to the beach. You could even invite your friends... and Trevor," I grumble and she crosses her arms, squishing the bouquet.

"I told you already, I'm not going to choose. So if you don't want to accept Trevor, then we should just end this here and now."

"No, no. That's not what I mean, Rylee. It's just hard to welcome someone new into our group. We don't even know the guy," I say and she relaxes.

"Well, then I think we might have to do something about that if you want this to go anywhere between us," she says with a shrug and I nod.

My phone keeps going off and I know it's Donny. Rylee is getting annoyed.

"Do you need to take that?" she asks, raising a brow, and I roll my eyes.

"It's Donny. I'm late. He won't start the movie until I'm there."

She laughs and shakes her head, smiling. "What movie are you guys watching? Is it something bloody and gruesome?"

"I wish," I grumble. "No, it's nothing like that, and honestly, I don't even want to tell you," I say and she looks hurt. "Fuck, I'm messing all of this up. I think tonight is Disney night. So, more than likely, Donny will start with *Tangled*, because he has a weird obsession with Mandy Moore. Then we will probably end the night with *Frozen* because he loves Kristen Bell," I say with a sigh, because I'm not looking forward to watching these movies again after seeing them over one-hundred times.

Rylee blinks for a moment and then throws her head back, laughing hysterically. "Oh my God, that's so Donny. I love Disney movies. We should all watch them sometime?" she asks, and I feel like an idiot for not inviting her to begin with. Maybe that would be good. All of us hanging out and watching some films.

"Donny gets in these moods around the Holidays, so I'm sure we will be having many more. We'd love for you to come, but you will have to fight with Mateo over who gets the best seat," I say with a smile and she nods.

"I love Christmas movies. Especially *Die Hard.*"

I clutch my chest and then drop to my knees exaggeratedly in front of her. "Marry me?" I ask, and her eyes go wide, letting out a little huffed sound of surprise. I give her a big smile, showing her I'm kidding, and she takes a breath.

"That was not funny," she grumbles, but I don't agree— that was hilarious. My phone goes off again and I groan.

"I really should go, but I'll text you about our date," I say and she holds up the flowers.

"Thanks again for these, Len."

I nod and she moves a little closer, and hesitantly brushes her lips against my cheek. Fuck, I really don't want to go, but my family needs me. She backs away and gives me a big smile before moving around me and walking inside.

I can't wipe the grin off my face as I race back over to my truck and grab the stuff for Donny and Teo. I shove into the apartment door and Donny is standing there with his arms crossed in front of him, pouting.

"You are two hours late, Mister. Now Colt says we only have time for one movie," he whines, and I roll my eyes as I hand him the massive bag of popcorn I got for him.

His green eyes widen and he pulls me into a huge hug. "Oh, you shouldn't have," he coos, then releases me and skips away. Mateo joins me at the door and grabs the big blanket.

"You're going to spoil his dinner, you know," he says and I grin.

"Sorry, Daddy." His eyes bug out and I can't hold in my laughter. I'm in a really good mood after my talk with Rylee. I hand Teo the flower, and he looks confused.

"I bought this for you. I figured you might like it, since I remembered your dad used to get one for your mom on special occasions," I mumble, starting to ramble. He doesn't say anything, and it's making me nervous.

"It was stupid. I can bring it back," I say, when he grabs me by the neck and kisses me hard.

"I love it, thank you," he mutters against my lips and I nod.

"You guys," Donny shouts and I roll my eyes.

"The prince is calling," I say and Teo huffs.

"Don't let him hear you call him that or he will want to be addressed only by that from now on," Colt says as he enters the room. "Pizza will be here soon. I also got some appetizers, since you made Donny wait so long and he's just withering away," he says with a scoff. I laugh and take the blanket back from Teo.

When I walk into the living room, Donny has it all set

up. He has three bowls on the table filled with snacks, and drinks lined up. He's also dragged two of our beds out of the rooms.

"Wow, this is quite the set-up," I comment and he smiles. I toss him the large, fuzzy blanket and he squeals.

It's so easy to make him happy. I don't know how someone could have ever tried to steal his light. He's like a kid hyped-up on sugar twenty-four-seven, who just wants to be loved. That's all any of us wants. Now that Rylee is back in our lives, I'm going to make it happen.

CHAPTER TWENTY-TWO

Mateo

I've pissed Colton off. There is no other reason I can think of for him to pair me with Rylee at the fucking SPCA. They all know I don't like cats. Can't fucking stand them. With their beady little eyes that always like to watch you. Even when you're taking a shit.

They are plotting something, and I won't be the one to fall for their evil schemes. Why didn't he send Donny here, or even Len. They love animals, and they probably wouldn't do something to piss off Rylee either.

I just know today is going to end in a fucking disaster. I try calling Colt again, but he's ignoring my fucking calls. I made one comment about how Rylee and I didn't kill ourselves while left alone in the hot tub, and now here I am.

I open the door and a little bell dings above my head. "Hi, you must be Mateo. I'm Denise. Thank you so much for volunteering today. We have so many kittens just needing some love and attention. Your partner has already arrived. She's in the cat room, last door on the left."

"Do you have any repairs you need done, or cleaning?" I ask, hoping she has a better job for me than just cuddling cats. I try not to shiver as I think about all the hair they leave everywhere, like viewable STDs, and the tiny little claws they use to climb on you.

I fucking hate cats!

"Oh, not at the moment, but thank you so much for offering. Enjoy yourself today," she says before dismissing me. I give her a forced smile, then move to where she pointed.

I walk down the hall looking for Rylee. She's not in the room that Denise said she was in. I pass a bunch of cages. It looks like maybe some new recruits have been brought in recently. One lunges at me, hissing and growling, and I squeal like a little girl as I jolt back.

I glance around to make sure no one caught that, and lo and behold, there's Rylee, laughing her ass off and crossing her legs like she's about to pee herself.

Just great. Now she's going to tell the others, and Donny's never going to let me live it down. She walks closer to me and points at the orange tabby, who looks more frightened of my high-pitched scream than I'm afraid of it. "Are you good?" she asks, and I cross my arms, puffing my chest up.

"Fine," I grumble, handing her the drink I got for her. She hesitates to take it and I huff. "It's not poisoned or laced with laxatives," I grunt, and she takes it.

"Thanks," she mumbles then hands it back to me. "Can you hold this? I was just looking for a bathroom," she says and I nod as she scurries away.

I wait outside the room for her, because like fuck am I going in there by myself. I watch as all the cats meow and scratch at the door. It's like they know I'm here, and they are plotting my demise.

The back of my neck prickles, and sweat drips down my temples. Someone touches my arm and I jump with a shriek. "Don't do that!" I snap, turning to face Rylee. She crosses her arms, bringing her tits up, and my eyes stop there.

"I called your name twice, Teo," she grumbles, then holds her hand out for her drink. I hand it to her then scratch my cheek. I need to shave.

"Sorry," I mutter, then move out of the way so she can open the door. Cats swarm us and I think I might pass out. My heart is racing and my hands start shaking. Rylee glances at me and I grimace as a gray tabby rubs against my ankle.

"Why are you here if you hate cats?" she asks as I shut the door. I shake my head and shrug.

"I think I pissed Colton off, but I'm not sure what I did. We had a good time watching movies and eating food last night. Well, until Flynn started to die, and Donny used my shirt as a tissue," I grunt and she stops petting the little white kitten.

"I'm sorry, what?" she barks with a laugh, and I can't help but to chuckle with her.

"Donny gets in these moods around the holidays. Someone called it seasonal depression. I don't know, but he becomes a little clingy around the people he loves, and he likes to watch movies that give him a reason to cry. He says it's more manly to get emotional watching a film, than just sitting on a couch and crying..." I trail off and move over to a cabinet. Sliding to my ass, I ignore the cat fight going on in the corner.

"I never would have known. Donny always seems so happy. Why do the holidays upset him?" she asks, but I shake my head.

"Not my story to tell, but anyways, we were watching *Tangled*. It's one of his favorites. He knows the words by heart, and pretends to be Flynn Ryder, or Eugene. I don't know if you've seen it, but he dies in the end before Rapunzel saves him."

Rylee sits next to me and all the cats run over to her. I clench my hands, gripping the top of my jeans, and take a breath.

We don't say anything else and it's kinda boring. I should take this time to talk with her. Make things better between us, but I'm at a loss for words. She laughs and takes pictures of a few cats as they play with a toy.

"Okay, I'm done," Rylee says, pulling my attention from a pile of kittens who are looking at me like I'm their dinner. She sits up on her knees and places a long-haired floof ball on my lap. "We are here to pet, love, and play with these innocent little babies. You are sitting there like you need to take a crap or something." She places two more cats near me and I tense up.

She sighs. "Do you want to play Twenty Questions while we sit here?" she asks, and I think it over. I've been trying to play nice and not set her off, but it's hard as I've been on edge since the moment I walked into this room.

There's a couch we could rest on, but there are too many cats claiming it.

"Yeah, we might as well. But keep those demon cats on your side," I say with a visible shiver, handing one of the cats back to her. It was starting to use my thigh as a scratching post.

"I just can't get over that you're scared of cats. You're what, six-foot-five, two-hundred pounds? Not to mention you're covered in tattoos," she says, running her gaze over me, stopping at my cock.

"I still owe you payback for what you pulled in the hot tub," I growl, inching closer to her. Her eyes widen and she bites her bottom lip. One of the cats hisses on the other side of the room and it pulls me away from the lust-filled thoughts I was having.

I groan and run my hand over my face, brushing off some of the fur. Fuck, my allergies are going to hate me later.

"My sister, Brenna, rescued a cat when we were little. That thing was pure evil, but she adored it. It used to attack me every time I walked past it. And it would watch me, plotting something. I don't like cats. Just because I'm a big guy, it doesn't mean that I'm not scared of things. I'm not invincible or something," I grumble and she's quiet for a minute.

"I'm scared of the dark. When I was younger, a man I trusted wanted to keep our relationship secret. People started to become suspicious, so to save himself, he shoved me into a small crawl space and left me there. He never came back. So yeah, me and the dark, or small, cramped spaces, do not mix well," she says with a little shrug, playing it off as if it no longer bothers her, but I can hear the tremor in her voice.

"What's his name? He's dead," I growl, making her laugh. I remember her mentioning that when she ripped us a new one after the televised performance. I felt sick and murderous then, too.

"He's not worth it, Teo. It was a long time ago. But don't shove me in any more locker rooms, 'kay?" She tries to joke, but now I feel like even more of a dick.

"Rylee," I start, but she cuts me off.

"So, first question. You mentioned a sister. Do you have any more siblings?" I look at her for a few minutes, and the way her eyes are glassy and her chest is moving, I know she doesn't want to talk about her past anymore.

I can respect that, but we will be tracking that dickbag down and removing his balls. I smile and look off at the wall, so she doesn't see how bloodthirsty I am. There's a poster of a kitten hanging from a tree, as if there wasn't enough cat memorabilia in this room.

"Yeah, I have two. Brenna is seventeen, and Nando is eight. He's my little buddy," I say with a grin.

"Are they coming to our next competition?" she asks and I shake my head, my mood instantly dropping again.

"Probably not. It's not really safe for them to be out in public at the moment," I grumble, then want to smack myself in the face. I can't believe I just told her that. There's just something about Rylee that makes me want to let my guard down.

"Safe? What do you mean? Is Missi after them too? Is it because you helped me?" She starts to ramble and I move closer to her.

"No, it's not because of you, Rylee. My uncle is dangerous. He likes to use my family against me, to get his own way."

She turns to face me and bites her bottom lip. She's quiet for a moment and I start to wonder if I said too much, maybe made her uncomfortable, before she finally speaks.

"If you need them to disappear, go somewhere safe—my room is empty. I don't know if you want them to go all the way to Florida, but I bet my mom could help yours get a job." She nibbles on her finger, and my heart aches at her offer.

The idea of sending them away has been on my mind for a while now. I have been trying to get the courage up to ask her for help, but here she is offering. "You would really do that? After everything I have done to you? You would be so selfless as to help my family? People you don't even know?"

I move closer to her and she sucks in a breath. "I'm such a fucking idiot," I mutter before placing my palms on both of her cheeks and pulling her lips to mine. I don't press hard or try to deepen the kiss. This is just a thank you.

I back away and she licks her lips. "I'm not the devil,

Mateo. If I'm able to help someone, I will," she whispers and I nod.

"I know. Thank you, Rylee. If you could ask your mom about helping my family, then yes. I would put them on a plane tonight," I say, and she pulls out her phone, sending a text.

"My mom's working, but she will probably respond soon." I sit back and take some deep breaths. I feel like a weight has been removed from my shoulders. I don't even care about the cat purring on my leg.

"How is your mom?" She gives me a big grin before telling me all about their plans for Christmas. "It sounds like it will be a fun time. Maybe I'll have to hitch a ride if my family is there too," I joke, and she looks off toward a huge cat tree.

I clear my throat. "So, the place you worked is good then? They treat their employees well?"

"Oh, yes. My mom has been working there since before I was born. I don't think she will ever quit," she says with a laugh, and the tension between us is finally starting to lessen. "It's not a bad job, and we had a free place to live. The owner of the hotel is like a grandpa to me. He would always bring me gifts on my birthday and Christmas."

She pulls herself to her feet and tosses her empty drink in the trash, then sits on the couch. I grudgingly stand and follow. As long as she's with me, the cats don't seem so bad.

"I think he's lonely. His son moved away before I was born, and I don't think he's ever come to visit."

"Wow, that's weird, and kind of sad," I mutter and she

rolls her eyes, then picks up a giant orange cat. Reminds me of that cartoon Garfield. He doesn't stay long.

"So what does your mother do?" she asks as I lean back against the fur-covered couch and rub my nose.

"She was a chef. She had her own restaurant and everything. But when my dad... died, she quit and decided to stay home and take care of us." I try not to show that I'm lying, and I avoid her eyes.

"Okay, next question," she says, and as I look at the amazing girl beside me, I can see why the guys are head over heels for her, and why I'm falling for her.

"Actually, Rylee, can I ask one?"

"You just did. You asked about my mom?" she says and I shake my head.

"No, you asked what my mom does. My turn," I say, a little snappy, so I take some deep breaths and calm myself. I don't want to fight with her.

She nods and I sigh. "Okay, forget the question. I'm just going to come out and say this. What we did to you was wrong. We should have just had a conversation with you, and not listened to what Colton and Donny overheard, but you have to understand... You're not the first girl that we thought was a gold digger." I take a breath and wait for her to snap back at me, but she just sits there and lets me continue. "Not to mention, the fact that you showed up here on campus, just made it even more suspicious." Rylee rolls her eyes and crosses her arms. Then she picks up a tiny black kitten with white paws and rubs her face into its fur.

"I worked at a hotel frequented by wealthy men. I have had plenty of chances to find some rich, moronic guy to be my sugar daddy, if that's what my intentions were. I had no desire then, and I have no desire now," she grumbles, getting up from the couch before taking off toward the exit. I groan, rubbing my cheeks. I swear there is hair all over me, and when I leave here, I'm going to need to disinfect myself.

"I know it probably doesn't mean much, but for what it's worth, Rylee, I am sorry," I say, and then don't follow her as she leaves the room.

CHAPTER TWENTY-THREE

Trevor

"First place goes to the Black Widows!" The whole room bursts into cheers, shouting and clapping, including me and Alex.

The Black Widows competed in a state competition today and, because our football team has an away game tomorrow in the same town where it was being held, we came to support them.

Alex is losing his shit, a massive smile on his face, as Serenity hugs Rylee. Happy tears stream down their faces, as the whole team steps up for their medals.

"They were fucking amazing!" Alex laughs happily. "And damn, did you see how high they tossed Rylee? I almost crapped my pants waiting to see if they would catch her!"

Yeah, that part wasn't my favorite. I mean, she did amazing, and watching her move like that, seeing her talent, fills me with so much pride for her. But I also don't like that her safety is left in the hands of these guys.

After Thanksgiving, things between Rylee and I have been progressing. We've gone on a few more dates this past week, and had some stolen kisses, but in moments like this, it makes me want more. I know we're only dating right now, but I want to be her boyfriend. I want to be able to do what Alex is going to do to his girlfriend as soon as we leave this room, pulling her into his arms and kissing her like crazy.

That's what I want to do with Rylee. That's what *they* get to do with her. Colton snatches Rylee out of Ren's hold, picking her up and spinning her around before putting her back down. He grabs her face in his hands and kisses her hard, right in front of everyone.

I try to ignore the white-hot jealousy coursing through my veins, and remember that Rylee wants me too. She told them that herself. I'm not going anywhere. I just need to relax and let Rylee take things at her pace. It's not about me.

"Come on," Alex says, grabbing my hand and pulling me out of the stadium. We go and wait to meet the team where they will be exiting from.

Other people join us. Some look like parents and siblings, standing around and waiting to congratulate their loved ones.

The team comes out, and we all clap and cheer. The moment Ren walks past Alex, he's pulling her into his arms and wastes no time before ramming his tongue down her throat.

"You guys killed it!" I congratulate Rylee as she stops in front of me. She looks so adorable in her uniform. Her hair is up in a ponytail, with a black and red bow on top. She also has some black and red glitter on her cheeks and eyelids, that sparkles in the light.

"Thank you!" she says, a permanent smile on her face. "God, the high I feel right now is amazing!" She takes me by surprise and wraps her arms around me. A happy thrill fills me as I wrap my arms around her, giving her a good squeeze. "I'm glad you could be here."

"I'm glad I could be, too," I say, kissing the top of her head, breathing her in.

"Can I ask you something?" she says, pulling back from my arms.

"Of course."

She bites her lower lip, her cheeks flushed from all the excitement. "Would it be too much to ask if you would come to my competitions?"

"No. Not at all. I'd love to be here for you."

"Really?" she asks, her face lighting up.

"I mean, I know we're not official or anything, but I'd like to be here for you. Like Alex is for Serenity," I say, my heart pounding in my chest as I wait for reaction.

"Like a boyfriend?" she asks, a small smile taking over her tempting lips.

"If that's what you want?" I ask. My whole body breaks out into a nervous sweat as I pray to all the Gods that she says yes.

"Is there going to be a question if I say yes?" She grins.

Holy shit. "Rylee Moore, will you make me the happiest guy and be my girlfriend?"

"Do you promise not to hurt me? Because I'm telling my mind to shut up and let us be happy for once, with the word yes on the tip of my tongue. Just please, don't break my heart."

There are tears in her eyes and my heart hurts for her. "I promise I will do everything in my power to never cause you any harm or heartache, Rylee," I say, cupping the back of her head. She looks up at me on the verge of tears. "I promise to handle your heart with the utmost care. Like the rare gem it is."

"You're so corny. I love it." She lets out a little laugh-cry. "Then yes, I'll be your girlfriend, Trevor."

A rush of joy fills me as I let out a whoop. Rylee laughs as I wrap my arms around her again, squeezing her tight. "You're so fucking amazing," I tell her before crashing my lips onto hers.

"What's got you so excited?" Alex says, coming to stand next to us with Ren under his arm.

"Trevor asked me to be his girlfriend," Rylee says, hugging my side. And when she places her head on my chest, I want to puff it out in pride.

"And what did you say?" Alex asks, eyes going wide.

"She said yes, duh," Serenity says. "I don't think he would be this happy if she turned him down."

"I said yes." Rylee laughs.

"So, if you two are official, what about them?" Alex says, looking over to the group of guys standing nearby, within listening distance. They heard everything, and Mateo and Donny do not look happy.

"Nothing's changed," Rylee says. "We've talked about it, and Trevor knows I'm exploring things with the guys."

"I do. And I told her I'm fine with it because I'm not going anywhere. As long as I have her, that's all that matters to me."

"Well, at least you have one good guy," Alex says, earning a slap on the chest.

"Be nice," both Ren and Rylee say at the same time.

Rylee gives me a kiss. "We need to get back to the team, but I can't wait for your game tomorrow."

"I can't wait either. Would it be too soon to ask if you would wear my letterman jacket?"

Her face lights up. "I'd love that."

A wave of relief takes over me. Taking off the jacket, I drape it over her shoulders and kiss her again before watching her go back over to the guys.

Mateo tosses his arm over Rylee's shoulder, earning a confused look from her. As they walk away, he glances over his shoulder at me with a smug grin.

I don't know what he's trying to do, but he's not going to get a rise out of me. She's my girlfriend now. I don't care what they do together, because at the end of the day, she's mine too. I'm not going anywhere.

"Dude," Alex says with a laugh as he claps my shoulder. "You got yourself a girlfriend! And an amazing one at that."

"She said yes, right?" I ask him. "Like, it wasn't in my head?"

"She said yes." He laughs. "I'm happy for you, bro. You

deserve it. After Robin, God I never thought you would agree to be with anyone else again."

The mention of my ex-girlfriend spoils the mood. The smile on my face drops as I remember what she did. Robin was my on and off again childhood best friend and girlfriend. Our parents were family friends, and we grew up together. She was my first everything. I came to school at Solidarity while she went to another college. I saw her on the weekends, and everything seemed perfect.

That was until I went to a party and found some football player balls-deep inside her. Robin wasn't the one. I knew that as we got older. So it wasn't like I was losing some great love. But we were really close, best friends over everything else. So seeing her betray me like that hurt really fucking bad.

When she realized I was in the room, she started to cry. Sobbing that she was sorry, and she loved me, just not in that way anymore, and she didn't know how to tell me. That she felt like we were better off as best friends than in a relationship.

I told her that I agreed, that I thought we would have been better off staying as friends, but that wasn't an option anymore because she lied to me, betrayed my trust. If she would have just talked to me, things would have been fine.

I think that's why I connect with Rylee. She's real, and she tells it like it is, no secrets, no lying.

"Hey, man. I'm sorry, I know how much Robin is a sore subject," Alex says, his voice softening.

"No, it's fine. Rylee isn't like Robin. She's been nothing

but open and honest with me since we met. I'm not worried about Rylee repeating what Robin did."

"But after what Robin did, are you really sure you're okay with your girlfriend having other boyfriends?" Alex asks. "I mean, I can try and talk her out of it. Make her see that you're the best guy to be with."

"No," I say, shaking my head as we exit the building. "None of this is a surprise to me. I knew what I was getting into when I started getting to know Rylee better. I think that's why I'm not bothered by it, like most would be. She's communicated what she wants, and how she feels, right from the start. I don't feel like I'm going to be blindsided by her, and as long as we keep a line of communication open, I think we'll be okay. So far, the guys haven't done more than give me some dirty looks."

Alex laughs. "I don't think they would dare try to fuck with you. Rylee would rip them a new one, and if they want a chance to earn her back, they won't do anything to risk that. That is, if they're smart enough. Jury is still out on that one."

"She's amazing." I laugh.

"She is."

CHAPTER TWENTY-FOUR

Rylee

"Do we have to go?" Donny mutters as we walk through the parking lot toward the stadium. "I don't like football."

"Look, they all came to our competition. It's only fair to show school spirit and be there to cheer them on."

"But we're not supposed to be there as cheerleaders today, it's our day off."

I can't help but smile. "Not like that. But we can sit in the stands and cheer like everyone else."

"You just wanna be there for your boyfriend," Mateo snips.

Biting my lower lip, I snuggle into Trevor's letterman jacket, inhaling his cologne. I stop, turning to face Mateo. "Yes, I want to be there for Trevor, and yes, he's my boyfriend. I've already made my feelings clear about how this will work, if you want to be with me. I'm not going to keep repeating myself. I understand if you feel jealous, it's a normal human reaction. But don't let it cause any more issues. I don't have time for it. I don't know what to tell you, Mateo. I have feelings for all of you, to various degrees. You know this. And if I didn't make myself clear before, I'm doing it now. Keep showing me you're not the bad guys, like I've grown to believe you were, and maybe we can have something. I'm not guaranteeing anything though."

"Except for Colton," Donny grumbles.

Taking Colton's hand, I weave my fingers through his, giving him a smile. He gives me one in return that makes my heart flutter. "Yeah, except for Colton," I tell Donny, but with my eyes on Colton. "And when he feels ready to ask me to be more like Trevor did, I'll give him the same answer."

Surprise takes over Colton's face, and I don't miss his eyes glossing over. His smile turns to one of hope and I just have to kiss him. Leaning up on my tip-toes, I kiss his soft lips, earning a little whimpered moan. "Ball's in your court, big guy," I whisper when we break the kiss.

His cheeks are pink and flushed as he sucks his lip into his mouth.

"Fine," Mateo huffs, pushing past us.

I watch him go, not sure how to feel. We shared a

moment at the shelter. He opened up to me, showing me a side to him that I didn't know existed. When he told me about his family, a lot of things clicked. There's still so much about him that I don't know, but I have a feeling it's not good.

After I left, I called my mom and asked her if she could get Mateo's mom a job at the hotel. She told me she would see what she could do, and called me back a few hours later telling me that a few other cleaners have quit, leaving their rooms open, and that her boss has agreed to give her a job. When I told Mateo, he seemed so relieved. I even told him that his sister could also work there, if she wanted to help out, like I did with my mom.

He thanked me and that was it. He's been pretty moody the past few days. I'm trying to not let it bother me. Maybe it's because he's upset to see his family go next week. But I'm not going to take his shitty behavior, if he keeps it up.

With Christmas only a few weeks away, I was going to ask if he wanted to spend the holidays there, to travel back together. He said he wanted more, but maybe he's changed his mind.

"He'll come around," Lennox says, placing a hand on my shoulder. "He's having a hard time dealing with his family leaving. He's worried about them, and rightfully so."

"I assumed as much, but that doesn't give him the right to be moody with me."

"No, it doesn't, but that's Mateo. He's a tough nut to crack. You'll understand him better the more time you spend around him," he says, giving me a smile.

"And what about you?" I ask, tilting my head to the side.

"What about me?" he replies, brows furrowing.

"When do I get to know more about you? Since the cabin, you've been so worried about the others getting back into my good graces, you haven't given yourself the time to get to know me. To get me alone."

He blinks at me then looks away. "I suppose you're right." He looks back at me. "They're my family, I want to see them happy. You mean the world to us, Rylee, and we all feel horrible for how we've treated you. And as much as we know we don't deserve another chance, it settles something inside us that you're willing to at least let us try to make things better."

My heart pounds in my chest as Lennox steps forward. Donny is on one side of me, Colton on the other with a little smile. I feel boxed in, but not trapped. And when Lennox cups my cheek, my eyes flutter closed. "This is me letting you know that I want you, Rylee. You're kind, loving, strong, and so fucking beautiful. When you agree to be mine, as well as the others, I'll be the happiest man in the world. But not now. I want to do things right. I want to be able to tell you the deepest parts of me. But I'm just not there yet." The emotion in his words makes the back of my eyes sting. "Just, please don't give up on me."

My eyes flutter open and I lick my lips. "I won't. As long as you don't hurt me again."

"Never." He puts his forehead to mine, and we stay like that for a moment. I try really fucking hard not to cry, but this moment, it's big. Donny rubs my back as Colton rubs his thumb over the side of my hand.

Cheering snaps us all out of our little bubble.

"We better get in there," I say, sniffing as I wipe some fallen tears from my eyes.

"Come on, sweet girl," Colton says, kissing the side of my head as he pulls me into his arms.

After we find our seats, we sit and wait in anticipation. The bleachers are packed with people chattering, the energy is wild. I'm not the biggest fan of football, but I enjoy it enough. And if it means supporting my best friend and boyfriend, I can deal.

Boyfriend. Just thinking of the word makes my heart swell. Trevor is amazing. Sometimes I think he's too good to be true. But then I remind myself not to allow my past trauma to let my mind overthink and ruin a good thing.

He makes me laugh, smile, and overall, he makes me feel wanted and safe. Something I've never felt with anyone before. But that doesn't change how I feel about the others. Colton has quickly taken over my heart too. And I meant what I said before. I'm just waiting for him to ask me to be his girlfriend and I'll say yes.

Some people might think I didn't make them grovel enough, or that I'm forgiving them too easily, but they don't see what I see. The hurt and pain before their eyes. Things that I'm now noticing, that contributed to the mistakes they made against me.

Alex has said more than once that I should make them suffer, make them pay the price for messing with me. But that's not who I am. The pranks were enough. Fun and harmless. Anything more, the guilt would eat at me. I'd rather take the higher road than act like Missi.

And I didn't just forgive them. Only one out of the four

of them has earned my trust. The others still have some work to do. But if they deem themselves worthy, then I'm not going to let anyone make me feel bad about giving them another chance.

Life is short, and I'd rather use that time being happy than being vindictive.

"Want some?" Colton asks, offering me some gummy bears that he brought with him.

"I'd love one," I say, opening my mouth. He chuckles and pops one in. "Thank you."

"Anything for you," he says, kissing me on my nose. I could get used to these gooey feelings.

"Gross," Missi scoffs from where she's sitting in front of us.

"Shut up, Missi," Donny says, kicking the back of her seat. "Jealous that Rylee has five guys, and you can't get one?"

"Donny," Lennox groans.

Missi spins around. "Five," she snorts. "Yeah, sorry, Donny. I'm not jealous that she can open her legs for a bunch of guys. That's called being a whore."

"Fuck you," Mateo snaps.

"Nah, but she will." Missi tips her head back and cackles like the witch she is.

"Don't bother wasting your time talking to her," I tell the guys. "She's not worth your breath."

Missi shoots me a glare. I just smile and flip her off.

"What a bitch," Serenity says, taking a seat next to me.

"Agreed. Where have you been?" I ask with a grin.

"Alex," she huffs. "I told him to wait until after the game,

but no, the fucker left the locker room, found me, then..."
She blushes and looks away.

"Then what?!" I ask with a laugh.

"Then he fucked me under the bleachers," she whispers.

"Oh my God." I shake my head. "He would."

"Not going to lie, it was hot knowing we could get caught at any moment."

"Naughty girl." I bump her shoulder.

"Says the girl who let a guy eat her out on a desk at school," she volleys back.

"Okay, fair point." I laugh. "The idea of being caught was thrilling."

We both laugh. Seconds later, the home team is announced. The other side of the stadium goes crazy, cheering for their team. Once it's our team's turn, we all stand up and shout, cheering and clapping. "Go Widows!" I scream, cupping my hands around my mouth.

The guys jog out onto the field and over to their coach. When I see Trevor, butterflies fill my belly. He looks up at me, his black hair flopping over his left eye. Flicking it back in that sexy way boys do, he gives me a toothy smile and waves.

I wave back, and when he sees me wearing his jacket, his smile gets wider. He's so cute.

The coach calls for his attention as they get into a huddle. "He's so cute," Serenity says. "He's got it bad for you."

"You think?" I ask. A part of me is still insecure when it comes to the sincerity of a guy's feelings.

"Oh, yeah." She laughs. "The way he talks about you when you're not around, it even makes me swoon."

"I'm crazy about her too," Colton mumbles.

"You are?" I ask, taking his hand.

"Of course I am," he says. "You're amazing, Rylee. Hell, just sitting next to you, holding your hand, is like winning the lottery."

"You're too sweet," I say, kissing his cheek. "I'm pretty crazy about you too." I lean in, brushing my lips against the shell of his ear. "I'm also pretty fond of what we did in your bedroom." I nip at his lobe, loving the little moan that slips from his lips.

"He totally has a hard on now." Donny laughs.

"Shut up," Colton says, slapping Donny. I giggle as I see him shift in his seat.

By the time half-time comes around, our team is in the lead.

"Look!" Serenity says, getting my attention. The crowd starts to murmur as I glance over and see Trevor walking up the stairs toward us.

"Hey, baby," he says, leaning forward, over Serenity. He cups the back of my head and kisses me hard. He smells of sweat and mint, and the way he plunges his tongue into my mouth, I'm a horny little mess.

"Hi," I say dreamily as we break apart.

"Sorry, I just missed you. Meet me after the game?" he asks, his crooked smile making my heart flutter.

"Mhhmm."

"See you after, baby. Just let me win this one for you

first." He kisses me again quickly as his coach shouts for him to get his ass back down to the field.

I'm a grinning fool as I watch him laugh, running back down the steps.

"Ok, he's good," Donny says.

"Yeah, he is," I whisper to myself.

The cheerleaders for the other team start to do their routine, and I realize they were one of the teams we competed against last night. The Vipers.

When they're done, everyone takes the time to use the bathroom, grab some food, and the teams do whatever they do with their coach.

"Ahh, who's that?" Colton asks, getting my attention from Ren. I look over to see what he's talking about. Trevor is off to the side, having what looks like a heated conversion with one of the cheerleaders from the other team.

"That would be Robin Reed, Trevor's ex," Missi says, looking over her shoulder at me with a cruel smile. "From what I heard, they were the IT couple in high school. Childhood besties. They called it quits in college. I guess Trevor wanted to play the field. But, from what I've heard, they were always expected to get back together when he was done having fun. So, I wouldn't hold your breath on him sticking around."

My stomach drops as my pulse picks up. Serenity is telling Missi off, but I can't hear them over the ringing in my ears.

"Hey," Mateo says, placing a hand on my leg as he leans over Colton. My eyes snap up to his, and tears I didn't know were there are already falling. His face softens as he brings his thumb up to wipe them away. "Don't listen to her. And don't make the same mistake we did. Talk to him first, hear his side of things, before you get yourself worked up."

He's right, but why is he trying to help Trevor? "You're right." I nod, wiping my eyes. "I can't overreact without knowing the truth."

"I might see him as competition, but I also see how much he means to you. I don't want to see you hurt, not ever again. And if he does end up hurting you, he'll be in a fucking wheelchair," Mateo growls, making me smile. "But give him the benefit of the doubt, unlike we did with you."

The game starts up again, but I can't sit still. My nerves are going wild, so I head out toward the concessions to get some fresh air.

As I'm leaving the bathroom, I bump into someone. "Sorry," I say. My eyes widen slightly when I see who I bumped into.

"No, it's totally my fault for not looking where I'm going," Robin says, giving me a smile. She has jet black hair and bright blue eyes. Almost like a female version of Trevor. "Hey, I know you. You're on the Black Widows, aren't you?"

"Ahh, yeah," I say.

"Congrats on the win. Totally bummed that we lost, but not surprised." She laughs. "Black Widows seem to always win any competition they enter."

"Colton does really good choreography," I say, smiling a little when I think about how passionate he is when it comes to cheer.

"Right, one of the guys on your team. Ugh, we need some hot cheerleaders on ours," she says. "I don't think my boyfriend would like that very much though. That's why I haven't bothered to transfer to your school. I wanna cheer, and he would be totally jealous and possessive with me being manhandled by the hotties on your team."

"And who's your boyfriend?" I ask, my heart threatening to explode in my chest.

"He's on your guys' football team, actually," she says, and I struggle to breathe. "His name is Trevor."

The way she stares me down tells me she knows I know him. That she saw Trevor kiss me. And her eyes flick down to the number and name on Trevor's jacket.

There's no fucking way I'm dealing with another Missi. I'm done playing nice with bitches who think that can mess with me.

I let out a humorless laugh. "Oh really? Because I'm pretty sure he's *my* boyfriend." She keeps the smile on her face, but I can see her eye twitch. "I don't know what game you're playing at, but it's not going to be with me. You're not welcome at my school or on my team. The flyer the guys base for is me, their girlfriend." Her eyes widen and I grin. "Yeah, that's right. Not only do I have one of the hottest football players at Solidarity as my boyfriend, but I have all the guys on the Black Widow team."

She goes to say something, but I cut her off. "And before you call me a whore, and all that mean girl bullshit I'm sure is floating around in your head, save it. You don't know me or my relationship with any of them. So, kindly get over the delusion that you're still with my boyfriend, and fuck off. I don't have time for attention-seeking bullies anymore."

With that, I shoulder check her and storm away. I'm so

fucking worked up, my body vibrating, that I go right to the guest locker room just in time to see the team heading toward it.

"Oh, boy," Alex says, looking at Trevor as they come to a stop. Trevor looks happy to see me, but it shifts into worry when he sees the anger radiating off me.

"Rylee, baby, are you okay? What happened?" Trevor asks, approaching me like you would a wild animal. I mean, I feel like one right now.

"I don't want to come off as some crazy girlfriend, but Trevor, I've been hurt too much to not worry. I met your ex."

"Fuck," he hisses, running a hand through his hair. "It's not what you think, Rylee."

"Then, please, tell me how it is, because she seems to be under the impression you're still together." I'm shaking a little, and even though I'm mad, Trevor takes a risk by wrapping his arm around my waist and pulling my body to his. He uses the other hand to grip my chin so that I'm looking at him. I hate the angry tears that fill my eyes, but I can't have this be too good to be true. I really fucking like him, and if he's playing me, I'm gonna lose it.

"Robin and I were childhood best friends. We dated for a while on and off as teenagers. When I came to Solidarity, she went to Verrando Academy. After a while, I realized that what I felt for her wasn't anything more than a strong friendship. I was going to tell her we were better off as friends. When I went to a party I knew she would be at, I found her fucking some other guy. The fact that she cheated on me, when all she had to do was tell me she felt the same way about our friendship, is what hurt. After that, we broke up and parted ways. I haven't seen or talked to her in years."

"Then why were you talking to her today?" I ask, my voice soft.

"She saw what I did, going up and kissing you. I guess she didn't like that, and felt the need to tell me she made a mistake. That she loved me and always has, and she was just confused back then. But, Rylee, I wasn't. I didn't love her that way. I've known her my whole life, and I'm more in love with you, after knowing you for only a month, than all the years I was with her."

I let out a little gasp at his words. "You love me?" I ask in disbelief.

"I do. Like, crazy in love with you." He gives me a grin that sends a wave of calm over me. "I know it's fast, but Rylee, you're everything to me. One thing that we have in common is that I hate liars. You're upfront, and honest with your feelings, so I know you're not keeping anything from me. And this, coming to me and asking me without accusing me of the worst, thank you. You have no idea how much it means to me that you waited to hear my side of the story."

"So, you don't want her?"

"No. Never again. You're it for me, Rylee. The little bit of time I've been with you has been the best time of my life. And I can't wait for everything that's still to come."

"And you love me?" I ask again, positive that my ears are playing tricks on me.

"More than what I think is healthy." He chuckles.

"I..."

"It's okay. You tell me when you feel you're ready. I just

want you to know how I feel. Whatever she said is a lie. Today was the first time in years that I've talked to her. I don't know what she's trying to accomplish, but I'm not taking the bait. I told her we would never be together again, and that I have a girlfriend. I know you don't have a reason to believe me after everything you've been through, but I hope you do."

"I do," I say. And its true. I can see it on his face, and the way he's talking to me.

Relief fills his face. "You do?"

"I do," I say again. "Sorry I came in here like an angry bull."

"Don't be. I find it kind of sexy when you're all worked up. But, how about next time, it's me teasing your sexy little body, and we leave all that hurtful stuff out of it?"

"I'd like that," I say.

He kisses me until my knees threaten to buckle. "Trevor!" the coach shouts. "Get your ass back out on the field!"

"Sit on the bench with Coach?" he asks me and I nod. I squeal as he picks me up. Wrapping my arms around his neck and my legs around his waist, I let him carry me back out onto the field.

I can hear the cat calls and the cheering as everyone watches, but my eyes find Robin's on the other side of the field. She looks pissed, and I let my petty show by giving her a smirk and a little wink for good measure. I deserve to be happy, and I'm not letting anyone get in my way again.

CHAPTER TWENTY-FIVE

Adonis

W hen we returned to campus, Rylee and Trevor went back to their dorm, and I have been going out of my mind. If she seriously sleeps with him before me, I'm going to go crazy. I have been head over heels for that girl since the moment she came to take my order.

I knew that she was my end game, until we fucked it all up. I'm so stupid. I always fuck something good up. I'm never going to get the girl. She has all the other guys, and now Trevor. Even Teo seems to be on good terms with her.

I sigh and throw another ball. I haven't had a dodgeball game in forever and I've been itchy. Mateo has MMA, Lennox has his smutty books and songwriting, Colton has his choreography, and I have anime and chucking balls at douchebags.

But lately, I haven't wanted to do anything. One of my many therapists once told me that I have seasonal depression, especially near the holidays. I know the guys have been trying to cheer me up, but I don't want to drag them down. They seem happy now.

I catch the red ball as it bounces back from the wall, then walk over to the equipment closet and put it back where it belongs. It's late and I know I should get some sleep, but the nightmares have increased, and I don't want to close my eyes.

I know that Lennox has noticed that I haven't been home the past few nights, but he hasn't said anything, and for that, I'm grateful. My grades are slipping, but I'll get them back up. I'm a closet nerd, but the lack of sleep isn't helping things.

I leave the gym and start the walk back to the cheer house. Felicia is sitting on the steps smoking. When she sees me, she tries to hide it behind her back and I laugh. "Busted," I joke and she groans.

"Do not tell Colton. I will never hear the end of it. But I needed one after the day I've had. Missi has been losing her shit since the game, and I am so over her crazy," she says, shaking her head and taking another puff.

I have never liked the smell of tobacco. It reminds me too much of him. "Your secret's safe with me, but hey, can you do me a favor too?" She tosses the cigarette on the ground and crushes it with her flip-flop.

"Yeah, what's up?"

"If Missi is going to go after Rylee again, can you just give one of us a heads up?" She rolls her eyes and nods.

"Yeah, Rylee doesn't deserve Missi's wrath. I'll let you know, but lately she's just been venting, and staying with her dad. Except tonight, she popped by to get some of her things."

"I hope she stays there for good. Thanks, Felicia," I say, then head up the steps into the silent house.

When I reach our apartment, Lennox has left the door unlocked and a note is taped to the wall where I usually hang my keys.

> Melatonin is on the counter with a bottle of water. I'm worried about you, Donny. Try and get some sleep. We love and care about you. You're not alone. If you need me, I'm in the next room.
> -Len

I sigh and wipe a tear from my eye. It's hard to explain how I'm feeling, so I usually just don't. I know Lennox has his own issues and nightmares, but I don't want to burden him with my fears.

No one needs to be haunted by my past as well.

His hands are on me again and I can't handle it. I scream and fight, but I'm too weak. He's too heavy. It's always the same. I fight and fight, as hard as I can, but I never win. I always end up broken and bloody in the end. So why bother anymore? I'm just a kid. This isn't how my life is supposed to be. I'm supposed to be protected and nurtured. Especially, from a man that's supposed to love and take care of me.

He leans over me once more, his breath reeking of stale cigars and alcohol. He was at the boys' club again. He only comes after me on the nights he has been out. I scream again, but his large, clammy hand covers my mouth, cutting off my air and making me gag.

"No, please, stop, Gran—"

I wake up with a jolt. I'm shivering, tears streaming down my face. Kicking the blankets off me, I ignore that I'm only in a pair of tight boxers, and slip on my shoes before racing out the door. I need to get away from here. Before he finds me again.

I sneak out into the dark night and run to her. She can make things better. She can make the nightmares disappear. I always sleep better when she's around. The dorm building isn't far, but my breathing is staggered and I'm close to passing out.

I just need to get to her. I close my eyes and picture her face, her smile, her laugh. I calm, but not much. I won't be okay until we're face to face.

I don't know when she became my safe space, but I need her. She can't ever leave us again.

I bang on the locked door until the night guard lets me in. She takes one look at me, and raises her eyebrows, but I can't deal with this right now. I push her aside and ignore her yelling and ordering me to come back. I'll deal with the consequences later.

I make it to Rylee's door and bang on it like I'm the police.

"If this is you drunk again, Lennox, I am going to beat your ass," Rylee growls from behind the door, and I wipe the tears from my face. Please, please, just open the door.

Finally, the door swings open and I lose it.

"Donny? What's wrong? What happened?" Rylee rushes to say, her voice a little groggy from sleep, as I fall to my knees once again in front of her. I bury my face into her stomach, breathing in her strawberry scent. I'm still shaking as she runs her nails through my hair.

"Don't let him get me," I whisper, flashes of my nightmare seeping in. But I don't think she can hear my mumbles. My head is still trapped in that hellish place. Even though I know I'm safe now, I still feel like I need her to protect me. She may not understand the draw I have to her, but she doesn't need to. She can be mad at me all she wants. I may be bigger and stronger, but that doesn't mean that I'm not still trapped in the memories of my past and needing comfort.

"Donny, you need to talk to me. Is it the guys? Did something happen? Was it Mateo's uncle?"

I look up at her and show her how broken I really am

inside. I can't keep my mask in place right now. She gasps and rubs her fingers under my eyes, but the tears keep falling.

"No, they are fine. I... I just... Can I stay with you tonight?" I ask in a whisper and she bites her lip, but eventually nods with a groan.

"Yeah," she says softly, then walks back to the bed, leaving me still on my knees. I climb to my feet and shut the door, making sure it's locked. Not that locks ever kept me safe. I notice we're alone. It's three AM, shouldn't Alex be here?

Why isn't he here? Does he just leave Rylee unprotected like this often? My heart races and my chest starts to heave. No, he can't do that. What if *he* gets her. I won't ever let anyone hurt my Cherry.

"Where is he?" I growl, and Rylee's green eyes widen.

"Who?" she asks, brows furrowing with confusion. "Donny, you're starting to freak me out. Maybe I should call the guys," she says, reaching for her phone on her side table. I rush over to her, shaking my head as I kick my shoes off.

"No, they will try to take me from you. I need you. I'll tell you, but I just need some cuddles first," I say, cracking a small smile and she huffs, then yawns. I'm scared to tell her about my demons. I like when she's in my arms, even when she's cute and grumpy.

"I was sleeping, Donny. I don't know what's going on, but if this is some trick or prank, right now isn't the time," she grumbles, then climbs back in her bed, leaving me at the edge.

"Where's Alex?" I ask, shuffling closer and laying down beside her.

"With Ren." She turns to face me. "Are you going to tell me what happened? This is the second time you've come to me amidst a panic attack." My eyes widen and I blow out a breath. "Yes, Donny, I know what an attack looks like."

"I can't tell you about the first time. That's not my story to confess," I whisper and she nods. My stories are bad enough without adding in Lennox's.

"Okay, and tonight, or this morning?" She sighs. I close my eyes and try to get up the courage to tell her one of my deepest, darkest secrets. But my heart starts to race and my chest begins to heave. I don't know if I'm going to be sick or pass out. I don't think I can do this...

"I can't. It's too soon. I haven't told the guys..." I pant and she places a palm on my cheek, wiping away my tears.

"Okay, then tell me why you're here. Why didn't you go to one of the others?"

"Isn't that obvious? Because I'm so fucking in love with you, Rylee, and you're the only one to make my pain go away, and the nightmares disappear." Her mouth opens as she sucks in a breath and I groan.

Placing my hand over my face, I grumble, "That's not how I wanted to tell you that I loved you." Warm fingers grip my hands and she pulls them away. God, why am I such a fuck up?

"Donny, look at me," she whispers, and I can see her green eyes are glassy. "You hurt me. I think, honestly, your betrayal was the worst, since I confided my deepest fear to you and you gave it to the others to use against me. If I was anyone else, I'd say I should make you face your greatest fear. Take you to the bird room at the zoo and let you stay there overnight, but I won't." She shakes her head and I cringe.

"I am so, so sorry, Rylee. For everything. I know I overreacted and never should have told the guys what I overheard until we had talked, but I was in a love bubble and when it suddenly burst... I..." *I felt like my world was ending, and after all I have been through, I wanted someone else to feel my suffering.*

"I told you my parents died when I was little," I begin and she nods. "I was sent to live with my father's parents... They weren't good people, Rylee. I don't remember what love is, because I haven't felt true love since my parents died... But in Florida, you made me laugh, and when you smiled, I felt like everything was falling into place. No one has ever made me feel like that before. I wanted to hold onto that."

I glance over her head and stare at the wall. "All the abuse and neglect was worth it because it led me to meet my best friends, my family, and then you. When I thought that it was all a trick, a lie... I shut down. It happens sometimes, and I know it's not an excuse for what we did, but I hope you can tell that I'm trying my hardest to make things better. I love you, Rylee. True, passionate, unfiltered."

She cuts off my rambling by gripping my chin and pulling my lips to hers. It's nothing wild like I have been imagining for months, but it means so much more than she will ever know. When she pulls back and waits for me to go on, I struggle to tell her the rest. I'm not ready.

"I struggle with depression, and lately I can't sleep. The night I stayed with you was my best night's rest in a while, and when I woke up from my nightmare, all I could think was..." I whisper and she moves closer to me. "I need you, Rylee Moore. I can't ever lose you again. I won't survive it," I tell her honestly, and she looks up at me for a few moments, then presses her lips softly to mine once more.

"Don't you ever hurt me again, Adonis Baros. I won't be giving any more second chances," she mumbles against my mouth, and I groan before kissing her deeper. Is this really happening? My cock hardens to steel and I know I'm about to make a fool out of myself.

I refuse to be a two-pump chump. I can at least make it to five... maybe six, if I think about naked grannies or some shit. Ugh, this is going to be a nightmare. I have waited so long for my dream girl, and here she is, kissing me, and I can't focus.

"What's wrong? Why did you stop kissing me?" Rylee pulls back to look at me and scrunches her nose. "Why do you look like you're about to run away or throw up?" I start to laugh and it's not deep manly chuckles. No, it's little, girlish giggles.

I'm not some virgin like Colton was, but I don't want to let Rylee down either. Sex has never meant anything to me, but with her, I have all these feelings and shit.

"Don't laugh." She nods, but I know she's going to think this is hilarious. "I'm trying not to come in my boxers," I grumble and she waits a minute, blinking her gorgeous emerald green eyes at me, before biting her bottom lip to hold in her smile. I know it's coming so I roll over and give her my back as she softly laughs.

"Donny, you're always surprising me," she says, touching my shoulder and trying to move me to where I was. I groan.

"I have been waiting for this moment for so long, and now that I'm here in your bed with the possibility of us fucking, I can't focus. What if I accidentally slip into the wrong hole? Or what if you don't like the things I do with my dick...?" I start to panic-ramble and Rylee sits up, then pulls her top off. She's braless and I sigh.

"Titty fucking you was one of my best moments," I whisper, talking to her tits before reaching up and playing with them. Rylee laughs and raises her eyebrow at me.

"We don't have to do anything, Donny," she starts, and I cut her off by leaning up and biting on one of her nipples. Hissing, she grabs my hair tight in her fingers and pulls. I moan loudly and she stops. That's not a punishment for me. I really like pain mixed with my pleasure.

I slide back and climb off the bed. Rylee gets onto her knees, her hand sliding down between her legs as her other one touches her breasts, watching me as I start to pace. My cock is sticking out the top band of my boxers, and I can't believe I'm even questioning this.

"Okay, I can do this. We can do this. Right, Lil D?" I ask my dick, and though Rylee is cracking up, she gives me a minute to process. I glance at her and she's pulling down her sleep shorts.

"Fuck, why are you not wearing panties? Go put some on right now!" I bark, and her eyes widen as she bites her lip, unsure whether to laugh or be confused. She doesn't move fast enough so I stomp over to her drawer and grab a black and pink lacy pair.

I toss them to her and she slips them on. Moving back to the bed, I place my hands on my hips. "Every time we're going to be together, you leave those on," I mumble and her nostrils flare. I know she wants to sass back at me as she lays down on the bed, but when I drop to my knees and shove my face in between her thighs, licking the lace, she moans and opens her legs wider for me.

"God, Donny," she mumbles and I growl, nipping the material and her clit. "Oh, fuck," she cries and jumps. "Why does that feel so good?" She whimpers. I rub my fingers over the lace, hard, making sure she can feel every bump and groove along her slit.

She's dripping for me and I want to... I sit up and rip a hole in the soaked lace before thrusting two fingers inside of her. "No, I really liked that pair," she moans and I laugh.

"I'll buy you a hundred new pairs, Cherry." I grunt before moving up to her lips and kissing her mouth. She groans as I finger-fuck her faster and curl my fingers up.

"Oh, my God," she cries as her tight pussy clenches my fingers. She's close, but I want to feel her finally grip my dick with those walls. At least if I cum too fast now, she will be with me.

"Do you need anything? I'm clean. I haven't been with anyone since before Florida," I murmur against her lips and she shakes her head. I sit up and kick my boxers off. My cock is leaking so much, I'm worried we're going to have a flood between the two of us.

It's okay, I'll plug her boat. I laugh at my inner thoughts, and Rylee sits up on her elbows. Her skin is flushed and glistening with a thin layer of sweat, and I just want to lick her all over. She runs her nails down my neck and pulls on my nipple piercing, making me hiss. My dick jumps and she smiles.

"I have been dreaming about this moment for way too long. I want you to ride me hard and dirty, leaving the panties on. I want the lace to grind against my cock as you cum. I want to feel the river of your juices all over it," I growl.

She grabs my shoulders and pushes me down so she can straddle me, and I kiss her again. I will never get tired of her lips on mine. My Cherry. I rub my dick along her slit, then press into the hole of her panties.

"God, you're so weird," she moans. I wiggle my way in and thrust up hard, ripping the hole bigger. These panties are trash, but they are mine. I don't care what anyone says. I'm making a new collection.

Gripping her hips, I pull her tits to my mouth and make sure they get enough attention too. I am a full supporter of breast exams, and I will help Rylee out any time she wants. "God, I want to marry your boobs." I groan as she moves back and forth on my lap.

Her moans cut off and she looks at me weird, pausing. "Wait, what?" she says with a breathless laugh, and I flip her, so she's on her back again.

Her nails trail along my shoulders and grip them tight as I start to fuck her into the mattress. I grind hard against her slit, and I know she's about to scream. I don't even try to gag her. I want everyone to know that she's mine... and I'm hers. I never fucking stopped, and I never will.

"God, Donny. Yes!" she cries out as I swirl my hips and grip her legs, pulling them over my shoulders. I'm about to explode, but I need her to come. My spine tingles and my vision blurs.

I think I'm hallucinating. This is better than I ever imagined. I never thought I would get the chance to connect with her in this way, and if I could write music or a poem like Lennox, I would.

I'd sing about rainbows and orgasms, and the way the stars have finally aligned just for this indescribable moment. I finally have my girl. And even though we've been through hell and back to get here, it was worth it. I'm not the same Donny as before.

She's changed me for the better. I just hope I can make her proud, and maybe she'll call me her boyfriend too one day.

My throat gets choked up and I clear it. I am not going to cry. No, I am going to blow my girl's damn world, so she keeps wanting a piece of me and Lil D. Thank God she can't read my mind right now.

"Come on, Cherry. I want you to choke my cock with this pretty pussy," I growl, and her eyes glaze with lust. For me. I did that.

I reach down and pinch her clit as I pull back and sit on my knees before I lean back, putting her in my lap. She looks like a sexy pretzel. It's a good thing my girl's flexible.

"Ow, oh, Donny," she whimpers as she wraps her arms around my neck. I shake my head.

"Grab your ankles and hold on tight." I grunt, then grab her hip with the hand not supporting her sexy back, and use her pussy like my personal jack-off machine. "So tight. So perfect. So mine." I groan as she starts to shake, her pussy leaking all over me. "Cum, now," I order, then release her hip and reach down, pinching her clit again.

I think my Cherry likes a little pain as much as I do.

"Oh fuck. Yes, Donny. Shit, I'm gonna... Yes!" She screams and explodes all over my cock, then releases her ankles and her legs fall open. I fall forward and come hard, almost blacking out. My cock jerks, sending so much pent-up cum into her that I can feel it leaking out as I continue to thrust my hips. I can feel Rylee shaking underneath me, panting as she begins running her nails through my hair.

"I don't know if this means that you forgive me, but I'll prove to you, Rylee, that I am, and always will be, yours," I mumble before rolling beside her and pulling her into my arms. She wiggles and removes her panties, then tosses them onto the floor.

"I need to clean up," she says and tries to move away.

"Just give me another minute," I say, and pull her onto my chest with a sigh. "I love you," I whisper, then kiss her sweaty head before finally falling asleep.

CHAPTER TWENTY-SIX

Lennox

I'm fucking dreading today. I wish I could just say fuck it all, and not care that all my belongings are about to be thrown away. But I have things from the guys and my grandparents that mean something to me.

"Are you sure about this?" I ask Teo as he grabs a dolly from the cheer house garage and tosses it in the bed of my truck. Grunting, he slams the hard shell tonneau cover I have closed, then moves over to the passenger side window, handing me a pack of garbage bags.

"I can drive," I say again for the third time. He reaches in and holds my hand.

"I know you can, Len, but I don't know what we're going to walk into when we get to your dad's house, so let me just take the lead on this." I nod with a sigh and he glances around to make sure the coast is clear, then leans in and kisses me.

It's early for a Saturday morning, and with finals and the holidays coming up, people are taking advantage of the extra sleep. I pull out my phone and send my mother a message. She swore back and forth last night that my dad was out of town, but I can never be sure if she's covering for him.

Colt and Donny offered to come too, but I didn't want it to seem like this was an ambush. I just want to get in, grab whatever means something, and get the fuck out. I have a shit ton of money from my inheritance that my father has no access to, so I can replace the meaningless things.

I watch as Teo shuts the garage door and walks back over to me. He's wearing some loose basketball shorts and a hoodie. His hair's a mess from my fingers gripping it this morning, and he has a smile on his face.

A lot of his stress and worries are gone now that his family is safe.

If I already didn't love Rylee, I would now. What she did for Teo's family was incredible, and completely selfless. I can't believe we ever judged her so wrong. She's a light in the darkness that needs to be taken care of and loved, and we almost ruined that.

I know she's close to forgiving us, but I think I still need some time to forgive myself.

Climbing into my truck, Teo grabs a pair of sunglasses that he leaves in the center console, slips them on, then gives me a glance. "Are you ready for this?" I nod, but honestly, no. I'm scared shitless. I thought my father was going to kill me the last time I saw him.

I don't know if I have a guardian angel or what, but it was fucking terrifying. I know if I ever have kids, I won't ever raise my voice or hand to them. I'll let one of the other guys do the punishments.

I couldn't live with myself if I turned into the monster that raised me.

Teo places his hand on my thigh and gives me a quick squeeze before turning the truck on and driving off campus. My dad lives about forty minutes away, up in the hills. We listen to some music and sing along, letting the salty breeze blow into the open windows.

The water is so clear and inviting, I'm tempted to just jump in and let the waves take me away. As we get closer, the beach roads turn into hills, and that prestigious, pompous fucking gate appears.

Mateo rolls his window down to talk to our guard, Henri. "You boys are here mighty early."

"Hey, Henri. Yeah, I was ordered to come get my things. Is my dad home?" I hold my breath, and for one moment, I pray that my mom told me the truth. That she wasn't covering for a man who has abused us all of my life.

"I haven't seen him. He left for a trip two days ago, but I wasn't on shift last night. So..." He trails off and I sigh, then nod.

"Thanks," Teo grunts, then heads up the driveway after

the gate opens. The mansion comes into view and I shudder. This is where I grew up, but it's never felt like a home. Mateo pulls up right in front and I have to laugh.

If my father saw my dirty truck parked here, he would lose his shit. I was always ordered to keep it in the garage, or in the staff parking lot. I couldn't tarnish his reputation, after all.

"The Lexus isn't here, so let's do this quickly," I mutter and Teo nods. I unbuckle and open my door, still holding the box of garbage bags in my hand. Teo moves to the back and unlatches the cover to grab the dolly.

I could have hired movers to do this, but I only want a few things. We don't have the room for all of my stuff.

Gregory, our butler, greets me at the top of the steps and opens the door for us. "Your father called and said he's going to be home in about an hour, so I suggest you try to get in and out fast, Master Crane," he tells us, as I move toward the grand staircase on the left.

"Thank you, Gregory. That is my plan," I reply, then haul ass up the steps.

When we reach the top, I snort at the huge painting that sits on the wall, of our fake ass happy smiles. My father had his hand on my shoulder and he was pinching me the whole time, making sure I didn't embarrass him. We sat there for over six hours.

"Fuck, this place gives me the creeps," Teo mumbles and I laugh.

"Yeah, I'll be glad to leave this house of horrors and never return again," I say as I walk down the hall to the last door and open it—my bedroom. It's spacious with a king-sized bed in the center on a platform.

I move over to my closet and click the light on. Mateo has some cardboard we brought to make boxes. I notice some empty totes up against the wall and smile.

Gregory must have left them there for me. I hand Teo the tape from my pocket and he gets started. "Grab all the watches and designer stuff from the top two drawers. They were my grandpa's." I point to where I'm talking and Mateo shakes his head.

"I sometimes forget how rich you are," he mutters, then dumps the stuff into a box. I peruse what's hanging and grab my most expensive suits. They are custom tailored, and I might need them at some point.

"Can you grab another box for all my shoes?" I ask and Teo nods, leaving me in the walk-in. I have an obsession with designer sneakers, and Donny, Colt, and I have the same size feet, so I know they would be pissed if I left them.

Digging to the back on the top shelf, I grab a small shoebox full of photos of the guys and me growing up. I hand it to Teo and he grins. I leave a lot of my clothes, but I do grab all my boxers and some basketball shorts.

Mateo would never admit it, but I know he's starting to wear through his clothes. The shorts will fit, but the tops would be extremely tight. He's too proud to ask any of us for help, but he will take my hand-me-downs.

"Grab some things for Colt too, and some sweatpants," I tell him and he sighs. "Baby, just do it. Otherwise, they will be thrown in the trash. My mother doesn't believe in donating used clothes to charity."

He moves over to the dressers and stuffs a bunch of clothing in the garbage bags.

"We need to hurry up. Is there anything else in here you want?" he asks, and I look around.

"No, but I do want some things from the bedroom and bathroom," I mumble, then move in that direction. It takes us five more minutes to get my stuff and then load up the truck. I made a stop in my studio and grabbed all of my guitars and notebooks, filling up the totes.

I was surprised my dad hadn't touched them yet. He never supported my passion for making music. I turn to shake Gregory's hand, and he scoffs before pulling me into a tight hug. He's been with my family since I was four, and he's helped me out many times.

"Take care, Master Crane. Ida and I will miss you," he says, and I find myself tearing up.

"Keep an eye on Mom. I wish she would just leave, but..." I trail off and he nods.

"Len, we need to go," Teo says, then comes and gives Gregory a quick hug goodbye too.

I'm climbing into the truck when my father's car comes speeding into the driveway, blocking us from leaving. I sigh and shake my head, closing my eyes. I was hoping to avoid this.

"Get in the truck, Lennox," Teo barks at me, and I open my eyes to see him clenching his fists. His face is turning red and he's pissed.

"No, he will press charges and ruin your life, Mateo. Don't do anything," I tell him, and he rolls his eyes at me.

Turning back around, I wait for my father to leave his car.

He moves around the back of my truck and peeks in. Probably making sure I'm not stealing any of his precious items. Like I would want any of his shit. I didn't even take any photos of my mom and him.

After today, I am renouncing that I'm his son. He should have never had children. Even if I was his pride and joy, and followed in his footsteps, he still would have been an abusive asshole. It took me a long time to come to terms with that. No matter what I did, he would never be happy.

"Finally came to get your shit. Good. And I see you brought your little fuck toy. How fucking sweet," he slurs, and I roll my eyes. He's already drunk. *Drinking and driving, how classy of him.* I haven't had a sip of alcohol in weeks, and sometimes I still crave it and struggle, but I'm glad I stopped.

I was turning into the man I despised. A person I don't want to be, or for the people I love to see. "Father," I greet and he sneers.

"I am not your father," he hisses. "I refuse to have a fairy as a son." I laugh, surprised his words are not breaking me like I thought they would.

"That's great. Then get the fuck out of the way so I can leave and never come back." He takes a menacing step toward me and tries to swing, but his aim is off. He leans farther to the right and falls onto the ground. An engine revs and I watch as Gregory pulls the car out of the way and parks it in his normal spot.

"You're pathetic. Just a washed up Super Bowl champion that's still stuck in his glory days. I can't wait for reality to hit, and you realize you've lost the best things in your life," I snap, moving closer to him.

"Don't come crying to me when he takes you for all your money and pride. I never should have let you associate with those kinds of people. They brainwashed you!" my dad shouts, still sitting on the ground and I laugh as Mateo moves closer. His shadow covering my father.

"The people who supposedly brainwashed me are some of the nicest, proudest, most loving folks I have ever met. You don't need to be rich to be a decent person. Even though they have little, they would give it all up to someone in need," I spit, and I'm losing my temper. How dare he try to demean Mateo's mom, and the people from the community center.

My dad tries to shift away as Mateo leans over him, with his arms crossed and a menacing snarl on his lips. "I love your son, and you're damn lucky he told me not to touch you, Sir. If you ever try to contact him, or come after him again, not only will you be dealing with me, but I'll put you in the fucking ground without batting an eye," he sneers. "And those people will help me hide my sins," he growls, and my feet lead me to him before my mind has caught up.

"I love you too," I tell him, then kiss him there right in front of my father, Gregory, and God. We ignore my father screaming insults at us and climb into my truck.

"Let's go home, babe. Maybe we can convince Rylee to watch a movie with us," I say, and Teo puts his sunglasses on and turns the key, starting the engine.

I wave to Gregory and he gives me a big smile before stomping over and pulling my father off the ground.

He's still spitting like a pissed off rattlesnake, and I don't even care. I did it. I stood up to the man who has controlled me for years, and walked away unharmed.

WE GET BACK to the house and Donny is just walking up the steps. He has a huge smile on his face, and he's not paying attention to anything.

"Yo, Donny," Teo yells, and I watch as he jumps, then grips his chest.

"You almost gave me a heart attack. But it's okay. If I died today, I'd die a very, very happy man." He tries to catch his breath, and something is different about him. I must have been staring too hard because he nods his head, like I'm supposed to know what that means.

"I think Rylee is forgiving me. She and I... we..." he trails off and then shakes his head. "Ya know what, I'm not even going to tell you. It was perfect and magical, and I will always remember it."

Teo throws his head back and starts laughing. I must be tired or still shocked from what happened at my dad's house, because things are just not clicking.

"Our little boy is now a man," Teo says, and my eyes go wide.

"No," I gasp. "She wouldn't. Colt is one thing, but you..."

"I'm in love, gentlemen, with the prettiest lady in all the land. With hair as red as apples, and skin as pure as snow, and tastes as good as cherries." He starts to ramble, and I don't know if I should congratulate him, or lock him in a psych ward.

"Hey, why is your truck full of shit?" he asks me, coming back down to earth, and I groan.

"I moved out of my parents' place. For good. I'm never going back. I grabbed a bunch of shit for all of us though. You and Colt can go through them. Help us bring everything inside."

"Fuck, yeah. Please tell me you grabbed all your Jordans. I think I'd cry if you left them," he says with a fake sniffle and I laugh. I'm in a really good mood, and all I want to do now is unload everything, then grab some food and chill.

Things are starting to look up for all of us. Rylee is coming around and beginning to forgive us. I'm finally free from my parents and their toxic bullshit. Now all we need to do is focus on cheer and the upcoming competitions. Oh, and keep an eye on Missi. I know she's plotting something.

There's no way her and the Dean are going to leave shit alone.

Colt and Donny dig through all the bags excitedly, and Mateo finally takes a few things for himself. I wish he would just accept help from us, his family, but I won't force him to change who he is.

I order some takeout and Donny tells us about his nightmare last night, leading him to Rylee's door. He won't talk about the sex, but that's okay. I'm just glad she was there to comfort him, and that she didn't turn him away.

"I want to get her something," he says and I groan.

"Donny, stop spending money. Rylee doesn't want to be

bought. The small gestures we've done are one thing, but if you get her something extravagant, she's just going to throw it back in your face," I mutter, and he rolls his eyes at me.

"You really want to win her over, go get her one of those demon cats. She was practically melting for them at the SPCA. Which I still fucking hate you all for," Teo grumbles and I laugh.

"We can't have pets in the dorm, so don't do that, Donny. Maybe one day we can move off campus. Get an apartment. Then you can get her a kitten," Colt suggests, but I can tell Donny has left the building. He's got a dopey smile on his face and his phone in his hand. He's not even touching the triple chocolate brownie that's on his lap.

"Donny, are you listening?" Teo barks, and Donny waves his hand.

"Yeah, yeah, no kittens until we move," he mumbles, but I know he's lying.

I glance over at Teo and he crosses his arms. He knows he fucked up, and it's going to be hilarious when this all comes back to bite him in the ass.

CHAPTER TWENTY-SEVEN

Adonis

I'm there before Denise even arrives. I'm so excited that I might piss myself. I can't believe I never thought of this before. Mateo is going to kill me, but it will be worth it to see the smile on Rylee's face.

"Wow, I don't think I have ever had someone offer me an absurd amount of money before just to arrive two hours before opening," she says as she pulls out her keys and unlocks the door.

"Donation. I made a donation. Don't make it dirty, now," I quip with a big smile. I'm practically vibrating. I shouldn't have had those two espressos and three donuts. I am going to be bouncing off the fucking walls today.

"I sent you some options last night. Did you have a baby in mind, or did you want to go play with them?" she asks me, moving over to the front counter. I stayed up all night looking through the photos, and I have my eyes set on two. But I can't get them both, so...

"I like Smokey and Ginger the best, but I can't decide. This is for my future wife. I think you met her. Rylee. She loves kittens, and I wanted to surprise her. I need one as feisty as she is, but who also likes to snuggle and comfort when she's had a bad day. One full of attitude, but also sweet." Denise looks at me and then starts to laugh, shaking her head.

"Oh, honey, you have it so bad for this girl. But I can see why you love her so much. She's an absolute doll, and the babies just adored her. That gruff man she came in with seemed like he was terrified," she says with a smile and I laugh.

"His sister traumatized him with a stray cat when he was a kid," I reply and she laughs too.

"Okay, well since we are here so early, how about you help me feed the kitties, and then you can get to know them?" I nod and follow her into a back room. She shows me where the food is and I get to work.

There's a black kitten with a star shape on its head that keeps hissing at me. "You would be perfect for Missi," I tell him, then hiss back. Finishing up with the cages, I move into a large cat room and get swarmed.

"Are you pussies hungry?" I coo, and they all meow and

start to fuss, tangling between my legs. I walk over to the bowls laid out and fill them, then take a seat on the floor. One of the kittens I was looking at adopting is in the mass of cats, getting stepped on. I wait and watch to see what it will do.

After a few seconds, it climbs on top of one of the others and smushes their face in the bowl of wet food. I laugh and clap, making a few of the other cats hiss and scurry away. "Oh, you are perfect for my Cherry," I coo, climbing to my feet and scooping up the fiery kitten.

I check the gender and smile. "You are going to be the best little girl for your mommy, aren't you?" She's a tiny ball of fluff with orange and white hair, and the greenest eyes that remind me of my girl's.

She squirms away from me at first, so I place her onto my shoulder and walk out of the room. "I think she's the one," I say to Denise and she laughs. The kitten is clinging to my skin, but I don't care.

"Are you sure? She can be a little wild at times," she says, moving closer to rub the kitten's nose. I nod and she claps.

"Well then, let's do some paperwork and I'll give you a list of things you need to buy, and of course, you will need to keep her shots up to date. We have a clinic here, or you can take her to your own vet." I keep nodding and smiling, but I'm not paying attention.

All I can think about is how much Rylee is going to love this little girl, and maybe the thank you kisses and sex afterwards. My cock twitches and I pray I don't get an erection here in the middle of the SPCA.

After twenty minutes, I am the proud co-parent of an

adorable baby kitten who is asleep in my hood. I've turned my hoodie around backwards so the hood could be in front of my face. I think I might get one of those cat-pouch hoodies.

The kitten is purring as we walk outside and climb into Lennox's truck. I plan to stop at a pet store, but first I need food. I buckle in and make sure the baby is safe, before pulling out of the parking lot and finding a coffee shop.

It's still early. I may have been a little too impatient having Denise come in at seven. I can't go inside the coffee shop, so I pull into the drive-thru and wait. There has to be fifteen cars here. My stomach grumbles and the kitten jumps.

"I hope you know that you're the luckiest cat alive. You're mommy is going to spoil you rotten, and you will have five daddies. Well, more like four. Mateo is scared of you little fluff balls. It's pretty funny actually."

I tell the cat all about the photoshoot, and when it's time to order my coffee and sandwich, I'm almost crying from laughing so hard. "We need to name you, but I'll wait until Rylee does it. So, for now, you will just be the cutest little floof that ever lived," I coo, and the guy at the drive-thru window gives me a weird look.

I take my food, then drive over to the local pet store. It doesn't open for another twenty minutes, so I remove the kitten from my hood and place her onto the passenger seat as I eat. She starts to meow and climb all over me to get to my bacon and I sigh.

"You're lucky you're so fucking cute. I don't share food with anyone," I grumble, breaking off a tiny piece and feeding it to her. She gives me those green eyes and I melt. "You're going to be trouble, I can already tell," I say and she meows, climbing up my arm to sit on my shoulder again.

She buries her little head in my messy hair and starts to suckle on my earlobe. It's very weird, but I did read that kittens who are weaned too early tend to do this. I turn some music on and lift her into my hands, spinning her around a little, making her dance with me.

She doesn't let me do it for long, and ends up pooping on me. "Oh, fuck, baby girl, that's so gross." I grab some napkins and clean us up, and she gives me a tiny meow.

The parking lot starts to fill, so I make sure her little bum is all clean, then place her back into my hood. I crack the windows to air it out, then shove all the trash into the empty food bag and open the door.

"No more bacon for you, miss kitty," I coo as we walk into the store. I toss the garbage away and grab a cart, then get to shopping.

We spend three hours trying collars on and picking out the fluffiest beds and the best toys. I may have gone overboard, but I don't care. When we check out, the kitten is purring sound asleep in my hood, and I don't even look at the total.

I pass my credit card over, then take all the bags and walk out of the store. My stomach is killing me, so after I load up the bed of the truck, I go in search of something to eat. I know Rylee is in class right now, so we have some time to kill. I'd take her back to the cheer house, but I don't want the guys knowing I did the opposite of what they told me to, until they see how happy and in love Rylee is.

When we get back to campus, I'm exhausted, and I think miss kitty needs to shit. She has been a nuisance the last twenty minutes, and I need to give her to Rylee and set up her litter box robot thing.

I pull up in front of the dorms and park. "Now, you need to be good and wait just a few minutes longer, okay? I promise, you are going to love your mommy." I crack open the truck door and grab all the bags I can handle, then head over to the dorm.

The kitten starts freaking out, so I drop the bags by a tree, and move her into my arms. She's not wearing her collar or leash, because I wanted Rylee to pick out what color she liked the best.

"Stop wiggling, baby. We're almost there," I coo, but she won't settle and soon she's leaping from my arms and darting across campus.

"No, fuck, come back," I'm about to lose my shit and my lunch. What if she gets hurt, or hit? I'm panicking and chasing after her when Rylee appears and crouches down, scooping her up into her arms.

She has the biggest smile on her face, and the kitten starts to purr instantly. I laugh and shake my head, trying to catch my breath. For a tiny thing, she's fast. I walk up to Rylee to tell her that I got the kitten for her, but she's going on about being chosen from the cat distribution system and she's smiling so big, I can't ruin that.

She will never know that I bought the kitten for her, and I'm okay with that. I nod and listen as she babbles about Peaches. I am so incredibly, hopelessly in love with this girl.

God, she's so fucking cute.

Today sucks. Officially sucks. I just hardly passed an assignment that I thought I had in the bag, only to find out the paper was meant to be on Australia, not Austria. And because someone else was assigned to that country, I lost points. I think it's bullshit, because it was a fucking good paper, but there is nothing I can do about it now.

Then Trevor had to cancel our movie date we had planned for tonight because he has the flu. I offered to go over there and help take care of him, but the man has too much pride for me to see him puke. I mean, it doesn't bother me, but he was insistent. Probably for the best; the last thing I need before exams next week is to get sick.

So, now I'm headed back to my dorm to study because I have nothing else to do. Serenity is at her parents' for supper. I tried texting the group chat with the guys, but everyone seems to be busy with something, and Donny didn't even bother answering.

Maybe a night in wouldn't be so bad.

As I'm stepping onto the path to my building, I hear a little high pitched meow. My eyes flick down to see the cutest little ball of orange fur running over to me.

"Oh my God!" I squeal, as I bend over and pick up the

little kitty. "Hi there, little man," I coo. "Oh my goodness, you're just the cutest!"

Have you ever seen something so cute that you have no idea how to process your feelings? Yeah, that's me right now.

"Where did you come from?" I say, looking around, but I don't see anyone who looks like they're in distress from losing a cat. And we're not allowed to have animals on this part of campus. Maybe this little dude is lost, and his mama's around here somewhere. "Is your mama around?" I ask him. He meows at me again and starts to purr.

"Dude, no. You can't do that." I groan. "I'm done for now. You're mine. I don't even care if your mama is around here somewhere. You look old enough to be away from her, and I'm sure as hell not leaving you out here." There's cars coming and going, and I'd hate myself if he got hurt. Also, I want him. Is it a him?

"Sorry," I apologize in advance, and lift up their bum. "Nope, not a dude. A pretty little princess, you are," I say, peppering her face with kisses. "A little peach of a thing. Oh! Peaches, that's your new name."

Movement causes me to look over. For a moment I think it's someone looking for Peaches, but I see it's just Donny. "Hey!" I say excitedly. "Look! Look what I found. She's so cute. Finally, the cat Gods have chosen me! I always wanted to be a part of the cat distribution system. And look, dreams do come true!" I laugh.

"Well, isn't he a cutie," Donny says as he stops next to me.

"She, it's a she. Her name is Peaches, like Princess Peach, and I'm her new mama. And before you ask, yes, I'm going to be that crazy white chick who makes their cat their whole life. Deal with it. She's my daughter now."

Donny smiles and shakes his head. "Well, congratulations mama. What are you going to do with her?"

"Good point," I say, brows furrowing. "I don't have anything for a cat. I'll have to see if Alex can watch her while I go to the store and grab some things. I hope he likes cats and isn't allergic because she's staying with me," I say, kissing the crap out of the cute little ball of fur.

"Ahh, I can go for you," Donny says.

"Are you sure?" I ask. "It would mean a lot. Here." I go to take money out of my purse, but he holds his hand out to me.

"Nah, I got it. Least I can do." Donny chuckles.

"No, I can't let you do that. Cat stuff has to be expensive," I say, brows furrowing.

"You work hard for your money. Save it. Let me do this for you. Please," he says, giving me his puppy dog eyes. "It's my way of helping this little lost soul."

"Thank you, Donny!" I say, grabbing the back of his neck and kissing him hard. He moans, sliding his hand through my hair, holding my head. His tongue slips in and over mine, and my moans join his. Fuck, I don't think I can get tired of kissing this man. It's still crazy we took that step. But God, this man was holding out on me. Donny might be an odd ball, but fuck, he knows how to work his dick.

I'm about to ask for another round from the other night when Peaches lets out a meow.

We break apart laughing and out of breath.

"You're gonna be a little diva, I can tell," Donny mutters. "Better not be pussy blocking me."

"Oh, shut up." I laugh. "Maybe she's hungry?"

"I'll go now and get everything. I'll be back soon. There's a pet store just down the street."

"Thank you!" I say again. He takes off and I look around, making sure no one sees me with Peaches as I tuck her into my purse. "Just until we get upstairs, okay? Be a good girl and keep quiet."

I make quick work of getting inside and upstairs. My heart is pounding by the time I get to my room. "Where's the fire?" Alex asks as I lock the door behind me.

"No fire," I say with a grin. "But we have a new roommate."

"What?" he asks, sitting up.

Peaches lets out a little meow as I pull her from my purse.

"Peaches meet Alex!"

"Oh my God," he says. And for a moment, I think he's going to freak out and get mad, but he jumps off the bed and snatches her from me. "Aren't you just the cutest little thing?!"

I stand there, surprised, as I watch this massive football player get all gooey over my new kitten.

"Well, I take it you're okay with us keeping her? Not that I'd be giving you much of a choice."

"You're not going anywhere, are you sweet girl?" he coos, ignoring me.

Alex and I sit on his bed and play with Peaches with a shoelace. About a half hour later, there's a knock on my door.

"Hey!" I say, letting Donny in.

"I got her everything she might need. Here's a bed, although I'm sure she will just sleep with you."

"Or me," Alex says, snuggling up to the cat.

Donny looks over at him with a raised brow but shakes his head and continues. "I got her a food and water dish, they're wider than most, so her whiskers don't get crushed. Here's a crap ton of toys. A few collars and leashes, as well as a harness. I couldn't choose. I also got her the best kitten food I could find, and this." He holds up a big box he has under his arm.

"What's that?"

"This is a little robot. Since you're going to be living in a tight space with her, I don't think you want to be smelling kitten pee and poop."

"I don't even wanna know how much you spent on that," I say, my heart filling with so much joy over what he's done for Peaches... and for me. "Thank you, Donny."

When he puts everything down, I jump into his arms.

He laughs, catching me and I kiss him hard.

"Hey, you two, no sex in front of the baby," Alex scolds us. We break the kiss and roll our eyes. "And don't think I didn't notice the fact that the room reeked of sex the other day."

My cheeks turn pink, but Donny just grins back smugly.

I guess today isn't as bad as I thought. I got a friggin kitten! And little Rylee's dreams are coming true.

I stay for a few hours with Alex and Rylee, playing with Peaches. I thought I was going to be busted when Alex commented that I was back really fast, given the only pet store nearby is about thirty minutes away.

I laughed and made up something random, then Peaches did the cutest yawn and all was forgotten. Rylee cuddled up on my lap as she snuggled the kitten and I felt complete. I didn't want to leave, but the messages from the guys were becoming insistent.

I need to get back and warn them not to tell Rylee I got her Peaches. She's so happy, and the way she's been openly kissing me in front of Alex... Ah, it's everything. I can't have them ruining that.

After I told Rylee that I would go to the store, I ended up taking a rest under the tree I left everything at. I probably looked weird just sitting there, scrolling on my phone surrounded by bags with the pet store label, but I don't care.

Seeing how excited and in love she is with Peaches, it's worth it. I just hope Alex gives her back to Rylee when I leave. He's been on FaceTime with Serenity for the past fifteen minutes as they coo over the baby together.

Rylee yawns and I turn her face toward mine for one more

kiss. I've been hard as a rock for an hour, and her wriggling on my lap is not helping. "I should go. I never told the guys I was coming here," I say with a groan as she moves again.

Her neck is flushed, and I know she's as turned on as I am. "Rain check?" I ask and she nods, then grips the back of my head and kisses me again until I'm about to strip her and fuck her in front of Alex.

Giggling, she leans back and blinks up at me. Alex grunts and shoves Peaches between us. "I'll see you at practice tomorrow," she says, then moves off my lap and gives the kitten love again.

I nod and fix my dick before climbing off the bed. I give Peaches another scratch behind the ears and kiss Rylee's forehead. "Bye, Cherry," I whisper, and she gives me a huge smile.

I leave the dorm and swing by the cafe for a late night snack. Missi and the girls are there, but I'm not in the mood. Felicia follows me back to the house and I groan. "Aren't you coming in?" she asks and I nod.

"Yeah, I just did something stupid, and I know Teo and Colt are going to hand me my ass," I say and she laughs, rolling her eyes.

"Donny, you are always doing something dumb. What'd ya do now?" I shake my head and shove past her.

"It's not a big deal. I'll see you later."

The moment I enter the house, I know I'm busted.

"So, do you have something to share with the class, Donny?" Len asks from the stove. He's mixing something in a pan.

"On a scale of one to ten, how pissed is he?" I grumble, and Colt laughs from behind me.

"If we hadn't received a selfie of Rylee with a huge smile on her face, we were going to make you sleep outside," he says, and I snort.

"About that, no one can tell Rylee that I adopted Peaches. The cat jumped out of my arms and took off. It was fate or something that Rylee found her." Mateo walks into the kitchen and grabs a plate. Len dishes up some pasta and grabs some for himself.

"So, let me get this straight. You went and adopted that evil spawn, and she's not even going to know it's from you?" Teo says then laughs.

"No, and she will never know, okay? It doesn't matter. All that matters is that she's happy."

CHAPTER TWENTY-EIGHT

Rylee

"My eyes, they burn!" I groan as I step out of my last exam before Christmas break.

"Well, you're done. You're free!" Trevor says with a chuckle as he scoops me up in his arms and spins me around. I giggle and kiss him. "Thanks for meeting me after," he tells me as he places me down on my feet. "I just really wanted to see you, since I can't for the next few weeks."

"I'm gonna miss you," I tell him as I snuggle in close.

"I'm going to miss you too. I hate that I have to leave

right after my last exam. But that's the joy of having divorced parents." He chuckles. "It's not too bad, but my dad has a big family, and they always want to see me before I head to my mom and stepdad's."

"It's okay. I hope you have a fun trip." I kiss him.

"I hope you do too. I know how excited you are to see your mom."

"I miss her like crazy." I smile. "Talking on the phone isn't enough. I'm due for some Mom snuggles."

He chuckles, kissing me again. "I better get going. My exam starts in fifteen, and I still gotta get to the building."

"Fine." I pout. "Kiss me one more time."

He gives me a dirty grin before grabbing my face and kissing me deeply. I moan, wanting more, but sadly it's over too soon. "Text and call me whenever you want," he tells me, giving me a butterfly kiss.

"I will. Bye," I say. Tears form in my eyes as I watch him walk away. I told myself I wouldn't fall hard for another guy, but between Trevor, Colton, and now even Donny, that's gone out the window.

"I should have known." Mateo's voice comes from behind me.

Turning around, I find him watching from a few feet away. "Excuse me?" I ask, confused.

"It's always about him. We have hardly seen you outside cheer for the past week. All of your free time has been spent with him." Mateo tosses his hand up in Trevor's direction.

"That's not true," I say, placing my hands on my hips. "I've seen Colton a few times, and Donny once."

"Not me though, and not Lennox," he argues.

"And not once did either of you text me to ask me to hang out!" I say, my voice getting louder. "I don't know what you think Colton and Donny did to get back into my good graces, but I'll refresh your memory. They showed me they had changed. They put in all the work, not me. Not once did I go crawling to them, because they didn't deserve that. They showed me how much *they* wanted *me*, how much they cared."

"I opened up." His nostrils flair. "I don't do that with just anyone."

"And I appreciate that. I'm glad you could see past your macho bullshit and show me a good side of you. But other than that, I haven't seen you try to spend time with me one-on-one, Mateo. Just because I'm on my way to forgiving some of the guys, doesn't mean you can stop working to show me that you're sorry."

His jaw ticks, eyes filled with fury. "And this fucker just gets to come out of nowhere and steal your heart? Are we not good enough? Is he always going to be number one in your life?"

"No!" I step up to him. "Stop thinking like that. Trevor has been nothing but kind and supportive. He's always been open and honest with me. And I did the same with him. He is my boyfriend because he showed me my worth."

"So what you're saying is, he's a better man than us? Than me?" He shakes his head. "Whatever, Rylee."

He turns around and storms off, leaving me fuming. "Stupid boys!" I shout, but he's too far away to hear me. "Ugh!"

The whole way back to my dorm, I'm in a pissy mood. I

was already sad about leaving Trevor longer than the guys. Now I just wanna slap the shit out of Mateo. I get it, he has his own baggage to deal with, but he has no right to act like that. I'd be stupid to not expect some jealousy, but he's not going to make me feel bad for being with someone who makes me happy. He could be one of those people, if he would just pull his head out of his damn ass!

"How was your—oh, that bad?" Alex asks as I step into the dorm room.

"Exam was fine. I'm pretty sure I did well. That's not what's got me all worked up," I huff, tossing my bookbag onto my bed and grabbing Peaches from Alex. I need some kitty cuddles. He looks like he's ready to protest, but gives me my cat and I join him on his bed.

"Trevor is leaving right after his last exam, and he came to say goodbye. I was bummed. Then Mateo was there, accusing me of liking Trevor more, and saying how Trevor is going to be number one in my heart, and ah." I groan.

Peaches climbs up my chest and starts to rub her face against mine, her purring makes me feel a little better.

"I mean, he's not wrong," Alex says.

"Shut up." I shoot him a glare.

He chuckles. "Look, I know you have your thing with Colton, and now Donny seems to have wormed his way back into your good graces, but I will always think Trevor is the best person for you."

"I know you do. You're my best friend, and these other guys hurt me. And now I'm dating your other best friend. But, Alex, I really like Trevor, like head over heels, but I feel the same about Colton. Sure, our relationship is different, but it doesn't mean I will like one more than the other."

"I don't know how you can do it. Dating more than one person has got to be a nightmare," he says, giving Peaches a head scratch.

"It's not going to be easy, but if everyone works at it, I can see it working. At least with Colton, and maybe Donny. From how Mateo acted today, I'm not too sure about him. I haven't even had much time with Lennox. I can see that he likes me. But he's been standing back and giving his friends a chance at happiness, forgetting about himself."

"Nope, we're not doing this," Alex says, taking the now sleeping kitty off me and placing her on his pillow. "We're going to get out of here and go shopping. No sadness, it's Christmas time."

"I do need to get a few last minute things," I tell him. I was waiting until my last check came in today. I'm thankful my boss is so understanding and gave me the time off.

"There we go," he says cheerfully, grabbing my hand and pulling me from the bed. "Off to it." He slaps my ass, making me yelp in surprise before laughing.

We spend the next few hours shopping. Most of the time it was me helping Alex get a million and one last minute gifts for Serenity. It's so adorable how much he loves her. Good thing he's going to be seeing her the day after Christmas, because I don't think he could go the full break without her.

I couldn't get too much because the tickets home and back were insanely priced, and I wanted to save as much money for gifts, so I'm only bringing a personal item and a carry on with me. I plan on doing my shopping for my mom when I get back to Florida, but I did get the guys, Trevor, Alex, and Serenity something.

"I think your bank account is yelling at you right now." I laugh as he struggles to get the trunk closed.

"Who cares as long as my girl is happy?" he grunts, jumping up to sit on the trunk to get it to shut. "Yes!" he shouts as it clicks closed.

"You're crazy." I laugh.

We get into the car and head back to campus. As we're pulling in, I see a familiar bike pulling out of the parking lot. Where is Mateo going at ten at night?

"Follow that bike," I tell Alex before I even have the time to think about what I'm saying.

"What?" he says, looking at me with furrowed brows.

"That's Mateo. I wanna see where he's going."

"Oh, I do love an adventure." Alex chuckles as he spins the car around. We shift with the movement, and I have to grab ahold of the assist handle.

The whole time we stay a few cars behind Mateo. Nerves flutter in my belly as the seconds tick by. What am I doing? I don't even know where he's going, or how far.

But when he pulls into the parking lot of what looks to be an old warehouse, my interest piques.

"Ahh, Rylee. This screams horror movie, serial killer," Alex says, parking on the side of the road in the dark.

"There are a bunch of cars. It's not like we've been lured out into the middle of nowhere alone to be killed." I roll my eyes.

"You can not go in there!" Alex says, but I'm already out the door before he can do or say anything more.

I curse myself for wearing a skirt as I try to quickly get close to the building without being seen.

Ducking behind a car, I watch Mateo get off his bike. He takes his helmet off and shakes out his dark hair. Fuck, he looks so sexy right now. He's in a leather jacket, his hair's a little sweaty, and I'm getting more turned on by the second.

Mateo heads inside the building. When the door opens, the quiet from the night goes from peaceful to having loud music drifting through the door.

Something tells me this is some kind of club. A few girls stumble out of the door as Mateo heads inside. They look like regular girls, so maybe I won't be too out of place.

Standing up, I smooth out my skirt and fix my hair before adjusting my tits so that they pull up, and I show some skin.

With a sway in my hips, I walk over to the door man, who's eyeing up the girls like they're his next meal. Gross.

"Hey there, big boy," I purr.

His head snaps over to me and a grin slowly takes over his lips. "Well, hello, doll face. What's a pretty little thing like you doing here?"

"What everyone else is here for, of course." I giggle, twirling a lock of my hair.

"Go on in. Cover is free for pretty little things like yourself." He licks his lips.

"You're too sweet. Thank you!" I say, slipping past him because I do not want that man to hit on me any longer.

As I walk inside, I'm hit by the heat of all the bodies in this place. It's packed. People are screaming and cheering over something going on inside. It's so loud it almost drowns out the music.

I weave my way through the crowd until I reach an open area. My brows jump as I take in the ring in the middle of the room. So, this is some kind of fighting club? And something tells me that someone like Mateo isn't just here to watch.

As one of the men in the ring goes down, the crowd goes wild, and the winner raises their arms in victory.

They clear the ring and the announcer steps in. "And there you have it, folks. Viper is the winner! Now, we have a club favorite here tonight. Let's hear it for Teo!"

The crowd once again goes insane, and that's when my question is answered when Mateo steps into the ring.

Fuck. Me. He's in a pair of sports shorts, and that's it. I take a moment to let my eyes wander down his body. I've seen him without his shirt on before. Half the time the guys practice without one, but there's something different about seeing him now, with his tattoos on display, his muscles bulging as he hops around the ring, jabbing at the air, that has me wanting a better seat.

I need to be in the front row for this.

Pushing my way to the front, I get a few shouts of protest. Part of me wants to tell them to fuck off, but the people in this place don't seem above stabbing me, so I keep my mouth shut.

There's a bunch of people pushed up against the ring, banging on the fence that surrounds it. I know it's stupid of me to get that close, but I do.

And just as I slip my way to the front, grabbing a hold of

the chain link fence, Mateo's eyes snap over to mine. The only tell-tale sign that he's reacting to the sight of me here is the slight widening of his eyes and the tick of his jaw. He quickly looks away as the announcer calls out Mateo's opponent.

Excited energy fills me as the two of them start fighting. This explains why he always has some sort of bruising when I see him at practice.

My heart starts to pound in my chest as I watch the way his body moves. He dodges the other guy's punches, getting a few of his own in before they start to dance around the ring.

My body breaks out into a sweat, my panties growing damp as a fire starts to burn in my belly. He's so fucking hot. He grunts and growls as he effectively beats this man to the ground, and as he delivers the finishing blow, he looks over at me with fire in his eyes, and I almost cum right then and there.

There seems to be a hell of a lot I don't know about this man, but this? This is something big, and I need answers if we're going to be anything in the future.

The announcer calls Mateo out as the winner, and the crowd screams so loud it's deafening. He doesn't stay for his victory, leaving the ring straight away.

I start to panic because everyone is pushing into me, crushing me into the fence. Fuck, this was a bad idea. A really fucking bad idea.

Just as I'm about to try and push my way out of here, Mateo has the guy who had me pinned to the ring on the ground. He's snarling down at the man and spits on him before his angry glare hits me. My eyes widen and I freeze. Oh, he's pissed, like really pissed—but why is it so *hot*?

I don't get any time to think as he grabs me by the arm and starts to pull me through the crowd.

He leads me out of the chaos and down a hall. Pushing an exit door open, he pulls me outside and slams me up against the wall next to it. The door crashes shut, cutting off the noise of the club.

"What the fuck are you doing here, Rylee?!" he roars in my face, his arm pinning me to the wall.

I don't say anything, my mind unable to form words right now. I think I'm going to pass out with how fast my heart is pounding.

"Answer me!" he shouts, making me flinch, kick-starting my brain.

"I saw you leaving on your bike, and impulsively, I had Alex follow you," I say, cringing back.

"Why the fuck would you do that? Why do you care where I go? This isn't a place for you, Rylee. You should have never come here. You're fucking lucky I took you out when I did, because the moment the fights are over, the guys in there would have gotten a good look at you and really bad shit would have gone down. And then I'd be in big shit because I would have had to kill anyone who fucking dared to put their hands on you."

His chest is heaving, his eyes wild, but damn, his words have me dripping.

"Sorry," is all I can come up with.

"Sorry doesn't mean shit, Rylee. This place is full of sick fuckers. Never come back here, do you understand me?"

"Okay." I nod my head. "But why are you here?"

He just stares at me for a moment, nostrils flaring. "I have no other choice right now. There's a lot about my life that I haven't told you. Not because I didn't want to be honest with you, but because I want to keep you safe. Promise me, Rylee, that you will never step foot in here again. I can't risk you."

"I promise," I say, licking my lips. My mind is trying to take this seriously, but my core is begging to be filled.

A slow smirk takes over his face as he takes a good look at my half lidded eyes. "Are you turned on, Rylee?" he asks me, and I blush.

I gasp as his hand slides between us and under my skirt, finding my drenched panties. He groans. "Fuck me, baby girl. You're fucking dripping for me, aren't you?"

I nod, my lips parting as he rubs his fingers over my panties. No point in lying, he can feel the evidence for himself. Watching him fight, it turned me on more than I've been in a while.

He moves his fingers away, and I almost whimper at the loss, but then he pulls my panties to the side and dips his fingers into my wet heat. I moan as he thrusts two deep inside me. He pumps his fingers a few times before pulling them out and bringing them to his mouth. I watch and whimper as he sucks my juices off.

His eyes roll back and my pussy pulses at the sight.

"Fuck, Rylee. You have no idea how long I've been wanting to taste you again," he growls, pressing his body into mine. I gasp when I feel his hard cock against my belly. His eyes are filled with fire, still pumped up from his fight.

"There's no taking my time with you right now. But mark my words, baby girl, next time I get you alone, I'm savoring your sweet pussy. Making sure I lick you well and good until you're soaking my face, then I'll clean that up too."

"Fuck," I breathe, trying to rub my thighs together.

"Oh, I plan on it." He chuckles, grabbing my thighs and lifting me up. I wrap my arms around his neck, and my legs around his waist. He pushes me back against the wall, grinding his cock against my wet center. "You drive me wild, Rylee. When I'm around you, I can't think straight." He runs the tip of his nose along my jawline. I take in a shuddering breath as my eyes close.

"I can't fucking breathe. We fucked up, Rylee, and we hate ourselves every day for it. And I've been a fool with how I've been handling everything after the cabin. But not anymore. I promise, from this day forward, I'm going to work to make you see the man I want to be for you, for Len. I'm in love with you, Rylee. I'd be stupid to keep lying to myself. You are mine. Fucking mine."

He snarls the last word as he thrusts up into me. My eyes fly open as I cry out. I was so in my own head at his words, that I didn't notice him taking himself out and lining up with my entrance.

He pushes into me again, my pussy slick with need for him. My nails claw at his back as he starts to fuck into me like an animal.

"This pussy." He groans, shoving his face into my neck. "So hot, so wet, so fucking tight. And mine."

My eyes roll back as I cling to him while he thrusts into me like a wild beast. He's big, so big, and it feels amazing.

"Mateo!" I shout when he adjusts me a little bit, hitting my sweet spot.

"That's it, baby girl. Scream my name. Let the whole fucking world know whose pussy this is. Who you belong to."

I hold on for the ride as he sucks and nips at my neck, his hips snapping up, sending his cock deep inside me with every thrust.

Sex with Mateo is exactly how I imagined it. Wild and dirty, just like he is. "Oh, fuck, yes," I moan as he slides one of his hands between us, bringing his fingers over my swollen clit. He starts to rub me with just the right pressure, making my back arch off the wall.

"Such a good girl, taking my cock so damn good. This pussy was made for me. I'm never going this long again without it." He grunts as he breathes heavily in my ear.

I'm so worked up from watching him fight, and the way he's talking to me, add in how amazing his piercing feel gliding against my inner walls, his cock so hot and thick, and I can feel my orgasm building already.

"I'm close," I whimper, grabbing a handful of his hair. I pull and he snarls, fucking me harder.

The brick wall is scraping my back, but I don't even care. God, this man can fuck. I can feel my juices covering where my thighs meet his.

Mateo grabs a handful of my ass, squeezing hard as he presses down on my clit. "Don't stop! Please! Please, Mateo, don't stop," I plead, as I feel the fire in my belly rising to an inferno.

"Never," he growls. "I'll never stop making you feel good,

Rylee. Only pleasure from us from now on, never pain."

"Oh, fuck!" I shout, as he bites down on my neck, pinching my clit at the same time.

I explode around him, my pussy gripping his cock like a vice as my walls flutter around his length. It's so powerful, everything goes black for a moment. I scream his name into the night air, not caring who can hear us, if anyone is around.

A second later, he slams into me one last time before letting out a roar as he cums. His cock pulses violently, sending jets of cum deep inside me. Stream after stream, he fills me with his hot seed until I can feel it leaking out of me, joining my own release.

We say nothing, just stay joined together for a moment as we catch our breath.

"Mateo," I whisper.

"Yeah," he says, pulling back to look at me, deep emotion swimming in his eyes.

"I'm glad to see you pulling your head out of your ass. I'm excited to see how things will be from now on," I say, a slow smile forming on my face. If he thinks that just because he can fuck my brains out and make me see stars, that I'm going to change, he has another thing coming.

He grins, shaking his head. "Always the brat, aren't you?"

"I just tell it like it is."

He pulls out of me, his cum leaving me with his cock and falling to the ground. "Fuck, that's hot," he chuckles as he kneels down, lifting my skirt. I look to see his cum trailing down my leg and I blush. He takes two fingers and swipes them up my leg, gathering his release before standing up. "Open," he says, and my brows rise. "I said, open."

Fuck me, is he really going to make me taste him? And why do I want to so badly?

Opening my mouth like he told me to, he sticks his fingers in. I suck his cum off, swirling my tongue around his finger to make sure I get every last drop.

A deep, sexy rumble leaves his chest as his eyes fill with heat. "So fucking perfect," he mumbles, more to himself.

"So, you fight?" I say, pointing out the obvious when he pulls his fingers free. I lick my lips, not minding his salty taste.

"I do," he says. "I have my reasons. Sometimes I enjoy it, sometimes I use it as a release, and other times..." He looks away. "I don't have much choice."

"I'm here to listen, whenever you want to tell me everything. I'm not going to judge you."

He looks back at me. "I know," he says, tucking a lock of my now wild hair behind my ear. "You're pretty amazing."

"I know," I joke, feeling a little nervous.

"So, Alex drove you?" he asks, and I curse.

"Shit, Alex," I groan. "Poor guy is probably worried sick about me."

"I can't leave just yet. I have another fight, but I need you to go. This place isn't for you, and I'd be worried about something happening to you if you stayed. I can't have that kind of distraction."

"Okay." I nod.

"I'll walk you back to the car."

Mateo picks me up and I wrap my body around him, tucking my face into his neck and grinning like a fool. I feel happy right now, high on the moment. Like everything is clicking into place. What I feel for him isn't quite love, not yet, but if he keeps showing me he cares, that he's sorry, I think it could lead to that. But I do feel for him, deeply.

He brings me to Alex's car and opens the door. He places me into the passenger's seat and buckles me in. "Take care of my girl, Alex," he warns him.

Alex looks at him in shock. "Ahh. I always do."

"Good." He nods, then cups my face. "Be a good girl, Rylee." He kisses me deeply and my toes curl. He nips at my lower lip when he pulls back, before giving me another quick kiss. "I'll text you when I'm home."

"Okay," I say in a dazed, breathy state.

Mateo shuts the car door and taps the top before jogging back to the warehouse.

"Okay," Alex teases in a girly voice, then chuckles as we pull away. "Look at you, blushing like a little church girl. And damn, Ry, you smell like a fucking whore house."

"Fuck off, I do not." I glare at him.

"Lies, all lies." He laughs. "I would ask what happened, but I have an idea. I don't need details."

"Just shut up and drive," I mutter, rolling my eyes and looking out the window. I can't help but smile as my body hums with everything that just happened.

One by one, these guys are showing me how much they fucked up. And although it might take some more time to find any sort of normalcy, I'm hoping that it's possible.

I've had a lot of hurt and pain in my past, and I think I'm due to be happy for once. Right? Or is that just some pipe dream by a young, naive girl?

CHAPTER TWENTY-NINE

Mateo

I finish my fights and rush out of the warehouse. People try to stop me and buy me beers. I made a lot of people money tonight, but I don't care. It's not like I ever see any of it. I reach my bike and give Anthony a chin nod.

I'm glad he's the only one around tonight. I don't need my uncle seeing Rylee. It's bad enough he's been threatening Lennox and the others. He's fucking pissed that he can't find my ma and brother. Brenna is laying low with her guy, and I hope she stays safe. I can't force her to leave, but she knows that I will always be here for her.

I grab my helmet and fix my jacket. I still smell like sex and sweat, and I need to shower. The last guy I fought, I think his name was Michealangelo—stupid fucking name, reminds me of that show with the turtles—got his blood all over me. He should know better that drugs will make your blood run thinner. Four hits and he was out cold.

I start my bike then get back on the road. I still can't believe Rylee showed up at the fight. My uncle had been harassing me for weeks about fighting, and I snuck out to shut him up.

I didn't tell the guys where I was going, but it wouldn't be hard for them to guess. I need to do something. My uncle needs to fucking go. He knows how to get to me. Threatening my family, and I know it wasn't an empty threat.

My dick twitches when I think about how good Rylee felt. She was better than I imagined, and watching my cum drip down her legs almost had me dropping to my knees to clean her up. I would have too, if I wasn't in a time crunch.

Next time, I'm going to have her in bed with me and Lennox. I'm lost in thought as I pull onto campus. I try to be quiet as I walk into the apartment, but I didn't have to bother. Len stands there in the kitchen, shirtless and with his arms crossed.

I walk over to him and kiss him hard until he's breathless. "I'm mad at you," he grunts against my lips and I smile. Backing away, I take off my jacket and toss it on a kitchen stool, then I slip off my shoes and tug my shirt over my head.

His nostrils flare and his eyes widen. "Why do you smell

like strawberries and sex?" I give him a smirk and lick my lips.

"I had a visitor tonight. A feisty redhead came to my fight," I start, and he throws his head back, laughing.

"No, she didn't," he says and I nod. My cock is hard from what I did tonight and he notices. Stepping closer to me, he drops into a crouch and runs his nose along the sweatpants I slipped on after the fight.

Humming, he nuzzles me. I groan as he reaches up and pulls my pants and boxers off before licking the base of my cock and sucking on my balls.

"You taste like her. Fucking delicious," he whispers before swallowing me down, sucking every drop of her from my cock. I grip his hair to make him choke and he pulls away with a smirk.

"I'm still mad at you, but thanks for the snack," he quips before climbing to his feet and walking down the hall toward his room.

I'm standing in the middle of the kitchen with my pants around my ankles in shock when Donny walks in. He snorts and shakes his head, laughing. "You just got major blue-balled, man," he says, as he grabs a bottle of water and walks back out.

What the fuck just happened?

THE NEXT MORNING I'm grumpy, and I don't want to do any Christmas shopping, but I need to grab a few things for the guys, and something special for Rylee. I don't have a lot of money, but after what she did for my mom, I need to thank her.

The shops are beyond crowded, and a lot of places are sold out, but I find a small charm bracelet that I think Rylee will like. I grab a paw print, a cheerleader, and a bucket of popcorn from the charms shelf and then pay for everything. We don't have many good memories yet, but I'm hoping to change that, and she can add to the bracelet.

The guys are easy to shop for, and soon I'm headed back to campus. I told Colton I would help him set up for the party tonight, and I know he's stressed. Missi fought to be in charge, and after the annual cheer sleepover disaster, she's no longer allowed to be a part of any planning.

Serves the bitch right. She's lucky I don't drop her off downtown. For the most part, she's been quiet, but I know it's just the calm before the storm. She's been staying with her dad, acting like Lennox didn't dump her ass in front of all her little friends, but I can tell, even the MUFFS are over her shit.

I even saw Ursula chatting with Rylee at practice the other day, and she wasn't being a bitch. I know it's our fault that Missi went after Rylee, but things have changed now, and so she needs to get with the fucking program.

I drop off my gifts at the apartment, and make sure to hide them from Donny. He's like a bloodhound sniffing out presents. Him and Nando used to team up and search every nook and cranny at my ma's house. Used to drive us all crazy.

Quickly changing into a pair of sweats and a zip-up hoodie, I leave the house and jog over to the administration building to get some supplies. Donny and Lennox are there waiting for me. "How many decorations do we really need?" I ask and Donny laughs.

"Such a Grinch. It's Christmas time. We need mistletoe, a tree, and tinsel." Donny starts to make a list and I groan.

"We have four hours to get all this done. This is so much shit for a party. Why are we doing this again?" I groan.

"It's tradition, and Colton insisted. Plus, this way we get to spend some time with Rylee without Trevor," Donny reminds me. "Help me grab shit to make wreaths too, and more lights."

Rolling my eyes at his excitement, I wish I had brought a cart. Biting my tongue at the complaints that want to roll off it, I tell my dick to get with the program. Just the mention of Rylee has me hardening. Not to mention, I've been turned on since Lennox left me blue-balled. It's not fair. I've jerked off, but it's just not the same. Unless I'm inside Rylee or my guy, my cock isn't having it.

"How are you feeling there, Teo?" Lennox teases as his eyes trail down to the imprint of my length in my sweats. "Planning on showing all the goods off to the world today, I see?"

Scowling, I shrug. "It's not my fault. The fucker's got a mind of its own."

Lennox snorts with laughter as he walks out the door with some lights. Struggling with my arms full, I trudge back and forth with supplies.

"Teo..." Donny grins as I bring the last of the Christmas shit in. He and Lennox abandoned me after the first trip.

Warily, I growl. "Uh-huh..."

"Lennox needs help getting the mistletoe up. Go help him," he teases.

"Will he kiss my dick if I catch him under one?" I grumble, making him snicker.

Dumping the decorations by Donny, I stalk Lennox. No one is in this area of the house, and I grab him around the neck and kiss him hard.

"Is this not how you're supposed to kiss under the mistletoe?" I grin. He chuckles and pushes me against the wall, ignoring the decorations. His hand is just closing over my cock when my phone rings.

"God... why?" I mutter. "What did I do to deserve this?" Pulling my phone from my pocket, I see it's my mom.

I take some deep breaths and answer. "Hey, Ma. How's vacation?" I say, just in case someone is listening to our call.

"It's been amazing. Nando is loving living right on the beach," she gushes, and I grin. She sounds happy, and like all the weight that's been pulling her down is gone. I owe Rylee more than some charm bracelet and orgasms.

I'll have to come up with something better. "That's great, Ma. I miss you though. Any plans for the holidays?" I have been thinking about maybe flying down with Rylee for the break. Donny and Len too. We need to make better memories where everything went to shit.

"Rylee's mom invited us to join her and her daughter. I guess our boss always has a big family meal for them. He's a sweet old man. Reminds me of your father," she says and I snort.

"Please don't tell me you're crushing on your boss, Ma," I grunt with a shudder and she laughs. I don't know when I last heard her sound so carefree.

"No, mijo, he's just a nice man. He's been so helpful to me and Nando. Is your girl there? I want to thank her again for everything. I can't wait til she's home and I can give her a big squeeze. You found yourself a winner, Teo."

Rylee chooses to walk into the room right then, and she gives me a huge smile. My heart starts to race and I grin back.

"Yeah, I think I'll keep her."

Teo is on the phone with his mom, and I'm almost done getting this tree in the stand. I was hoping to get Rylee to help me decorate, just the two of us. Colton and Donny are in the kitchen decorating cookies, and I know Teo will be in there soon to make sure they are edible.

"Hey," Ursula says as she brings in the tote full of ornaments. She's been quiet lately, and not following Missi's direction. I think the team is starting to realize that Rylee isn't the devil-incarnate, and that Missi is just a fucking psycho.

"Hey, thanks, Urs," I say as she drops it in front of the

tree. She opens the lid and laughs. A lot of the decorations are homemade from the children's center, but there are a few that Donny purchased. He calls them his NSFW ornaments.

She picks up a giant silicone dildo that has a white ribbon strung through it to look like cum and quickly drops it. "God, what is wrong with that dude?" She mutters under her breath about Donny and I laugh.

Rylee walks into the room and gives me a wave. Ursula rolls her eyes and leaves.

"So, what can I help with?" she asks, peeking into the ornaments then bursting out in giggles.

I smile and she holds her stomach. "Let me guess, Donny?" I nod and she calms down.

"I was hoping you'd want to decorate the tree with me?" She wipes her eyes and smiles.

"Yes, I love doing the tree with my mom. I was sad to miss out this year. We always make hot cocoa and blast Christmas music. One year, I'd like to go somewhere that has snow. Have one of those white Christmases like in the movies," she says as I start to untangle a string of lights.

"That sounds nice, and something we can definitely plan for," I say, getting frustrated. Rylee drops one of Donny's special ornaments back into the tote, then moves closer to help me. "Here, I have nails, let me try to get the knot out," she says, and I hand her the ball of lights. Loud laughter comes from the kitchen and I smile.

"What are the others up to?" Rylee asks and I point to the door.

"Colt and Donny are decorating cookies for tonight. Teo is baking them, because he is a little anal about his grandma's recipe. Last year, Donny ate all the dough, then tried to make more so he wasn't caught. He used cayenne powder instead of cinnamon. It was disgusting."

Rylee giggles and shakes her head. Her hair is down and curled, and she's already dressed for the party, wearing a dark green sweater dress. My dick hardens and I lick my lips remembering the taste of her and Teo that I licked from his cock last night.

I know we haven't reached that stage yet, and that's okay, but I can't wait until I can bend her over the couch again and eat her until she's screaming my name and dripping down my chin.

"What about you? Do you have any Christmas traditions?" Rylee asks as she hands me the untangled lights with a big smile, snapping me out of my dirty thoughts. I don't want to dim her mood, so I make something up that I once saw in a movie. I'll tell her one day about my family.

"We don't have many. My dad is busy and my mom is always preoccupied, but we do get to open one present on Christmas Eve. It's usually a new pair of pajamas and a movie for all of us to watch together. It's been a few years since we've done that, but I always looked forward to those two hours we would spend without phones or distractions," I say, wishing that could have been true.

Christmas was always spent with Gregory and Ida. My dad was never home, and my mom was usually wasted or sleeping off her high. "Now, Mateo's family has the best Christmas. His mom would go all out with food, gifts, and surprises. You and him are lucky to have amazing parents," I say, then climb on the ladder and start laying the lights on the branches.

"I'm excited to meet her in a few days. Are you guys still thinking about coming with me to Florida?" she asks, and I shrug. Mateo talked about it, but nothing has been decided.

"Would that be okay if we did? We wouldn't want to intrude on time with your mom." She bends over and grabs one of the handprints and hangs it onto a branch.

"I think I'd like it if we could all spend some time together away from school," she mumbles, and I cover my mouth to hide my smile. Finishing the lights, I climb off the ladder and help her place the ornaments.

"Those kids really love you and idolize you," Rylee says as she looks at all the decorations the children made us. There is one that's my favorite. I point toward it.

"This one a little girl named Kenna made for us. She was in foster care, and her new family didn't want her. We found her sleeping in the back room one night. There was a bad storm, and the woman in charge of the community center called Donny asking if he would go make sure all the windows were closed. He found her and..." Rylee is looking up at me with those emerald green eyes, and I can tell they are wary. "He took her to Teo's mom, and they helped her find a real family. She sent us that as a thank you." It's a glass heart with a photo of her and her puppy inside. She had used puffy paint on the back to write us a note.

"That's, wow... That's actually really sweet," she says, clearing her throat, and I have to roll my eyes.

"I know we fucked up. We treated you like shit, and for that, I will always be sorry. But, deep down, we're not evil,

Rylee. We have huge hearts, and those kids mean everything to us. That place saved all of our lives in one way or another."

"Hey, I didn't mean to make you upset, Lennox. But you have to understand, after everything you all put me through, I thought those guys I met at the hotel were fake. Just a facade you put up to sleep with me." Rylee sighs. "It's nice to see that it wasn't a dream, or something I saw through rose-colored glasses."

I nod, because I can see why she'd think that. "No, it was all real. We just took a wrong turn, and it led to all of this. I really hope we can get back on track. Maybe seeing who we really are, where we came from, will help you see it."

Rylee nods. "I really hope I can, because these," she says, gesturing to the tree, "are people I would be proud to know."

I wanted to have time with her because I've been an ass, but I didn't want her to see so much. I want to hide my broken pieces from her, and instead she's chipping away without realizing. Biting my lip, I decide to give her something as I decorate the tree.

"I lied..." I confess in a mutter as I hang a snowflake on the tree. It's a combination of dildos and children's ornaments, and my lips twitch as I allow myself to really look at it.

"That's a surprise," Rylee snarks and I shake my head. She's such a brat. It's nice to see her backbone and spirit. "What did you lie about?"

"Ry... this community center saved our lives. We each had cheer, but it gave us a place to escape to when we needed it. When life sucked ass, we'd go help, or tutor, or do something to allow us to survive until the next day. You may see a bunch of assholes who tortured you, but maybe the real question you should ask is, who made us this way?"

Deciding the tree is done, I step back. Fuck, this talk didn't go the way I expected, but nothing really does with this girl.

Turning toward me, Rylee grabs my hand before I can walk away. "Hey... all I ever wanted was for you to be real with me. Thank you."

Blinking, I nod, acting on impulse and kissing the palm of her hand. "I'm going to get dressed, I'll see you in a bit. It isn't easy for any of us to talk about this, so we bury it. It's why Donny finds you when he doesn't sleep well. You're a safe place for him to land, even when you hated him. I know this will all take time, but I want to get there with you," I explain.

Rylee's face softens, and I smile as I walk away from her. Only it feels more like I'm walking toward a new opportunity, because I feel lighter than I ever have.

The doorbell rings as I come back out of my room, people flooding the house, and I open it. Here we go...

THERE'S PUNCH, beer, and a ton of alcohol flowing, but strangely, I don't have the urge to drink as I watch everyone enjoying themselves. People are taking advantage of the mistletoe, and I smirk as I stand next to Teo while they make out.

"Don't smile like that. I have plans to corner you under some later," he rumbles, and I curse as my dick gets hard.

"Fuck, baby, don't threaten me with a good time," I tease him.

"Dammit, you still owe me after leaving me with a hard on and no relief," he mutters as Donny sings Christmas songs on the karaoke machine with Felicia.

Donny is really going to town on *Jingle Bell Rock*. I always forget he can sing until he starts singing Christmas songs. He loves this holiday. Hence the crazy decorations, and the boozy punch.

"You had your dick inside of Rylee," I remind him, pinching his ass. Teo hisses and I grin.

I'm so glad I decided to drop Missi and be true to my feelings. It's been harder and harder to ignore how much I hurt Mateo with my fake relationship with her.

"You could have me inside of you soon, if you're a good boy," he teases, and I groan as my dick twitches.

Rylee chooses that moment to join us. She's got a cup in her hand and she gives me a big smile.

"Having fun?" I ask and she nods, then steps closer to me until her breasts are pressed against my chest. She bats her eyelashes at me and smirks when she feels my dick twitch.

"We could be having more... maybe in private?" she suggests, and Teo snorts into his cup. I glance at him and he's staring at us.

I clear my throat. "Do you mean just us or..." I leave it open, waiting for her to tell me what she wants. I don't think we're ready to go that next step, but I wouldn't say no if she wanted to include me with Teo.

She bites her lip and leans up on her tippy toes to whisper in my ear. "What if I said I wanted Teo to fuck me hard into the couch from behind as I swallowed your cock whole?" she says, and I legit gulp.

"Now?" I squeak, and Teo throws his head back, laughing. Why am I so nervous? She nods and steps away, taking my hand.

THE NIGHT GETS crazy and wild, and pretty soon, I'm in need of a break. Teo goes to get us some drinks and I plop down on a chair.

Colton eyes me, a smile gracing his usual grouchy face. "Thanks for helping with all of this," he says, leaning against the wall. He seems strangely relaxed as he watches everyone enjoying themselves.

"Did you get laid too and not tell anyone?" I ask, my brow raising.

"Nah, I'm just happy everything is starting to go well. Where's Rylee?" he asks, and I blink slowly.

Shit. Looking around, I realize I don't see her. She said she wanted to go hang out with Ren and Alex. There's Christmas themed drinking games outside, and I open the back door as the guys follow me. I can still hear Donny, and I shake my head at the enthusiastic fucker.

Beer pong is in the right corner, but I don't see her. Continuing walking, I glance over at The Christmas

Alphabet Game table, I see Rylee taking a shot as everyone cheers. The game is simple: you have to say a Christmas-related name, song, or item, and the person who hesitates has to take a shot. They're taking shots of some awful cinnamon alcohol, and I wince as she shudders.

"Rylee is going to need to be carried out of here soon," I grumble over my shoulder.

"I didn't even see her walk out here," Teo says as the next round starts. There's singing added to this one, and you have to sing the first line of the song if you choose that as your alphabet selection.

Walking over, I see Rylee grin as she sings her line, safe from taking another shot. Alex fails this time, and he takes a shot, groaning dramatically at the taste.

"It's not that bad," crows a girl who seems way too sober, and hasn't had to take a shot.

Alex sticks his tongue out, and I shake my head.

"We better keep an eye on her." Teo sighs, stepping into a spot left open when someone leaves.

I'm not drinking, so I cross my arms with Colton next to me as I watch the game continue. It's actually really funny being the sober one for a change, as everyone acts like an idiot.

The next half hour continues on before Rylee taps out after another brutal shot. Grabbing a bottle of water for her, she gives me a brilliant smile before going off to dance with Donny.

Pizza is delivered soon after, and I bring a pie out to Rylee and the guys. Coaxing her into eating, she takes a big bite and moans, and I thank God there's no one close enough to hear her. I may need to kick their asses. Why are her happy food sounds so similar to when she cums?

Teo and Colton adjust themselves, and I chuckle as I eat, grateful I'm not the only one affected.

"Hey, I think I should take her home soon. Missi is staring her down, and I don't need any drama," Colt says as Rylee gets a little too close to the edge of the pool.

I nod. "Yeah, let's do gifts first though."

"Hey, baby," Teo calls out to Rylee and she scrunches her nose. Fuck, she's cute.

"I'm not your baby, Mateo Russo," she quips, and Alex laughs. Serenity grabs Rylee's arm and tugs her over to us.

"Let's go do gifts at our place," I suggest and she nods, stumbling over toward the door.

I grab the other guys and we head after her. I hope she likes what I got her. It's not much, but after Mateo came home smelling like her last night, I was up half the night writing a song.

I'm not going to play it for her until we're alone, but I want her to have the lyrics. Alex and Ren break off to go dance while we help Rylee downstairs to our place. She sits on the couch and starts to laugh.

"Donny, you need to chill out on the naughty decorations," she says, and I chuckle with her. He has mistletoe dicks hanging everywhere. Taking a seat next to her, he pulls her into a hot kiss until she moans.

My cock twitches and I sigh. She's way too drunk for us to have any group fun. I smack Donny on the back of his head, and he pulls away from her looking love-drunk. He gives me a glare, and Teo hands out the gifts.

I watch as she rips open the paper excitedly and gasps at the bracelet Teo bought her.

"Wow, thank you," she murmurs and Teo shrugs, trying to look unaffected as she stands and gives him a quick kiss. I hand her my song and she reads it, smiling.

"I think we need to have some one-on-one time soon, Len," she tells me and I agree, pressing a soft kiss onto her lips.

She hands us a bag with matching shirts, and I laugh as I read what's on them. *Our Flyer Is Better Than Yours.*

"These are perfect. Thanks, Cherry," Donny says, then leans in to kiss her again. Ugh, my dick is never going to go down.

Rylee starts to yawn, and she looks like she's about to fall over. Colt walks closer to us and takes her arm.

"How about I walk you home?" he asks and she nods.

We say our goodbyes and then watch as she leaves. Donny sighs.

"I'm going to marry that girl someday," he says with a wink, then heads back up to the party. I glance over at Teo and he seems to be thinking really hard.

"She's perfect for us. We can't lose her again," he mutters, and I reach out to touch his arm.

"We won't. Let's go dance," I suggest and he nods.

MATEO COMES CLOSER to me as we dance, and I can't fight it anymore. I grab the back of his neck and kiss him. He tangles his tongue with mine and grinds against my hardening cock. Gasps sound around us, but I ignore them. Donny whoops and I smile against Teo's plump lips.

"What the fuck?!" someone shrills beside us, and I know exactly who it is. Mateo backs away and I turn my head to glance at Missi. She's holding a red plastic cup full of punch, and her nails have punctured the sides from her crushing it in her hand. Red liquid drips down her wrists to the floor, and someone cuts the music off. I look back over at Teo.

"Are you ready for this, baby?" I ask with a smirk and he grins, crossing those tattooed muscular arms across his chest.

"So what, you're gay? That's why you wouldn't sleep with me?!" Missi shouts, and I tip my head back and laugh.

"Trust me, Mis. Me being bisexual had nothing to do with me not wanting to sleep with you," I snap, curling my lip. "You are the most psychotic, evil, manipulative bitch I have ever met. My dick would shrivel just at the thought of you touching it." I watch as her face turns red and she starts to shake.

"I will fucking destroy you, Lennox Crane. This is all that whore's fault. She made you this way!" she screams, and Fatima comes up from behind her and pulls her out of the room. She's yelling and fighting, and Donny starts to clap.

"Now *that* was awesome!" he shouts, and Teo comes over to give me one more kiss in front of everyone.

"Does anyone care that we're fucking?" he shouts, looking at the rest of our team and their friends. Ursula is drunk and she moves closer to us.

"I think it's hot as fuck. Rylee's a lucky slut," she slurs, then leaves the room following Missi and Fatima. Felicia's crying from laughing so hard, and she holds up her cup to us to say cheers.

"So now that everyone knows about you and Teo, do you think it's time to announce that we're all in Rylee's harem?" Donny asks and we all lose it, laughing until our stomachs hurt. I feel free and happy. Things are finally starting to come together.

I'm hungover and pissed the fuck off! I can't believe those assholes think that they can play me like that and I'll just take it. I've been quiet and acting subservient, but now? Oh, I'm going to fucking destroy them, and their little slut too.

They think she's safe, but they have no clue what we have in store for her. I don't bother with any makeup, and I put on one of those dresses Daddy likes. I need him to listen to me and help. I want that bitch gone. Off my team for good, and back to her little hovel, wherever she came from.

I don't bother stopping to talk to his secretary as I shuffle over to his door. It's cracked open and I can hear him yelling with someone on the phone. "I don't care what you need to do. We cannot let this steroid debacle get out!" he shouts, then slams something against his wall.

I wait a few more moments as he makes another call. "Jenson, I need you to call one of your buddies from the police station and get us a dog. I want a full search in the football and cheerleading locker rooms. We will find the person selling steroids."

I pull out my phone and text Kyle. I think I just figured out the perfect way to get that little slut gone for good.

"Baby, this is so boring," Kyle whines as he kisses my neck again. We're hiding in the practice gym under the bleachers. I wish I could get closer, but if Kyle would just shut the fuck up then I could hear everything going on.

Coach Williams is fighting with my daddy and his police friend as they tear apart the locker room. "Shh, I promise to make it up to you later," I tell Kyle, as he runs his hands up the back of my thighs and under my dress. I bite my lip to hide my moan when his fingers reach my panties.

"How about I just bend you over and slip inside as we wait," he grumbles, and shivers run down my spine. I am so fucking horny thinking about how I'm going to ruin that little whore's life, that one thrust from him will have me cumming on his cock.

Someone shouts from inside the other room and I smile.

Game over, bitch!

CHAPTER THIRTY

Rylee

I can't believe it's Christmas break already. The past few months have felt more like years. So much has happened, and a lot of it was more like a nightmare. But for the first time in a long time, I'm happy.

Things with the guys are going well. I'm falling in love, laughing, and smiling more than I ever have. I thought my past with Chaz and Demon, plus what happened with the guys, would cause me to close my heart off, but I'm glad it didn't.

Not everyone is a horrible person, and not everything is

black and white. I know a lot of people, if they were in my shoes, would have cut the guys out of their lives for good and not given them a second chance. And maybe I'm a fool for not doing that, but I don't regret it.

Underneath are men who've been wronged in life, in some really messed up ways. They didn't choose the life that they were given, and I don't believe they should continue to be punished for their mistakes if they show that they are willing and have changed.

So, this new year will start off good. I'll go home for Christmas break, visit with my mom, and when I come back, it will be a fresh start for me and the guys. We'll really start to date, and spend more time together outside of school and cheer. Maybe I can even convince them to get to know Trevor better, so he can join our little group, and I don't have to have our relationship so separate from the others.

The Christmas party was amazing, and just what I needed with them. We exchanged our gifts and the guys spoiled me like crazy. They didn't have to, and I made sure they knew that, but I loved everything anyway.

They loved my gifts too, even though I thought there wasn't anything special about them. Yet the smiles on their faces said they didn't care what they got, just who it came from. And that made me like them even more.

Trevor and I video chatted this morning. He told me that his dad was taking him on a skiing trip, and that he's headed to the mountains and won't have any reception. He wanted to let me know, so I didn't worry if he didn't get back to me, and he wanted to see my face one last time.

I miss him already, but I'm planning on keeping myself

busy with mom, and the guys, if they decide to come after all. "You better be good for Alex while I'm gone," I tell Peaches as I give her head a scratch. Alex is going to take her for the break because his place isn't too far from school.

I suggested bringing her to a boarding place, and he looked at me in horror. Told me no baby of his would be staying all alone, and he was taking her. As adorable as I think he is with her, he better remember she's mine. I will cut him if he tries to take my little girl.

She just purrs, rubbing her head against my hand. "I'm gonna miss you too," I say, smiling with tears in my eyes.

I've never had so many people in my life before, and none that I cared about this much. The feeling is indescribable, to have so many people care about me. Sometimes I think it's all too good to be true.

I'm trying not to think about it, like the other shoe is going to drop. But this is me, and I never get to be this happy for long.

There's a knock on the door as I'm zipping up my suitcase. "Coming!" I shout. I'm making sure I have everything ready for my flight tomorrow, but the guys are having an end of semester party. They stayed behind to get ready, and Alex is there helping Serenity. I told them I'd meet them after I finished packing and got ready.

Maybe they couldn't wait and came to meet me.

Opening the door, I don't find one of my guys. "Dean Kondom," I say, a wave of dread taking over me. I hate this man with a passion. Just being around him makes me want to puke.

He gives me a cruel, sickening smile as he pushes his way

into my room. "Hey!" I say as panic rises. He locked the door behind him, making sure to stand in front of it.

Fuck, I have no way out. My head starts to spin, my body breaking out in a sweat. "What do you want?" I ask, trying to sound strong.

I don't know what he wants, but the look on his face tells me it's nothing good. I could scream for help, but the building is empty with everyone leaving for break.

My eyes dart over to my phone. If I'm quick enough, I could dive for it, but I don't think I'd be able to make a call in time. Fuck, fuck, fuck! Maybe I'm overthinking. Maybe he just wants to talk. God, please let it only be that.

"You're a naughty girl, Rylee. I knew you would be trouble from the moment you got here. You come here, show up my daughter, and take everything from her that she worked so hard for."

"I didn't do anything to Missi!" I argue. "She's the one who has been messing with me. She tried to kidnap me and drown me!"

He just rolls his eyes. "You young girls are so dramatic. Grow up, Rylee. You're clearly the bad apple of the bunch. You know, drug enhancements are forbidden at this school. I thought you had natural talent, but you've been taking steroids all along," he says, giving me this fake ass disappointed look as he shakes his head.

"What are you talking about?! I don't do steroids," I say, brows furrowing. What the fuck is this man on?

"Then why did we find a whole bunch in your locker at the gym? Are you selling them? I know you're in need of money, but drug dealing is illegal, and is grounds for expulsion."

"I don't know what you're talking about," I say, my head starting to pound as I try to wrap my thoughts around what he's saying. "I've never been around steroids. Never touched them a day in my life. So whatever you think is happening, you have it wrong."

"Oh, I don't think so. You had your chance to leave, Rylee. But you're a stubborn girl who is so, so foolish. As of right now, you are expelled from Solidarity Academy. You are to leave the premises and never return."

"What?!" I shout. "I didn't do anything!"

His smile turns sinister and fear claws up my throat. "Maybe, maybe not. But that's what the school board is going to believe when I show them what we found in your locker. There's no fighting this, Rylee."

"I'm not leaving. I deserve a chance to defend myself, to prove I'm not guilty." This has Missi written all over it. Fucking bitch. I knew her being quiet and staying away was bullshit. She was planning something all along. God, I'm so stupid for not seeing it.

"No, you won't be doing any of that." He chuckles. "But here is what you are going to do. You're going to write a note to your little boyfriends. Tell them that coming here was a mistake, that you're homesick, and you won't be coming back. You're also going to tell them not to contact you, and that it's over. Tell them it's for the best."

Like fuck I am! As he's been talking, I've been slowly inching toward my phone that's sitting on my desk.

"Go on!" he shouts, nodding to my desk. "Write it."

I scramble over there and pull out a piece of paper and a pen. I feel him watching me, but he stays by the door. With one hand I write out the note like he asked, as I carefully reach for my phone with the other.

Once I have it, I keep it close to my body and angle myself so that he can't see my other hand moving. Just as I'm done writing the note, I open my lock screen and search for Colton's number.

I write out a quick text that says 911, and just as I'm about to send it, my phone is snatched from my hand. "You little bitch!" he roars as he tosses my phone against the wall, making it shatter to the ground. My arms shoot up, trying to protect myself from him.

I'm gonna puke. God, why isn't my fight or flight kicking in? I lost my shit when the guys took me. Why am I freezing up, cowering like a weak person?

He grabs me by the shirt, fisting it in his hands before throwing me up against the wall. I cry out as my head bounces off from the force.

"Why can't you ever just do what you're fucking told?!"

"I-I'm sorry."

"Oh, you will be," he says, shoving his phone in my face. "See this?" he asks, pressing play.

My eyes widen in shock, as moaning plays throughout the speakers. "Where did you get that?" I ask, watching a video of the guys fucking me from the summer. The one my ex took.

"Oh, I have my ways. Looks like your little ex was just dying to get his hands on some cash. This video isn't the only thing I own. Now. Listen good, and listen closely. You are going to take this ticket and get on the flight that leaves in the next hour. You're not going to look back. You're done at this school. And you will not contact those boys. It's in your best interest to just pretend you never came here. And if you don't, I will show everything I have to the media. I will not only ruin your reputation, but the boys' reputation too. They will lose everything they've worked hard for, all because you can't do what you're told."

He grabs something out of his pocket and thrusts it against my chest. "There's a cab waiting for you. Already prepaid. It's time to go."

I bite the inside of my cheek so hard that blood pools on my tongue as I try my damnedest to hold myself together. I will not cry. I will not break in front of this monster.

Like father, like daughter.

I can't believe this man is in charge of a whole school. He should be locked up.

Letting go of me, I stumble over to the bed and grab my bag and purse.

He watches me, following me the whole way down to the lobby of the dorm and out front where the cab is waiting. It feels like my knees are going to give out, as my body starts to shake from everything that's happening.

Fighting with him wouldn't be the smart move. I don't think he would hesitate to hurt me. He knows I have no leg to stand on. I'm some poor girl here on a scholarship, and he's got money and connections. No one would believe me.

The guys would.

He throws my bag into the back of the trunk before ripping the door open. He shoves me in, and I almost smash my face on the seat. "You take her to the airport, do you understand me?" he tells the driver. "No stops."

He looks back at me and smiles that fucked up smile again. "Don't try anything, Rylee. I have eyes everywhere."

With that, he shuts the door and the car immediately starts to move, the locks pressing down, trapping me inside.

As the seconds tick by, my mind starts to play catch up on what just happened.

My hand flies to my mouth as I hold back a sob. This can't be happening. When I knew everything was too good to be true, I didn't think this would be the end result. I thought maybe I'd get my heart broken, or have to move on from one or all of the guys. But I'd get over it. I'd keep going with school, and lean on my friends.

But this is so much worse. I'm about to lose everything because I can't risk that video getting out. I feel the same way now that I did when Chaz came to me with the photos and videos.

The Dean made it very clear he would ruin them if I said anything. And even if the guys won't care about the video getting out, it doesn't change the fact that the Dean can take everything they worked for away from them.

He would do to them what he's doing to me. Make up a lie, plant evidence to make them look guilty.

No, I'm not worth losing all of that.

Looking out the window, I try to hold back the sounds, but the tears fall free. I don't want to lose them. Even after everything we've been through, I still care for them. It hurts to think of never talking to them again, never seeing them again. My heart is fucking shattering inside me, the pieces stabbing me like little knives as I struggle to breath. My whole world is crashing down, and I have never felt so helpless in my life.

I don't know how I'm going to be able to keep them away. If they know me, really know me, they won't believe that note. None of what he made me write would ever sound like it came from me.

Fuck, part of me wants them to know I wouldn't give up on them that easily. To just pack up and go without any warning. I have no idea how I'm going to do it, but it has to be over.

Everything I've worked for, fought for, is all gone. Months of dealing with Missi was all for nothing. She got what she wanted—me gone. And I've never hated myself more in my life than I do right now.

DO YOU WANT MORE?

Whew! How are we all doing? Yeah, I know, I'm a wreck too, but it's okay. Book three isn't that far away. One click now.

Raise 'Em Up, Book three of Solidarity Academy will be coming soon!
We are estimating around fall time!

https://books2read.com/SolidarityAcademy3

Want to come chat about the book?
Join the Spoilers group.

https://www.facebook.com/groups/795817792071406/?rcf=share_group_link

EXTRA SCENE

"Now?" I squeak, and Teo throws his head back, laughing. Why am I so nervous? She nods and steps away, taking my hand. I let her lead me to a random guest room off the side of the kitchen.

Teo follows and makes sure the door is locked. She sits on the bed and looks around, then pouts.

"There's no couch. I guess I'll just have to go for a ride," she purrs and opens her legs, showing me her red lace panties.

Finishing her drink, she sets it onto the floor. "How

much have you had to drink?" I ask, because I don't want her to regret this. We're finally starting to make progress.

She huffs and crosses her legs. "I'm a little tipsy, Len. But I know exactly what I'm doing," she reassures me, and I nod before moving closer and bending so her lips are within reach of mine.

I hover a breath away from her until she moans and grabs the back of my neck, pulling us together. I kiss her hard and deep, tangling our tongues together.

Teo comes up behind me and grips Rylee's hips, pulling her up to grind against me. I groan against her lips, and she whimpers when I pull away.

The room smells like her and Teo mixed together, and I know it's going to drive me crazy.

"Are we really doing this?" I check, and by the way her green eyes are dilated with lust and she's wiggling on my erection, I would say the answer is yes.

"Please, but first I want to watch you two together. That night in Florida was a tease," she says with a sigh. Teo laughs behind me, and I glance at him from over my shoulder. Taking my throat with his hand, he pulls my lips to his, groaning as I immediately submit to him.

"Fuck, why is that so hot?" Rylee mumbles as she watches. I don't let things get too heated and reluctantly pull away, only to kiss Rylee.

"Tell us what you want, baby," I coo, moving my mouth from hers to trail kisses along her jaw and collarbone. She squirms and softly moans.

"You on this bed. I want to ride your tattooed cock, while Teo fucks your tight ass." She whimpers as my hand trails down her body to her soaked panties. I slip them to the side and rub her clit as she continues to tell me how dirty she wants us to be.

"Hmm, you're soaked, baby girl. Baby, taste," I tell Teo, and I lift my fingers to his mouth. He groans and I unwrap Rylee's legs from my waist and move aside so he can taste her properly. One thing my guy loves is giving head, and I have no complaints.

I stand and start stripping, watching as Teo has Rylee on the edge. She's digging her nails into the back of his head, and he's groaning in ecstasy. Moving over to the side of the bed, I lean over and whisper into Rylee's ear.

"See what you do to our guy? How he's willing to drop to his knees and serve his queen," I growl, kissing her neck as she sucks in a breath and moans louder.

She reaches over and grabs my cock, tugging it slowly, and my knees shake. God, I'd forgotten how much I've missed her touch. She moves a little faster and I pull away from her, then kiss her pout.

"I am not coming all over your hand, baby girl," I grunt and Teo stops licking her slit and looks up at me. His lips are glistening, his hair is a mess, and his cheeks are red from her grinding against his face. But it's his eyes that get me.

He looks happy. At peace. I know he's been wanting us together for a long time now, and tonight I'm going to make sure all his fantasies are fulfilled.

I had forgotten how delicious Rylee tasted, and I don't want to stop, but this isn't just about us. Len is here too, and he's being a good boy, waiting for me to have my snack before interrupting us.

Rylee is close. Her moans are getting louder and her thighs are squeezing my head like a watermelon. I want to fuck her, but I won't. Tonight is about her and Lennox. I will take his tight little ass like she said.

"I am not coming all over your hand, baby girl." Len grunts and I pull away from Rylee. She whimpers and I smirk, licking my lips. Len groans and I stand up, then move over to him and kiss him hard.

He licks inside my mouth, taking all of her juices. His cock is hard and rubbing against my shirt. Reaching down, I grip him tight and jerk him off for a few seconds until he's putty in my hands. Moaning from the bed breaks our kiss up, and I glance over to see that Rylee is now, and thrusting two fingers deep into her pussy. Damn, isn't that a pretty sight. My mouth waters for another taste, but I'm going to wait until she's full of my guys cum first.

"Get on the bed, baby, and let her ride this cock," I growl, releasing him. Rylee whines and I smirk. Lennox almost trips as he rushes to get into position, and I try not to laugh at how eager he is.

Not that I can blame him. He's the only one who hasn't had sex with Rylee again since Florida. He lays down on the bed, and Rylee gives me a little grin. "Aren't you going to order me too?" Spreading her thighs wider, she removes her fingers and holds them up for me.

"Are you looking for a red ass, baby girl?" I growl, stomping over to the bed and sucking her cream from her fingers with a groan. She gasps as I lick in between her fingers, careful not to waste a drop.

Lennox moans from beside us and I turn to him. He's got his cock in his hand and he's stroking it slowly. Pre-cum beads on the tip and I lean over Rylee to lick it up, before moving back and kissing her hard.

Gripping her hair tight, I hold her where I want her until she's panting into my mouth. "Get naked and then ride our boy until he fills you with his cum," I order, and her eyes flash with defiance, but she sighs.

"Fine, but I want to watch as you fuck him," she huffs, then crosses her arms. Len laughs, and I don't hesitate to grab her hips and flip her until her stomach is on the mattress. Her ass is just waiting for my hand to mark it.

Gripping her panties, I slide them over her plump ass, and down her legs, tossing them onto the floor, before I lean down and press a kiss against her creamy skin. She moans and wiggles her ass, tempting me. I nip her flesh, then soothe it with a lick.

A moan leaves Len's lips, and I look up to see her sucking his cock. "Such a naughty girl," I mutter as my palm makes contact with her right ass cheek. She whimpers and I smile as her skin begins to turn pink.

"Fuck, Teo, I'm about to come in her mouth if you don't hurry up," Len groans and I nod. I smack her other cheek, then grab her hips and line my cock up. We don't have any lube, and if I'm going to fuck Lennox's ass, I need to make sure my dick is slick.

"Oh, fuck," Rylee moans, releasing Len's cock from her lips as I bottom out, and then thrust a few more times before pulling away. Len takes some deep breaths before grabbing her and pulling her onto his cock. She sits there, then surprises us and spins around to face me.

"Jesus," Len shouts and groans as she begins to rock. I climb up onto the bed until I'm between his legs as he bends his knees. Rylee gives me a smile, biting her bottom lip and I chuckle.

"That was mean, baby girl," I say before grabbing the back of her throat and pulling her lips to mine. She opens her mouth for me and I suck on her tongue, making her shiver.

"Fuck! Whatever you're doing, don't stop," Len moans. "She's gripping my cock in a choke hold," he pants. Not removing my lips from hers, I reach down and rub my cock along Len's hole.

"No, baby. If you fuck me, I'm going to explode," he whimpers and Rylee laughs. Pulling back from my mouth, she gives me a wink.

"Do it," she mouths quietly, and I grin. Gently pushing inside him, he clenches around my tip, trying to keep me out. Rylee swivels her hips as Len digs his nails into her skin, breathing hard.

She's still wearing her dress, and that just isn't going to work. "Take it off or I'm going to rip to shreds," I growl and her emerald eyes get wide. I know she wants to talk back to me. She's my brat for a reason. "Now, or I pull out," I warn, and she purses her lips. After a slight hesitation, she sits back onto Len's lap and rips her dress over her head.

Adding to our pile of clothes on the floor, I shake my head as she raises her eyebrow at me. "You okay, baby? I need to move," I groan to Len, and he licks his lips, nodding. I thrust in a little deeper and my head falls back in pleasure. Rylee kisses my throat as she continues to ride Len's cock. Her moans grow louder and with every breath she pants onto my skin my hips get faster until I'm fucking Len hard and fast.

"Fuck, fuck," she starts to chant and I know she's close. Len's eyes are squeezed shut tight and he's biting his lip. I grab his legs and wrap them around my lap, so he can sit on me.

"Teo, God, you're so deep," Len groans and I nod. Rylee stops moving and stares at where my cock is stuffing Lennox.

"That's so hot," she moans, her eyes starting to roll back. But I don't want her to cum. She needs to wait for Len and me.

"Turn around baby," I tell Rylee as she whines, but listens, climbing off of him, then sitting back down. I can't resist smacking her ass, and she jumps, turning back to look at me with a glare. I grab Len's thigh and massage it as I pump into him slowly.

She rubs the tip of his cock against her clit and groans, before sliding him back inside her soaked pussy. Len grabs her hips as she leans down to kiss him.

Watching the two of them together while he's squeezing me so tight has my vision going fuzzy. I'm not going to last much longer. I bend down and press my lips to Rylee's spine. She shudders and Len groans.

Thrusting my hips I fuck into him hard and fast, then lean over Rylee and grab his throat, cutting off his air. His eyes roll back as I reach down and rub Rylee's clit.

"Oh, yes, fuck." She explodes, yelling and I know even with the music playing in the next room, people have to know we are fucking in here.

I let Len breath as he cums so hard my cock is being strangled, causing my orgasm. I groan loud and deep and Rylee giggles as she tries to catch her breath. She's laying on his chest as I rest my forehead on her sweat-soaked back.

"That was..." she trails off and I smile against her skin, pressing a kiss.

If this is what our future looks like, then I'm going to be very happy and extremely sated.

Whew! Yeah I need a cold shower now. How about you?

ACKNOWLEDGMENTS

There are so many people to Thank and usually, we make a page of Acknowledgements, but this time around we're just going to say:

Thank you to our editor Emma. You are amazing!

Thank you to November Sweets for once again formatting our baby. We're so blessed to have you in our lives!

And thank you to our amazing alphas, betas, street, and ARC teams! You guys are the real rockstars! We wouldn't be anywhere without y'all!

MORE FROM AMBER NICOLE

Reverse Harem:
    Alistar Academy Duet:
    The Forest Witch Lies
    https://books2read.com/alistar1

His Little Devil (Book 2) (Coming Soon!)

Forever Changed Duet: Completed!

Forever Changed

https://books2read.com/foreverchanged1

Forever Yours
    https://books2read.com/foreverchanged2

Kelly Cove Secrets: Mermaid Co- Write with Chelsii Klein

The Storm Beneath The Waves

https://bit.ly/StormBeneaththeWaves

Solidarity Academy: Cheerleading Bully Academy RH Co-write with Alisha Williams

Book One: Knock 'Em Down

https://books2read.com/Solidarityacademy1

Book Two: Take 'Em Out

https://books2read.com/Solidarityacademy2

Book Three: Raise 'Em Up

https://books2read.com/SolidarityAcademy3

Forbidden Truths Duet:

Forbidden Lies

https://books2read.com/Forbidden-Truths

Forbidden Secrets:

https://books2read.com/Forbidden-Truths-02

Quiet Confessions Duet:

Quiet Confessions Part One

https://books2read.com/quietconfessions

Quiet Confessions Part Two

https://books2read.com/QuietConfessions2

Locked Hearts, Locked Souls Society Book One (Co-write with Jenn Bullard)

https://books2read.com/Lockedsouls1

Locked Promises, Locked Souls Society Book Two

https://books2read.com/LockedSouls2

FF, Dark, Bully, Stepsister Romance:

The Midnight Confessions, Part One

https://books2read.com/TMC1

The Midnight Confessions, Part Two

https://books2read.com/TMC02

The Midnight Confessions, Part Three

https://books2read.com/TMC03

Shared World:

Karma (Dressed to Kill)

https://books2read.com/DTK-Karma

Link to Facebook group

If you want to come hang out with me and talk about books, come—join my author's group!

https://www.facebook.com/groups/ambernicolereaders group/?ref=share

ABOUT AUTHOR AMBER NICOLE

Before accompanying her military husband across the United States, Amber Nicole was born and raised in upstate NY. An avid reader and baker, she always has something cooking, whether in the kitchen or in her mind. She is well known for her international best selling duet *Forever Changed,* and she has a wide range of tropes to choose from. Whether it be why choose, MF, MM, FF, paranormal, or contemporary.

She also has two incredible children who help inspire her every day and a husband that pushes her to follow her dreams. She's an animal lover and has many of her own.

Stay tuned for more from this incredible author.

MORE FROM ALISHA WILLIAMS

Emerald Lake Prep
Book One: Second Chances
Book Two: Into The Unknown
Book Three: Shattered Pieces
Book Four: Redemption Found

Blood Empire
Book One: Rising Queen
Book Two: Crowned Queen
Book Three: Savage Queen

Silver Valley University
Book One: Hidden Secrets
Book Two: Secrets Revealed
Book Three: Secrets Embraced

ONGOING SERIES

Angelic Academy
Book One: Tainted Wings
Book Two: Tainted Bonds
Book Three: Tainted Hearts (coming soon)

Black Venom Crew:
Book One: Little Bird
Book Two: Venomous Queen

Boys Of Kingston Academy:
Tantalizing Kings

STANDALONES

We Are Worthy- A sweet and steamy omegaverse.
We Are Destiny A steamy omegaverse
If You Go Into The woods- Steamy MF Shifter Novella
A Mid Nights Bloody Dream (TBD)
Knot Going Anywhere (TBD)
Fated To Save Her

CO-WRITES

Solidarity Academy
Knock 'Em Down: Book One
Take 'Em Out: Book Two

Lost Between The Pages
Mad For The Sea Witch

Wild Thorn Ranch
Marshall

Wild Child

ANTHOLOGIES

Jingle My Balls : A Gay & Merry LGBTQ Charity Anthology
In The Heat Of The Moment: A Charity Anthology
Ours to Keep: A Why Choose Anthology Romance
Beach Shots & Monster Knots: A Monster Romance
Anthology

SHARED WORLDS: A NIGHT OF RAPTURE AND PRIDE

Naomi (Dressed to Kill)

Made in the USA
Monee, IL
07 July 2023

38787221R00233